INTO THE FOREST DEEP

Into The Forest Deep

An Ever After Tales Collection

ROBYN TOCKER

Pete's Press

First Printing, 2024 by Pete's Press

In honour of my aunt Marcia.
Your words of wisdom are engraved on my heart.

PROLOGUE

The woods stared at Greta.

The twisted branches bent in the cool breeze, their gnarled roots peeking out at her from the safety of the underbrush. She felt their penetrating gaze as her daughter's laughter rang in her ears. The young mother took a deep breath and forced herself to look away from the place that had fuelled her nightmares for years.

Isla, five years old with her pale blonde hair flying behind her like a sail, ran past Greta. Hans' six-year-old son Lukas was right on her heels, his bushy black curls easy to follow in the bright afternoon sun. Between the two of them, Greta barely managed to stay standing.

Her father's front door swung shut, the heavy wood thumping loudly in the quiet woods that surrounded the village of Lobkovice. He smiled at his grandchildren and waved to Hans as he ran after the children. When he looked at Greta, he sighed.

"What are you thinking, my little Gretel?"

She ignored the woods' stare.

"Papa, you haven't called me that since I was a child," she chided quietly. "I wish you would move away from here. We could take you to the market to celebrate your birthday if you just accepted my offer."

"And live on that cobbled street of yours with all those fancy cottages and nosy neighbours?" the old man said with a huff. He shook his head, his greying hair ruffling in the breeze. "No, daughter. My place is here. A wood carver has no purpose without his trees."

Greta could feel the woods' stare. The hair on the back of her neck stood up.

"You can't stay here alone. What if you have an accident, or get lost in the woods?"

Her father laughed. His scarred hands took one of her pale ones and squeezed.

"If I were to get lost, it would be my own doing. I know these trees better than I know the lines on my hands. I don't need bread-crumbs."

It slipped out so innocently Greta almost missed it. Her father's eyes widened. No one had spoken of that time in years. Greta remembered how smart she thought Hans was for finding a way around their stepmother's cruelty. If only the birds hadn't decided a breadcrumb trail made a delicious meal. She knew one day she and Hans would have to tell their children exactly what happened, but as far as Greta was concerned, that was many years away. She took a shaky breath.

The wind picked up and the woods seemed to take a big breath, expanding closer to the cottage. Greta took a step away from the shadowy outlines of the branches.

"Papa, please. Think about it. If you won't come to the village with me, at least go to Hans' farm. He's got so much land now; there would be room for you there. The sheep would give you something to do." She bent her head down towards her father's. "You and I both know Sarah needs all the help she can get."

Greta only felt slightly guilty for shoving their father onto her brother's doorstep. It was hard enough to be the doting daughter when memories of her childhood crept up. Hans was lucky; he wasn't expected to be a caretaker for their father, not like she was.

Her father stroked his chin. She noticed the start of his wiry beard. *A sure sign winter is coming.* Her father only ever grew a beard when the wind started to bite.

"It's true the farm is a lot for her to manage, but I can't impose. I'd just be another mouth to feed. And with a growing boy, that's the last thing she needs," he said, shaking his head. "I'm better off here. I want to spend at least one more birthday in my own house before I'm dropped onto someone's doorstep."

"Fine. But if you insist on being so stubborn, I'm going to get our maid Helen to come check on you every day."

Her father blustered about the waste of time, but Greta wouldn't budge.

"Jacob will be done with the mines in a few weeks. He'll be busy setting up his smithy, but he'll be home every night. I won't need as much help around the house as I used to. Isla isn't as much of a handful either," she said with a smirk. "I'm sure Helen would love an excuse to be outside every day."

Her father stared at her for a moment then shook his head. "You're as stubborn as your mother."

She bent down and kissed his scratchy cheek. "Not half as stubborn as you."

He opened his mouth but Hans, panting heavily, interrupted.

"Have you seen Isla?" he asked.

Greta's heart stuttered. "I thought she was with you and Lukas."

Hans put a hand on his broad chest as he tried to catch his breath. "She was, but I lost track of them by the chicken coop. When I found Lukas, he was alone."

The three adults looked at Lukas, who stood hiding partially behind his father. His little hands gripped the back of Hans' shirt. Greta's heart rammed against her ribs.

"Lukas, where did Isla go?" she asked.

Lukas' cheeks were dusty with dirt, and she saw grass sticking out of his dark cloud of hair. Panting, he pointed to the woods.

"S-She said she saw something. I couldn't catch her."

Greta rose to her full height and stared at the woods. Its branches shook with laughter. *Yes,* it seemed to say, *I have her, just as I had you all those years ago. And you know where I led you then, don't you?*

Greta's breath caught in her throat. "The witch," she whispered.

She ran into the woods before Hans could yell "wait!"

The trees of her father's woods had grown closer together over the years. The familiar scent of pine and moss threw her back to her childhood. Before her stepmother's scheming, before breadcrumb trails and a witch's cottage, Greta had loved these woods. It was her haven from her stepmother's temper and her father's ignorance and hunger and pain and every bad thing that she could remember growing up. But since she and Hans had escaped the witch's cottage, she had not stepped foot on this overgrown ground.

With her daughter's laughter ringing in her ears, Greta pushed aside branches and ignored how the bushes caught on her brown skirts. Tearing holes and losing stripes of embroidery, she kept going, looking for any sign of her precious girl.

"Isla! Isla," she called, frantic.

Nothing.

Greta stopped beside a large oak and leaned against it as she caught her breath. She squinted in the dim light. Streaks of sunlight tried to get through the canopy of trees. Greta swallowed and listened. Sandgrouse and an alpine swift twittered. A red squirrel jumped from branch to branch above her head. Greta closed her eyes, remembering how her woods used to sound all those years ago. She pushed aside the snapping twigs and fallen acorns, the whistling wind and crinkle of dead leaves, until she came upon a sound that shouldn't be there. The sound of a little girl rolling on the ground as she tried to catch something. Greta opened her eyes wide and ran towards the noise.

She cleared a fallen log in the middle of her path and ran another half mile before she found Isla lying on the grass, staring at something in her hand. Greta used her last burst of energy to tumble down in front of Isla and wrap her tight in her arms. Isla gasped.

"Mama! Let go, I can't breathe!"

"I am *never* letting go of you again, do you hear me?" Greta said as she buried her head against her daughter's soft hair. She inhaled the smell of soap and lavender.

After another frantic moment passed, Greta loosened her grip enough to look her daughter in the eye.

"What were you thinking, Isla? You know you're not allowed to go into the woods alone!"

Isla stared at her lap. "I know, but . . . I saw something! A big something. It was black and green and brown and it moved funny. And I just had to find it!" She looked up at her mother. "I wanted Lukas to come, but he's too slow."

"And did you find this something?"

"No, I found a lady."

Greta's hands shook. "A lady?"

"She was old, like Grandfather, but she walked funny. She gave me this."

Isla held out a pale purple crystal tied to a piece of string.

Greta paled. In her mind, she was immediately thrust back to the witch's cottage, up the stairs and into the attic. The pale purple crystal glared at her, twinkling in the moonlight. As if to say, *Remember me?* Greta swallowed thickly. She wished she could forget.

Greta snatched the crystal from her daughter and tossed it as far as she could into the woods.

"Mama! That's mine!"

Greta grabbed Isla's arms and held them tight. "What did the woman say to you?"

Isla's eyes were full of tears. "I want my necklace back! The lady gave it to me as a present."

"What did she *say*, Isla?"

"She said she would come find me again when I was ready. But she wouldn't say ready for what."

Greta scooped her daughter up and ignored her cries for the crystal. She couldn't run with Isla weighing her down, but she kept a steady pace as she made her way back to her father's cottage.

"Listen to me, Isla. You must *never* go into the woods again, do you hear me?"

"But Mama!" she whined.

"Never, Isla! You'll understand when you're older."
The woods stared at Greta as she retreated, and she stared back.

~ 1 ~

LUKAS

The steps to the front porch creaked as Lukas settled with his back against one post and one of his legs propped against the other. He had blocked the entrance to the front door, but the sun hit his block of wood just right.

"Lighting is everything, my boy. If you're going to let the wood talk to you, you must see where it wants you to go," his grandpa's words echoed in his memory.

Lukas tied his bushy hair back with a strip of worn leather and tucked a stray curl behind his ear. As he held the small block of pine in his hands, he closed his eyes and tried to see where the wood wanted his knife to go. He initially picked this block from his father's scrap pile for its scent, but he sensed the wood knew it was destined for more than kindling.

With an idea in mind, Lukas began cutting away at the wood to find what was hidden underneath. Inside, his mother had the house smelling of porridge and fresh bread. His stomach gurgled, but he ignored it. His hazel eyes followed the path laid out for him by the wood and he remembered his grandfather's instructions.

"Don't leave a project half-finished. Lunch can wait. The wood cannot."

I should have written these things down. It had been a year since his grandfather had passed away, and although he had tried to

~ 7 ~

commit most of the woodcarver's tricks to memory, Lukas feared one day he would wake up and have forgotten them all in the night. When he was younger, Lukas hadn't noticed a strain between Hans and his father, but as he got older, he knew there was something separating the two men, not that they ever shared what it was with Lukas. Despite the tension, Lukas knew he was lucky to have had his grandfather for so long. By eighteen, many of his childhood friends barely had one parent still alive, whether from a deadly accident or illness, let alone a grandparent.

A lesser kestrel called above the farmhouse. Lukas didn't glance up to see it gliding through the late summer clouds. He wished it would go away so the larks would come back to the front yard. Although his father Hans farmed many acres for grain and kept a large section for his sheep and few cows, their front yard was Sarah's creation. With blooming wildflowers and a gated herb garden to the left of the house, Sarah had cultivated this area into something she could manage. Lukas helped where he could, but as a grown man, Hans expected him to spend more time in the fields with their Racka sheep herd and less time picking vegetables out of the backyard garden.

Lukas didn't cut deep enough and sent a splinter shooting towards the yard. He frowned. The wooden bear didn't look quite as fierce as it had a moment before. With a sigh, he put the block of wood on the porch and got to his feet. His morning chores were done, but his carving would have to wait. *If Papa catches me sitting around, it'll be another lecture over supper.* He'd had enough of those this week.

The family milking cow huffed when she saw Lukas coming around the corner. She was one of three barn residents, and she would have been out in the field if she wasn't close to giving birth. Before leaving for the fields, Hans had instructed Lukas to keep her in the outdoor pen for the day.

"She needs the sunshine like the rest of us," Hans had said.

Bella, the Hungarian Grey cow, was still chewing her way through breakfast. Lukas hopped the four-foot wooden fence into the pen and ran his hands over her pale grey sides and flanks. He steered clear of her pointed horns, each measuring at least a foot on either side of her head. This wasn't her first calf, but Hans had raised her from a newborn when her mother died giving birth. Entrusting his favourite creature to his son was no small matter, even if Lukas would rather be carving a new project than doting on an old cow.

"Well, Bella, think you're going to show us your baby soon?" he asked quietly, keeping his voice low and soft.

The cow just swished her tail. Lukas chuckled.

"You're right. Better wait until Papa is back with the sheep. He would hate to miss it."

Lukas opened the door that separated the pen from the interior of the barn and went to check on the horses. Hans was one of the better farmers in the area, but he didn't spend more than he could afford. Lukas had mentioned in passing wanting new tools for woodcarving and received only a raised eyebrow in reply. He had let that subject drop. With summer clipping along at a trot and the fall harvest on everyone's mind, Lukas knew the last thing Hans was thinking about was his son's hobby.

It's not a hobby! he wanted to say. *I love carving. It's one of the only things that brings me joy.* Well, that wasn't necessarily true. Lukas did love the farm; he liked helping his mother in the garden and spending time with the animals. He just wasn't sure he wanted to spend the rest of his life on the same plot of land.

The Noniusz horses didn't even flick their black tails when they heard Lukas shuffling around the dimly lit barn. He sidestepped a fresh pile of manure, hoping not to get any on his boots. The top floor held bales of hay while the bottom, in addition to Bella and the horses, stored tools, scrap metal, and other odds and ends that Hans couldn't find a better place for. Hans had various work-shops scattered about the farmyard; one for blacksmithing, one for metalworking, another for general repairs. He was known to be a jack-of-all-trades farmer and many local producers would stop by when they knew Hans was back with the sheep to ask his advice or to get his help on a project. Although he generally kept to himself, Hans was never one to turn away a neighbour.

Lukas rubbed Rowan's nose as he walked by his stall. The black horse stood over seventeen hands high, large for a Noniusz, and while he was an exceptional working horse, he could be grouchy if his mealtimes were interrupted. Lukas smirked.

"Don't worry Rowan, I won't take away your mash. You and Gerdie can frolic to your hearts' content this afternoon in the meadow. I won't need you to help me in the fields today."

Gerdie was the other Noniusz, a young mare even darker than Rowan, standing fifteen hands high. She was only four years old but exactly what the family needed for their weekly trips to the market. She was technically Sarah's horse, but Lukas had always had a soft spot for her. On his way out of the barn, he snuck half an apple into her stall and smiled as he heard her munching on it.

Lukas' stomach gurgled. He glanced at the sky. *Too early for lunch, but maybe Mama won't miss a slice or two of bread.* He jogged around the back of the house to the front door and went inside his child-hood home.

Hans had started to build this cottage a year before he asked Sarah to marry him. By the time the wedding ceremony was over, he was able to drive them to their new home in the country. A large kitchen and living space made up most of the main floor, but a door separated the main bedroom for Hans and Sarah. When Lukas was a baby, his crib was nestled in their room, but once he was old enough, he went up to the loft and hadn't left since. In addition to Lukas, the loft also stored extra quilts, crates, and other odds and ends Sarah hadn't found space for. Hans had also dug out a root cellar below for vegetable storage during the winter. Sarah used to tell Lukas when he was little that, having grown up in the village, it took her time to get used to country living, but she managed. Lukas had tried to picture growing up like his cousin Isla had, surrounded by people and constant noise. *I would go mad.*

Inside, he saw Sarah mixing something in a large bowl at the kitchen table. Her cream apron kept most of the flour off her pale blue dress, but it did nothing to hide her pregnant belly. She looked up from her work, her straight brown hair pulled back in a ponytail, and smiled at her son.

"You're just in time to taste the bread. I made an extra loaf for you."

Lukas' stomach gurgled again. They both laughed. He rolled up the sleeves of his loose, cream shirt and went over to her, taking the bowl out of her hands.

"You really should be resting, you know. Papa won't be happy to see you working so hard in this heat."

Sarah chuckled. "Oh, don't worry, I already got my lecture before he finished breakfast this morning."

She sat down at the table as Lukas finished mixing the ingredients for what looked to be raspberry pie. She and Lukas had already picked the bushes once and would have to do it again soon if they didn't want to lose the delicious fruit to the birds.

"He's right, you know. Even Constance said you need to take it easy with this baby."

Sarah leaned back against her chair, resting her hands on her swollen stomach.

"I *have* been taking it easy! Do you know how hard it is to stay in bed for five months?" She shook her head. "I promised your father after today I would go back on bed rest, but for now there's simply too much to do! This baby will be here before we know it and I've got a list of chores longer than my leg to get done before then."

Lukas put the bowl down on the table and sat across from his mother. When his parents initially told him Sarah was going to have a baby, he hadn't exactly expected the news. By now, Lukas was used to being an only child. The thought of his parents conceiving his new brother or sister was not something he wanted to dwell on either, but it was too late for that. Over the last several months, Lukas had grown to accept his family's new reality and had done his best to help Sarah whenever he could, especially when Hans was away. As the days passed, Lukas was growing more and more excited to meet the new addition. *I just hope it's a boy.* He didn't think he could handle a little sister, especially if she were anything like Isla.

"Why don't I go to the market for you this afternoon? It's only going to get hotter, and you can't ride Gerdie in your condition."

Sarah brushed back the loose hairs that had fallen from her ponytail. "Would you, Lukas? That would be such a big help. I only need a few things."

She pushed herself up and waddled to the kitchen counter. She grabbed the list and handed him a large woven basket.

"Fill this with the last of the sweet potatoes and some of the turnips and carrots. Frau Nagy loves them and you're more likely to get a better deal on the fabric."

Lukas smiled as he rolled his eyes. "I know, Mama. I've done this before."

She kissed his cheek. "I only meddle because I care."

"I love you, too," he said as he headed for the door.

"Wait!" she said, then handed him the loaf of bread wrapped in a cloth. "For the road. You can't barter on an empty stomach."

He gave her a quick hug then went out the door.

"Make sure you have a nap!" he called as he headed around the corner to the outside cellar door where the harvested vegetables were kept.

By the time he saddled Gerdie and left the farm, his stomach was rioting. Lukas shoved a huge chunk of the loaf in his mouth and ate the rest on the way to the village. His family lived a few miles away from the village, but it was far enough that no one wandered over unexpectedly.

The nearest village to Hans' farm, Lobkovice, was protected by Krystof Popel the Younger, whose home, aptly titled Lobkovice

Castle, Lukas used to play in when he was younger. That was before Popel decided his son Isaiah and daughter Aliz should be raised with children of their own class, not "dirty village children who looked to have been raised by wolves" (a direct quote). Lukas shook away the memory of Isaiah and Aliz and focused back on the dusty road that led to the village.

Lobkovice held about a hundred cottages, a church, dozens of shops, and a towering hall used for meetings and social gatherings. Lukas and Isla went to the fall harvest dance last year in that hall and while it was fun, Lukas always felt crowded whenever he stepped into the village. He supposed his father had felt the same way, hence why farm life had been so appealing to him all those years ago.

The market was set up in the main square every day. Many permanent shops were located right across from the square, giving easy access to local traders and merchants passing through. Lukas trotted to the tavern and tied Gerdie up in the shade. He patted her neck and tossed her the other half of the apple still in his pocket.

"Stay in the shade, girl. I'll be back soon," Lukas said then left with his basket of goodies for Frau Nagy.

Along the way, he spotted his aunt Greta. For as long as Lukas could remember, his aunt had towered over most of the women and many of the men in the village. Although her hair had darkened and grey hairs streaked through it, nothing much had changed about her since Lukas was a child. From what Lukas had observed over the years, her stature and commanding tone often got her what she wanted, except when it came to her father. Growing up, Lukas remembered the arguments his aunt and grandfather used to get into about him leaving his cottage. Since his grandfather's passing, Lukas had noticed she had shifted her temper towards her daughter.

Lukas bowed his head. "Good afternoon, Auntie."

"Good day to you, Lukas! Running errands for your mother, I see." She shook her head, her cream bonnet hiding her thick hair.

"How is she doing? Isla told me Constance's daughter had been by last week." She folded her arms across her chest, covering the bodice of her plain, dark brown dress.

"Szilvia came to check on Mama, but it was nothing serious. She just wanted to make sure Mama was following Constance's instructions."

"And is she?"

Lukas smirked. "You know Mama."

"I don't see why she wouldn't. If she's going to get herself in such a precarious position at her age, the least she could do is listen to her healers."

Lukas ignored his aunt's criticism and instead asked where Isla was. Greta huffed, her thin lips pressed into a frown.

"Off with Szilvia, no doubt. Or worse yet, that boy. You know how she likes to tax my patience. I can barely keep track of her. I would have thought by now she would have outgrown her childish behaviour. Lord knows how much I could use her help at home."

Lukas doubted that very much. Greta ran a small, efficient town-house and only kept a handful of staff. After Jacob had left the mines and opened his own blacksmith shop, specializing in identifying jewels and valuable minerals, Greta took in a few orders of sewing to bring in extra money. Isla wasn't known for her embroidery, so he doubted Greta needed Isla for that. *She just wants to keep an eye on her, as she always has.* Ever since Isla had run off into the woods when they were children, Greta hadn't let Isla out of her sight, if she could help it. Not until she turned fourteen, at least, and became much harder to control. Isla's fiery spirit usually got her into trouble, but Lukas liked that about his cousin.

"If I see her, I'll be sure to send her your way," Lukas promised.

Greta smiled and squeezed his arm. "You're such a good lad. Your mother is a lucky woman." The church bell rang the hour. Greta's brow furrowed. "One o'clock already? Where does the day go?" She kissed his cheek again. "Goodbye, Lukas! Give my greetings to your mother."

"I will," he said as he waved goodbye.

Lukas made quick time getting to Frau Nagy's fabric shop. It was a quaint townhouse with her shop in the front and her house behind, separated by a bolted door. Fabrics of every colour, thickness, and texture were neatly organized throughout the shop. As the owner, Frau Nagy ran a tight ship. Her daughters used to help before they married, moved, and had babies of their own, and with her husband dead and buried five years ago, the woman was left to manage her affairs herself.

As predicted, the gruff woman was easily pacified by the offer of fresh produce and gave Lukas the desired fabric at a decent price. She was a short woman, her grey hair pulled back in a tight bun. She folded the fabric and placed it in the basket after wrapping it in a protective cloth. Her stature always privately amused Lukas, since her name meant "tall" and she was the furthest thing from it. Her spectacles slid down her nose as she lifted the stack of fabric into the basket.

"Almost time?" she asked.

"Won't be long now. We should be ready when the baby arrives."

"Good. Tell your mother to wash her belly in sheep's milk every night. It will keep the skin from stretching."

"I made sure to pass along your advice the last time I was here. Mama thanks you for it," Lukas replied, a thin smile on his lips.

Frau Nagy let slip one of her rare smiles. "No need for thanks. After seven babes, I ought to know what gets rid of wrinkles." She chuckled. "Off with you, now. Sarah will want to get started sewing before night falls."

Lukas bowed his head then left Frau Nagy's store. He glanced up at the sun to see how much time he had left when he felt something solid run into his back. He stumbled forward and almost dropped the basket.

"Oh, I'm terribly sorry!" the person said.

Lukas turned to find a familiar face. He brushed the dirt from his brown trousers and blushed as Miriam stood behind him.

"You didn't drop anything, did you?" she asked, wringing her hands.

"N-No, I'm fine," Lukas stammered. He swallowed thickly as he took in the young woman he first met as a boy. Her uncle's farm neighboured Lukas', and with so many children, Miriam's mother often sent her older children to her brother's farm. Both were kept busy, so there wasn't much time for more than a passing glance, a shy smile, blushing cheeks, and rushed conversations over the fence. A few months ago, she'd moved out of the village to her uncle's farm permanently. Unfortunately, due to their busy schedules, he hadn't been able to stop by for a visit.

"Are you alright?" he asked, drawing himself away from his childhood memories.

Miriam's long, black hair was tied back in a braid, and it bounced as she nodded.

"I really should watch where I'm going. Auntie rushed me out the door to get to Frau Nagy's before she closes and I'm just so scatterbrained I completely forgot what she wanted and—" Miriam paused, her blue eyes focusing on Lukas' blushing face. "I'm rambling, aren't I?"

Lukas smiled. "A little."

Miriam blushed even darker. "No wonder my sisters tease me. I make a fool of myself every time I . . ." she trailed off.

Lukas raised an eyebrow. "Every time you what?"

Before she could answer, Frau Nagy stuck her head out her door. "Either come in and buy something or move along! I don't need you children blocking my shop," she said then slammed the door shut.

Miriam glared at the door. "Children! Huh!" She shook her head then looked back at Lukas. "I had better get in there before she locks the door. It was good seeing you, Lukas. Uncle and Auntie send their greetings, too. So sorry about running into you!" She hurried inside, her olive green dress brushing up against him as she slipped beside, then past him. Lukas stood there a moment, dazed, then gave his head a shake and headed for Gerdie.

Just as he was half a block from Gerdie, he saw a stall set up by the baker's shop. Lukas didn't recognize it, but he couldn't forget the scent of roasted cocoa beans. Lukas paused and stared at the large bag staring at him. His mouth watered as he thought of the crushed beans becoming his mother's famous hot chocolate, a drink Lukas had loved ever since he was a little boy. It had been months since he had found any beans at the market.

He met the man's gaze, his grey mustache covering most of his mouth. "How much?"

"Twenty forints."

Lukas nearly choked on the amount. He fished around his pocket for the bills. "Fifteen," he counter-offered.

The man shook his head. "I'll go as low as eighteen. My master almost lost his ship to get these. Half the crew didn't make it."

Lukas wasn't sure whether to believe the man or not, but he knew Sarah would be pleased to see the beans. He paid the eighteen forints then headed home.

As Lukas was riding up his farm's lane, the sun was just starting to set. He dropped the basket off on the porch then got Gerdie settled in her stall, making sure to top up her food and brush her down before heading to Rowan's stall. The muscular horse kicked the stall door, impatient as ever. Lukas patted Rowan's flank and gave him a pre-supper snack.

"You better have been good while I was gone, Ro. I'll never hear the end of it if I find out you kicked another hole in the wall."

As Lukas approached the house, he expected to hear his mother preparing supper. The familiar sounds of the table being set and pots boiling was missing, causing Lukas' stomach to tighten. He shook his head. *Maybe she took my advice and is resting.* Lukas grabbed the basket on the top step then headed inside. Sarah was nowhere to be seen. Lukas put the basket on the bare kitchen table and went to the closed bedroom door. Behind it, he heard the creaking of a bed and a groan growing louder and louder.

Lukas had rarely stepped inside his parents' room since his nightmares had stopped when he was eight. When he opened his parents' bedroom door, the same four-poster bed was pushed against the back wall, the dressers as tidy as ever, and the window open, causing the pale curtains to flutter in the breeze. Lukas' heart stopped mid-beat when he saw his mother.

Sarah was lying on the bed, the sheets tangled around her legs. The bed was soaked with sweat. Sarah's hair was plastered to her forehead. She gripped the sheets tight as she arched her back. That was when he realized the animalistic groan was coming from her. He rushed to her side and grabbed one of her hands.

"Mama, what happened? Is it the baby?"

Sarah cried out. She grabbed her belly with both hands and held it as if she was trying to keep it from splitting open.

"It's coming," she panted. "Too soon," she moaned.

She opened her eyes and tears rolled down her cheeks as she looked at Lukas. "Go get the midwife. I don't know how much longer we have."

Lukas got to his shaking feet.

"I can't just leave you like this!" He looked at the fireplace and tossed a few logs on the dying embers. "Do you need water? Towels? Anything?"

"Lukas!" she shouted as another contraction hit her. "Go!"

He tossed one last look at her then ran, leaving his mother wailing in her room. He forgot about the cocoa beans entirely.

~ 2 ~

ISLA

"For someone who spends so much time with flowers, you're awful at weaving flower crowns, you know that?" said Szilvia from her side of the table.

Isla stuck her tongue out at her friend. Isla brushed her pale blonde hair from her eyes and attempted to attach another marigold to her crown. She had found the flowers easily enough, but weaving them wasn't her strongest skill. Szilvia had complained when Isla found them; she had searched that same area for a half hour and came up empty.

"For someone who spends hours with herbs, you think you would know how to season your meat better."

Szilvia gasped, placing a hand over her heart. "How dare you?" The young healer's dark auburn hair glowed as the light from the fireplace lit her up from behind.

"That's the last time I prepare dinner for *you*!" Szilvia said.

Isla smirked as she nudged Szilvia's foot with hers underneath the table. "My stomach thanks you." She narrowly dodged a stick tossed at her head.

The two girls continued with their weaving. The midwife, Constance, had left them with a long list of tasks to complete before the sun set. As usual, they had completed them early and although weaving wasn't technically one of them, Isla would do anything to put off going home to her mother, even if it meant inventing chores like flower crowns and daisy chains.

"At least when Mama asks, we can say we'll give them away at the fall dance," Szilvia had said when they were gathering the flowers earlier. No matter that the dance was weeks away. The crowns wouldn't make it until then. But Isla was sure they would find a use for the decorative headpieces before they completely wilted. The village children wouldn't turn them away.

Their baskets, once overflowing with mushrooms, bay leaves, parsley, and other wild herbs Constance had yet to transplant to her backyard garden, sat empty on the table. Before weaving, the girls had placed their findings into the appropriate crates, waiting for Constance's approval. Next spring, Constance would use the seeds and plant them in her own garden. Until then, the girls would have to keep collecting the items for Constance's elixirs.

Isla secretly hoped the seeds wouldn't take next spring. She loved the weekly trips into the woods. Isla had been drawn to the overgrown trees and thick brush since childhood. It was a good thing her mother had yet to find out about her wanderings. Her time with Constance and Szilvia would no doubt come to an end.

Isla glanced at the clock on the fireplace's mantle. *I can probably get away with staying another hour or two. Mama won't expect me to be on time for supper.* Greta rarely expected Isla to be on time for anything.

Constance's cottage was on the outskirts of Lobkovice close enough to come by horse but far enough that it was the perfect sanctuary for two teenage girls who wanted to learn more about medicine. Isla had started pestering Constance four years ago for lessons. She had grown up alongside Szilvia, much to Greta's dismay. Isla's mother had higher aspirations for her daughter than a healer, even though Isla believed there was no greater calling than to help others. Despite Greta's attempts to refine her daughter into a young lady, separating Isla from Szilvia hadn't worked.

"No wonder the Chief Steward doesn't want his daughter around you. You're practically wild!" Greta had bemoaned to a younger Isla.

It wasn't hard to convince Constance, who was practically Isla's second mother, to teach her all that she knew about medicine.

Isla didn't care what her mother thought of Szilvia or Constance. Greta, like most of the village women, respected Constance's wisdom, but never befriended her. The men appreciated her skills, but they didn't trust her. Isla had seen it in their eyes when she helped Constance during a birth. The men, if allowed to stay, watched her closely. Female relatives usually helped during the heat of the moment, but once the baby came, they forgot Constance was there. Isla had tried to speak up for Constance once, but the older woman had merely shaken her head.

"They've made up their minds, my dear. Let them be. They know where to go when trouble comes knocking, and that's what matters."

Constance and her quiet wisdom reminded Isla of her aunt Sarah. Although Constance was a decade older than her aunt, Constance had a strong spirit that inspired confidence in her patients. Isla hoped to be like her one day.

Isla frowned at her flower crown. The marigolds were already starting to fall off. She tossed it onto the table with a huff.

"I give up! Give me herbs to crush or oils to mix. Flower crowns?" She shook her head. "My demise."

Szilvia picked up Isla's failed attempt with a chuckle. "It's better than your last one. At least four have stayed together!"

"You're not helping."

Szilvia just shrugged. Isla went to the fireplace and stirred the cauldron full of soup. "Constance should like this for supper. When do you think she'll be back?"

Szilvia shrugged. "Who knows? The Millers' farm is a few hours from here and you know how sickly those poor babies are. I probably won't see her until morning."

"Do you want me to keep you company?"

"Your mother would throw a fit," Szilvia reminded her. "You've already stayed the night three times this week."

"When does my mother *not* throw a fit?"

Szilvia shook her head with a chuckle. "You could stay at Erik's. Or has his mother caught you there already?"

Isla blushed, shaking her head. "You know he spends most of his time at the Chief Steward's castle. Isaiah apparently has a lot of work for him," she said as she rolled her eyes.

In addition to the Chief Steward's children and Szilvia, Isla had spent many childhood and early teenage days with Erik, the youngest child of the village butcher. It was his jokes that first attracted Isla to him. Over the years though, the two had spent more and more time together, until two years ago when their friendship turned to romance. She blushed as she remembered kissing him for the first time on Lukas' farm after they had helped with the harvest that year. Since then, the two had been inseparable. Except when he was at the castle.

Szilvia chuckled. "Oh yes, I'm sure the Chief Steward's son is just *dying* for a last-minute hunt, or needs his horse looked at, or whatever useless chore Isaiah has come up with."

Isla smirked but said nothing. She had liked Isaiah well enough when they were children. He had an astounding imagination. Many afternoons were spent playing games Isla had never heard of before. But when the Chief Steward commanded his son to his side, taking Isaiah's younger sister with him, everything changed. A year later, when Isaiah returned to his father's castle, he acted as though Isla and Szilvia never existed. Or if he acknowledged them, it was as a royal did a peasant. Isla wasn't sure why Erik was allowed to be treated like a friend, or why Erik still *wanted* to be Isaiah's friend after how he had treated the girls, but she didn't make a fuss. Or at least, not much of one. The arguments never ended in Erik stopping his work at the castle, so what was the point?

Szilvia got up and slipped her hand into Isla's. "You can stay if you like," she said, noticing how quiet Isla was.

Isla shook her head with a small smile. "No, thank you though. You're right. Mama would be angry if I didn't come home." It wasn't as if the midwife's loft could comfortably fit an extra body, anyway. Constance's cottage was plain but sturdy, stuffed to the rafters with supplies. Szilvia slept in the loft with various tools, pots, and boxes, while Constance kept her chamber on the main level, the door always shut.

"Will he be back today at least?" asked Szilvia as the girls sat down at the table again.

Isla picked up Constance's calico cat, Anna, off the mat in front of the fireplace. She growled at being disturbed but settled in Isla's arms. Isla stroked her soft head and sighed.

"Who knows. I hope so, as does his mother, but Isaiah always seems to have a reason to keep him at the castle. I'd go over there myself and see what was going on if I didn't think I'd be thrown out."

Szilvia shook her head. "I got a letter from Aliz yesterday. She said she'll be back soon from the capital." Her cheeks turned bright red.

Isla grinned. "What, her father is actually letting her leave the hopeful suitors for more than a day?"

Although all three girls used to be friends, Szilvia was the only one who stayed in touch with the Chief Steward's daughter. Isla knew about the letters, but other than that, she didn't know how deep the friendship went. In the last six years, Aliz had only left the capital of Hungary twice. As Szilvia avoided Isla's gaze, Isla suspected there was more than friendship between them.

"I suppose he's realized she misses home more than she wants a husband," said Szilvia. She made quick work of Isla's failed flower crown then got up and placed it on Isla's head. Her brown eyes sparkled as she smiled at Isla.

"Now you have a present for your mother, so she won't be as upset when you miss supper."

Isla was about to state her unwillingness to part with the crown when someone pounded on the door. Szilvia hurried to open it, stepping over a few more cats, stacks of books, pots, pans, and baskets of herbs. When she opened it, Isla's eyes widened to see her cousin Lukas standing there. He trembled in the doorway. Isla had never seen him so pale before. She got to her feet, Anna still in her arms.

"What happened? Is it Uncle Hans?"

"Where's Constance? My mother—it's the baby. She needs Constance."

Szilvia looked in dismay at Isla then turned back to Lukas. "She's out with another patient right now."

Lukas' shoulders sank. "When will she get back?"

Isla put Anna down. "It could be as late as tomorrow."

"Mama doesn't have that kind of time! She needs Constance now."

Szilvia and Isla exchanged a glance. Isla nodded. Szilvia left the entranceway and headed to the backroom. Isla went over and took Lukas' hands in hers.

"We can help. Szilvia and I have been at hundreds of births."

Lukas frowned. "My mother needs a real midwife, not two apprentices." He winced. "I'm sorry, that was rude." He shook his head. "I'm just . . . Are you sure?"

Szilvia came back to the main room with a basket full of supplies. Constance always kept an extra one made up just in case. "We're all you've got, I'm afraid."

Lukas looked between the two of them then nodded. "Come on, then. I brought Rowan."

"Rowan!" Isla exclaimed. "How did you convince the lazy thing to come?"

Lukas ran over to Rowan and held up the feedbag. "A little grain goes a long way. Come on! My mother needs you."

Lukas boosted Isla up first then helped Szilvia onto Rowan's broad back. It was a tight fit, but with no other horse, it would have to do. Szilvia held onto Isla's waist as Lukas swung himself up and took the reins. They were off at a gallop before Isla could take a breath.

When they reached Hans' farm, Isla could hear her aunt crying from the porch. Her palms started to sweat. She took a deep breath, remembering Constance's instructions.

"You have to be calm, no matter what. The mother needs you to give her your strength, and you can't do that if you're panicking," Constance had said when Isla attended her first birth.

Isla flexed her shaking hands then followed Lukas and Szilvia inside. She headed for the linen closet as Lukas led Szilvia to the bedroom. Although both girls had been trained in midwifery, Szilvia had more of a talent for it. Isla's gift lay in ointments, lotions, and poultices, which she hoped she wouldn't need.

With an armful of sheets, Isla hurried to Sarah. When she got inside her aunt's room, she dumped the fabric at the foot of the bed and looked around. She immediately shut the open window. She turned to find Lukas building up the fire. She went to Szilvia's side.

"What do you need?" she asked quietly.

Szilvia felt Sarah's stomach, putting pressure in certain places, and retreating when Sarah moaned in pain. "Hot water. Lots of it," she murmured. "If you have anything for pain, get it ready."

Isla nodded. She went to where her aunt had pressed her head into the pillows and brushed back her damp hair. Isla smiled. "We've got you, *néni*. Soon you'll be holding your baby."

Sarah opened her eyes, her lower lip trembling. "It's too early," she whimpered. "I've never felt this kind of pain before."

"Nonsense, Sarah! I've seen Constance deliver babies a few weeks younger than this and they grow up to be healthy boys and girls," said Szilvia. She covered Sarah's lower body with a sheet. "Lukas, can you help me lift up your mother? I want to get these sheets off the bed."

Isla left the door open behind her as she headed to the kitchen. Pot after pot of water was filled and boiled over the kitchen fireplace. Lukas came just in time to take one of the three pots. He hadn't yet regained his colour, but Isla was glad to see he had stopped shaking. She grinned at him.

"Don't worry, Lukas. Your mother is in good hands."

He nodded but his frown remained. "She's right, though. It's too early, isn't it?"

Isla shrugged as they made their way to the bedroom. "It's hard to say. Szilvia wasn't wrong when she said younger babies have survived. But I won't lie to you, Lukas. There is always a chance. If you can't be calm, there's no shame in that, but you can't be in the room with us if so. Your mother needs to focus on the baby, and she can't do that if you're fretting."

Lukas drew back his shoulders. "I can help."

"Then come on. We've got to deliver your baby sister."

"Brother!" Lukas insisted. "I told you no sisters."

Isla laughed. They entered the stuffy room and saw Szilvia adjusting Sarah's pillows. Sarah was lying on a fresh set of sheets and although she was as pale as Lukas, she seemed to have regained some of her strength. Isla set down one of the pots of water and took the other from Lukas.

"Can you grab the last one?" she asked.

Lukas nodded and left the women alone.

"Try to get some rest, Sarah. We'll have you up and walking in a little while," said Szilvia. She left Sarah on the bed and joined Isla by the window.

"Well?" asked Isla.

Szilvia shook her head. "There's nothing obvious. Her water did break, but why so early I can't say. It could be any number of things." She glanced at Sarah. "The babe's making its way down, but she won't be ready for hours. I'm going to get her walking and see if we can speed things along."

"Should we send for Hans?"

Szilvia bit her lip. The freckles that ran across her nose and cheeks darkened as the room got hotter.

"Let's see how she does. If she quickens then we'll send Lukas. I don't want him to miss this, but I don't want to panic him, either."

"I'll get the pain medicine ready."

She went to move around Szilvia, but her friend grabbed her hand.

"I might need an extra set of hands when the labour really starts. Are you sure you can help?"

Isla glanced at her aunt's bulging frame in the bed. For years she had studied under Constance so she could help people. She glanced at Szilvia. "I wouldn't be a good healer if I couldn't help someone I love."

Szilvia held her gaze then nodded. "If you need a break, take it."

Isla squeezed her hand tight then left the room.

Lukas wasn't in the kitchen. Isla frowned at the pot of cooling water. *Two pots should be enough.* Isla set another pot on the fire and moved the boiled one onto the stove. She tossed a few logs in the stove and got a fire going for stew. As she waited for both pots to boil, she grabbed her herbs for the pain medicine. While chopping, she heard the front door slam shut. Lukas hurried inside, shrugging off his light jacket.

"I forgot to feed the chickens," he explained. He saw the pot and winced. "Sorry. Do you want me to take it now?"

She shook her head. "You can chop vegetables. I thought I'd make a stew for supper. Sarah's going to need her strength, and you must be starving."

Lukas fetched potatoes, carrots, turnips, peas, beans, and onions from the cellar. They chopped together in silence, each listening carefully to whatever thump or shuffle sounded from the bedroom. As Isla mashed the peppermint leaves, Lukas seasoned the stew and searched for the raspberry pie he claimed Sarah had made earlier. Isla was about to joke about Sarah's appetite getting the better of her, when she heard the bedroom door open.

"Isla, can you come here for a moment?"

Isla grabbed the small bowl with the medicine and shot Lukas a hopeful grin. "Sounds like we're getting close!"

Lukas ran his hand through his messy hair. "Should I come with you?"

"Do you really want to see your mother in the midst of labour?"

Lukas paled. "Call if you need me."

A wave of hot air hit Isla's face when she entered Sarah's room. She nudged the door shut with her hip and headed over to where Szilvia sat between Sarah's raised legs. Sarah moaned as another contraction came. Szilvia stared between Sarah's legs.

"You're doing wonderfully, Sarah. Just a little longer." When she saw Isla she nodded her over. "Give her some of that, then come here. I need your opinion," she murmured.

Isla spooned a generous amount of the medicine into her aunt's mouth. She left the bowl on the bedside table then joined Szilvia. She rolled up her navy skirts and pulled back her blonde hair into a ponytail. From what she could see, the baby hadn't crowned yet.

"How much longer?" she asked quietly.

Szilvia shook her head. "It doesn't matter how long if the baby comes out backwards."

Isla blinked. "What?"

Szilvia grabbed Isla's hand with her bloody one. "Feel."

Isla never imagined she would have her hand inside her aunt, but she quickly got over it when she felt ten tiny toes instead of a head. She felt the blood drain from her face.

"Damn it," she cursed.

Szilvia licked her lips. "I think I could move him if I had enough pressure on the outside."

Isla's eyes widened. "Have you done that before?"

"Once, but I've seen Mama do it a dozen times. If I don't do it, I'm afraid the baby will get stuck. I don't want to cut her unless I absolutely have to."

"What do you need me to do?"

Szilvia smiled at Isla then looked at the pregnant woman.

"Sarah, your baby has gotten a little turned around in here, but don't worry, Isla and I know what to do. When I give the word, Isla is going to press on the top of your belly so I can help your baby along. It's going to hurt, but it will help your child. Do you understand?"

Sarah propped herself up on her elbows to look at the girls.

"Do what you have to. Just hurry," she said with a moan. "I don't know how much longer I can do this. Where's Hans? He should be here."

Isla glanced at Szilvia. She nodded. Isla went to the door as Szilvia untied the long sleeves from her bodice, leaving her arms bare. She washed her arms up to her elbows in one of the pots of water. "Get some fat, if you can. That might help."

Isla rushed past Lukas and grabbed a bowl full of congealed animal fat from the pantry where Sarah stored it for cooking and cleaning. Lukas was right behind her when she turned around with the bowl in hand.

"What's going on?"

Should I tell him? She looked at the bedroom door. Isla took a deep breath then met Lukas' worried gaze.

"The baby is turned around. Szilvia and I are going to fix it, but you should get Hans."

Lukas paled. "Will she die?"

"I don't know, Lukas. We're doing everything we can."

Lukas' Adam's apple bobbed as he swallowed. She saw tears in his eyes as he looked at his mother's bedroom door. "Can I say goodbye first?"

"Make it quick. We have to do it soon."

Her cousin grabbed his coat on the way. Isla stirred the stew Lukas had put together, giving it a taste as she waited for him to return. She covered the pot and removed it from the stove. She stirred up the coals in the fireplace then put the stew there to keep warm for when Lukas and Hans arrived. She heard Lukas shut the bedroom door. He stopped and kissed Isla on the cheek.

"I'll be back soon." He then left, slamming the front door behind him.

Isla glanced at her aunt's bedroom, her heart pounding against her ribs.

$$\sim 3 \sim$$

LUKAS

Lukas hadn't ridden Rowan this hard in years.

The horse huffed in protest as Lukas pushed him faster towards the grazing field for Hans' flock of sheep. It was at least a mile from the homestead, but to Lukas it seemed like a day's ride.

When Rowan turned the bend and left the dirt road behind for grassy meadows, Lukas leaned further forward in the saddle, rising on his feet so his backside no longer touched the leather. He patted Rowan's neck.

"Just a little further, Ro. You'll get a big bag of oats all to yourself when this is over."

The mention of oats seemed to spur on the temperamental horse. His ears flicked forward, and Rowan picked up the pace.

As he searched the field for any sign of his father, or the sheep, Lukas' mind kept spinning back to his mother. He couldn't get her screams out of his head. Tears pricked the corners of his eyes. He couldn't imagine what kind of pain she was in, or how afraid she was.

If she's as scared as I am, I'm glad I got Isla and Szilvia.

The fields surrounding Hans' homestead were used to grow crops and for grazing, depending on the time of year. Lukas suspected his father had taken the sheep to the farther field that hadn't been tilled yet. Lukas would have done the same if he had taken the sheep that day. He shook his head, berating himself for not taking the animals himself.

Papa should be home with Mama. She needs him.

Lukas doubted Hans would be as panicked as he was right now.

Lukas was beginning to doubt which field his father had picked when he spotted Hans amidst the sheep just ahead. The flock of sixty – a mix of ewes, lambs, and the lead ram – were grazing around Hans. Their spiral horns stood out amongst the tall grass, their grey wool protecting them from the chilly breeze. Hans' cap was pushed further up his head, revealing where he was starting to go bald. His salt and pepper hair peeked out from the brown wool cap; Lukas could spot the shadow of a beard appearing on his father's chin. Hans' dark grey trousers were dusted with stalks of grass, as was his brown tunic and vest.

"Papa!" Lukas shouted. "Papa!"

Hans lifted his head. That was when Lukas spotted the lamb in his father's arms. From his perch on Rowan's back, it looked newly born. He ordered Rowan to stop just in front of Hans. Lukas coughed from the dust. Hans took off his cap and attempted to shake the debris from his face.

"What is it, Lukas? You look like you've seen a ghost."

"It's Mama," he said, his breaths coming in short bursts. He cleared his throat. "It's the baby."

Hans' dark brown eyes widened, emphasizing the wrinkles in the corners of his eyes. "Now?" he whispered. He shook his head. "Are you sure?"

Lukas nodded. "Isla and Szilvia are already there."

Hans swore. He placed the lamb back with its mother then mounted Rowan. He settled in behind his son. "We'd best be going, then. I don't want to miss my second child's birth."

Lukas would have laughed if he wasn't so scared. It was a running joke in the family of how Hans had been out tending the sheep when Sarah went into labour with Lukas almost two decades ago. Thankfully, Constance had been making her rounds that day and heard Sarah's screams. Hans arrived just in time to see newborn Lukas curled up in his mother's arms, fast asleep.

Lukas pushed Rowan as hard as he could, but the horse was tiring. When the farm came into view, Lukas could have wept with relief. Rowan hadn't even come to a full stop when Hans dismounted. He nearly skinned his knee, but Lukas saw Hans catch himself then run up the front steps of the farmhouse. Lukas couldn't hear his mother screaming from outside, but he couldn't hear a baby, either. Lukas swallowed thickly.

Rowan neighed and stomped his left front leg. Lukas shook his head then got off. Reins in hand, he led Rowan to the stables and did the quickest wipe down he had ever done. He didn't forget about Rowan's oats.

Hans had left the front door open. Lukas took a few deep breaths to calm his racing heart then headed inside.

Lukas was hit with a wall of heat. Despite the open door, the farmhouse was sickeningly hot. He wiped his sweaty forehead then headed to the bedroom. He still didn't hear anything. His heart beat faster.

As he got closer to his parents' room, he could hear voices, but they were quiet. The bedroom door was partially open. Through the gap, he saw Hans kneeling by Sarah's face as she laid on the bed. Szilvia was by the fire, her back to Hans. Isla was on Sarah's other side, wiping Sarah's face with a cloth. Lukas' hand trembled as he opened the door wider.

Isla was the first to spot him. He expected to see a smile light up her face, or at least a look of relief that the birth was over. But his cousin had never been good at hiding her emotions. Lukas could see the tear tracks on her cheeks.

Lukas fully stepped into the bedroom. The heat was even more oppressive. He slowly went over to the bed. When he looked at his mother, his heart nearly broke. She was so pale; he could see the veins in her arms and neck. He did his best to ignore the pungent scent of blood in the air. He watched her chest as she took one shaky breath at a time. Lukas clenched his hands into fists at his side.

Sarah opened her eyes and turned her head slightly to look at her son. "Lukas," she whispered, her voice raspy. "My sweet boy. I love you so much."

Lukas blinked as tears welled up in his eyes. "I love you, too Mama."

Sarah shook her head, the smile fading. "Promise me you'll look after your father. You'll need each other."

"We need you too, Mama." He knelt down beside his father, who he realized now had buried his head in his hands, sobs wracking his body.

Lukas took Sarah's hand in his. "*I* need you."

Sarah squeezed his hand, all her remaining strength in that tight embrace. "I won't be far. I'll be watching over you." She closed her eyes then loosened her grip on his hand.

A few more breaths, and Sarah died.

Hans moaned aloud when he realized his wife was gone. It was the sound that came from someone whose soul was being ripped from their body, a sound that no words could fully describe. He wrapped his dead wife in his arms and held her as he begged for her to come back.

"This wasn't supposed to happen!" Hans exclaimed.

Lukas got up and backed away from his father's grief. A chill came over his body and he sought out the fire. It was then that he remembered the baby.

Szilvia had cleaned up the blood and other fluids from the newborn and wrapped it in a clean blanket. She turned to face Lukas as he came up beside them. Isla went to Lukas' other side.

"A boy?" Lukas asked, his voice thick with tears. As he stared at his little brother, he realized the baby wasn't breathing. He met Szilvia's stare. "Dead?" he whispered, horrified.

Szilvia nodded, tears running down her cheeks. "Stillborn. There was nothing we could do." She swallowed. "She named him Adam."

"Adam," Lukas repeated. He stared at his brother's dark, curly hair and pale skin. His eyes were shut, and would never open. Lukas wanted to scream.

All of this, for what? Mama, dead. The baby, dead. He clenched his hands into fists. His eyes welled up with tears. What was he supposed to do now?

"I'm so sorry, Lukas," Isla said, her arms folded over her chest. She came over to the fireplace and stood beside him. Lukas noticed from the knees down, her dress was covered in blood and other liquids Lukas didn't want to think about.

"What happened?" he asked, his voice thick with tears.

Szilvia shook her head. "The ba—Adam was coming out backwards. I flipped him, but he never took a breath. Once he was out, your mother lost too much blood. There was nothing I could do." She wiped a tear. "I'm sorry, Lukas."

Lukas squeezed Szilvia's shoulder. "You did everything you could, just as you said. It's not your fault."

"It's all so unfair," Isla muttered. "I can't understand why God would—"

"Don't talk about God," Lukas growled, surprised by his own anger. "God wouldn't allow this to happen, not if He cared."

Szilvia took Lukas' hand from her shoulder and guided him to the door. "Why don't you sit down for a bit? Eat something. Isla and I will tidy up."

"Shouldn't we send for the pastor?"

Isla's eyes watered again. "There's no rush."

Lukas looked to his father, who was still prostrate on the bed, weeping. "What about Papa?"

"I'll talk to him. He needs time," Isla said. She urged Lukas to the door. "Rest. We'll take care of it."

Lukas remembered the sheep had been left in the field. They would be fine for a few hours, but Lukas would have to get them before dark. He focused on putting one foot in front of the other.

He closed the front door firmly. He turned around to see Hans head straight for that very door.

"Where are you going, Papa?"

"To the fields," Hans answered gruffly, his back to his son.

"But what about Mama and Adam? Don't you want to be here when the pastor comes?"

Hans stopped at the door, his hand on the rusting handle, then looked back at Lukas. He had never seen his father look so sad.

"I can't, Lukas. I just can't." Hans' voice cracked on the last word. Without waiting for a response, he left the house, slamming the door behind him.

Lukas stared at where his father once stood, unsure what to do. He thought of his mother, dead in her bed, his baby brother, cold and pale and dead too, and his father, running as far as he could from the farm. Lukas blinked away tears as his heart constricted.

Now what?

$$\sim 4 \sim$$

ISLA

Here lies Sarah Baláž, loving wife and mother, with son Adam Baláž. Cherished beyond measure.

Isla read her aunt and cousin's shared tombstone for the seventh time as she waited for her mother to finish receiving condolences from the villagers. Dressed head to toe in black, Greta looked the perfect image of a grieving sister-in-law. Isla remembered the countless hours her mother had spent criticizing Sarah's management of the farm, her parenting style, and a long list of other things Greta thought she could do better. Isla was amazed at how quickly her mother could find no fault in death, with a sister-in-law she had lectured constantly in life.

Greta sighed heavily as the wind picked up in the church's graveyard. "She was a wonderful woman. And to lose the baby, too! I can't imagine what Lukas will do without her."

Isla narrowed her eyes, staring harder at the tombstone. She knew that tone. Her mother was scheming, and Isla wanted to be far away before Greta's plans reached her.

No doubt they'll involve me. Any excuse to get me away from Erik, Szilvia, and Constance.

Isla still couldn't believe her aunt and baby cousin were dead. She went to sleep remembering the day of Adam's birth and always woke up in a cold sweat. So much had happened in such a short time. It didn't feel real.

Turning Adam had been the easy part. Szilvia really had done everything right – Isla had watched Constance do it enough times to know no step was missed. But Isla did wonder if the girls had missed something *else*. She just couldn't believe that her aunt would bleed out for no reason, other than "it happens." When Constance had said that with a sad shake of her head, Isla had wanted to throw something.

It's not fair.

By the time Szilvia and Isla could address the bleeding, the blood had already soaked the sheet through, getting down into the mattress. Isla remembered trying to soak up the blood with whatever rag she could, but it wasn't enough. She had prayed and prayed Lukas would come back in time. That was the only prayer God heard that day.

Isla shook her head, forcing herself back to the present. The wind picked up again, sending a shiver down Isla's spine. Her thin, dark grey dress was meant for boiling herbs, not solemn ceremonies, but it was the best Isla could do on short notice. Only a few days had passed since Sarah's death, and Greta had wasted no time making the arrangements. For once, Isla was grateful for her mother. Left without his mother, and with Hans nowhere to be seen, Lukas was in no shape to plan the funeral.

Hans had returned with the sheep the day after Sarah's death, but he hadn't stayed long. He packed a bag, then left again for the fields. Isla had stayed the night and she had heard Lukas and his father arguing about Hans' plan.

"The sheep can wait! I need you here. I can't run this place by myself!"

Isla hadn't made out Hans' reply, but she did hear the front door slam again.

Hans hadn't returned for the funeral.

Isla looked up from the gravesite and saw Lukas nearby. He was talking with the village baker and his family. His shoulders were hunched and from what she could see, his hands were shoved deep in his pockets. It looked as though he was barely holding himself together. Not that she could blame him. The baker's wife offered him a basket of fresh bread and rolls. These weren't the only gifts for the family, but Isla suspected they would be eaten the quickest. Her stomach gurgled faintly.

Szilvia came to her side and weaved her arm through Isla's.

"It was a lovely service," Szilvia said quietly. "You can tell how loved Sarah was."

Isla nodded. "She was the kindest woman I knew." She glanced at her mother. "When I was little, sometimes I used to wish she was my mother."

Isla swallowed hard . She knew it was an ungrateful thought but growing up with Greta had been trying at the best of times. Isla used to go for frequent sleepovers at Lukas' home for years, before she became brave enough to ask Constance. Sarah always seemed to know just what to say to make Isla feel better – a trait Greta had never had.

Szilvia squeezed Isla's arm. "Would you like to come over for tea?"

"I can't. Mama needs to discuss something with me," Isla said with a heavy sigh. "I can only imagine what."

Szilvia nodded. "Mama and I will leave the door unlocked, just in case." She kissed her friend's cheek then left, heading back for home, where Constance waited. She had had too many patients to come to the service, but she had sent Szilvia along with some tonics to put in their tea, ones especially good for tiredness and anxiety.

Greta came over to her daughter, her black cloak wrapped tightly around her shoulders. "Come, Isla. We must head home. Your father has already left with the guests' gifts." She waved Lukas over.

Isla dutifully followed her mother, falling into step beside Lukas. The basket of bread swung at his side. Isla looped her arm through his and squeezed. He glanced at her, tears in his eyes. By the time they reached the townhouse, Isla took the basket from him and put it on the kitchen table. She steered him towards the main fireplace and sat him down on the couch. Greta went over to the stove to boil a kettle for tea. While her mother was distracted, Isla took his hands in hers.

"What do you need?" she asked quietly.

"Nothing." He shook his head, running a hand through his tangled hair. She suspected he hadn't brushed it that morning. "Nothing you can do, anyway."

The kettle whistled. Isla knew time was running out. "We can slip out the backdoor. Whatever she has to say can wait another day."

Lukas smirked, the first thing that looked like a smile in days. "The last thing I need is her angry with me."

Isla would have said more, but Greta came over with a tray in hand. She balanced four mugs and a steaming kettle atop it. Isla stepped away from the couch, giving her mother space to place the tray on the short table in front of it. Greta said nothing as she passed around the mugs. Her father's mug lay unclaimed on the tray. Isla wondered what was taking her papa so long with the gifts.

Perhaps he wants to avoid this as much as I do.

Isla settled beside Lukas, the plush couch offering comfort to her tired body. She hadn't slept well these last few days, and she suspected neither had Lukas. The dark circles under his eyes hid little.

"Well?" Isla said, the silence unnerving her.

Greta stood by the fireplace, leaning her tall frame against the mantle. The flames cast shadows across her face, highlighting the wrinkles starting to spread across her forehead and cheeks.

"I thought he would come," Greta said quietly, almost to herself.

Isla raised an eyebrow. "Who, Mama?"

Greta shook her head and turned away from the flames. "Never mind." She took a long sip of tea. She faced Lukas. "Did your father give any indication when he would come back?"

Lukas shook his head. He stared at the mug, avoiding Greta's gaze.

"We'll need to find some help for the farm, then. You can't manage it all by yourself. Until my brother comes to his senses, we'll have to do our best to keep the place running. Or you could just stay here."

Isla glanced at Lukas. He rubbed a hand over his face. "And what would we do with the farm if I did stay?"

"Sell it."

"Out from under Uncle Hans' nose? Could you even do that?" Isla asked. She hated to think of the farm being sold, but she understood if Lukas didn't want to carry the burden of the farm on his shoulders. *He's barely older than me.*

"I appreciate the concern, but I'm not selling the farm. Papa would never forgive me if I did," said Lukas.

Greta scoffed. "His forgiveness is the last thing you should be worrying about. If anything, he should be begging for your forgiveness. To leave you after losing your mother . . ." Greta shook her head. "He's running away, as he always does. It's not up to you to manage his affairs."

Lukas met Greta's stare. The anger in his eyes sent a shiver down Isla's spine. "Mama would want me to keep the farm. I'll see if I can find help, but I won't hear talk of selling it. We have to at least give Papa time to come back."

Isla placed her hand on Lukas' arm as she looked at her mother.

"I can help. Until Uncle Hans comes home."

Greta sighed. "That could be weeks, Isla. You can't stay there and miss your training. You know what Constance would say."

"I'll make it work. At least let me go for a few days. I'll talk to Constance. Perhaps we can come up with a different arrangement."

"If you're serious about this healing business—"

"Mama, I don't want to argue right now," Isla snapped. She and Greta had fought enough about Isla's decision to become a healer. She grabbed Lukas' hand. "Can I go or not?"

Greta didn't say anything for a moment then sighed. "Fine. One week, then we must come up with a new plan. A long term one," she said, staring at Lukas at the end.

Lukas nodded as he stood. He finished the last of his tea, placing the empty mug on the tray. "I'll bring the cot out from storage. It'll be warm in front of the fire. See you tonight?" he asked as he looked back at Isla.

She nodded, flashing him a confident smile. "It'll be like old times, when we used to have sleepovers."

Lukas smiled, but it didn't reach his eyes. He kissed Greta goodbye then left.

Greta crossed her arms as she stared at her daughter still sitting on the couch. "I don't know what your plan is, but you had better be on your best behaviour at the farm. Lukas thinks he can manage on his own, but he's grieving. He doesn't know what he needs. We must be the voice of reason."

"We? Don't you mean you?"

Greta shook her head. "Don't start with me, Isla. It's been a long day. Now, promise me you won't have Erik over while you're with Lukas. *Promise.*"

Isla blushed. "You think I offered my help just so I could spend time with Erik without a chaperone?" She got off the couch. "If I wanted to see Erik, I would just go to the castle." She brushed past her mother, her anger curling in her belly like a snake.

"You know how I feel about him, Isla!" Greta called as Isla stomped across the spacious room to the door separating her room from the main area of the house.

Isla slammed the door in response.

Once safe in her room, she sighed. She had left the window open, the thick curtains blowing in the breeze. She closed the window then went to her dresser, pulling out enough clothes to last a week. She doubted Hans would be back in a few days like Lukas hoped. Secretly, she knew Greta was right. But she wasn't about to give her mother the satisfaction of taking her side. At least if she was at the farm, she could help Lukas come up with a plan to save his childhood home. Or find a way to stall Greta.

Isla's bedroom had white-washed walls and sprigs of rosemary, thyme, lavender, and a few other plants hanging from the ceiling. As they dried, they filled her room with calming scents, exactly what she needed when she and Greta fought.

Her bed was to the right of the window against the wall, a side table underneath the window, and a large rug covered most of the hardwood floor. She had weaved it herself when she was twelve, and although it was starting to come apart, she didn't want to get rid of it just yet.

Inside her dresser, she pulled out a small wooden box where she kept her few precious items, including letters from Erik. Isla suspected her mother went through her room every few months. Greta hadn't found the letters yet, but the last thing she needed was to come home and find Erik's treasured words burning in the fireplace.

I'll have to send a message to him when I'm at Lukas'. He should be back before I'm home.

As she tied the string of her bag shut, there came a knock at her bedroom door. It sounded too heavy to be her mother's rapping.

"Come in!"

Greta's father Jacob stuck his head in. "Ready to go?"

Isla raised an eyebrow. "Are you coming with me?"

Jacob shrugged, his wide shoulders stiff from his years in the mines. "I could use the walk. And I thought I could check on the fences while I'm there. Your uncle mentioned something about a broken board or two a week ago. I can't remember where it is, but I'm sure I'll find it."

Isla shook her head. "I'm a big girl, you know. I can walk myself."

Jacob stepped fully inside his daughter's room. He had to duck to fit through the doorway. His height hadn't helped him in the mines, but he was one of the few men in the village taller than Greta. Isla secretly suspected that was one the reasons Greta chose to marry Jacob. He took Isla's bag from her and kissed her forehead.

"You'll always be my little girl. Now come along, before it gets dark."

Isla didn't say goodbye to Greta on her way out. Jacob didn't say anything about it. He had learned years ago not to get in the middle of their arguments.

As they made their way to Hans' farm, Isla felt a tingling sensation working its way up her back. She shook her head, thinking it was the wind, but the breeze had quieted to the point where Isla barely felt it. The tingling continued, sinking down her shoulders towards her hands. Isla licked her lips, feeling more unsettled with each step. Usually, she only got this feeling when she came across a plant she needed for a tonic, but even then, it usually wasn't this intense.

When they passed the woods where her grandfather used to live, Isla stopped in her tracks. The branches waved at her, and she could swear she heard something.

Come play, come play! a voice called.

Isla took a deep breath, but it caught in her chest. She had heard that voice, once. Long ago. She shook her head, unsure if she was imagining things.

Come, come! the voice said again. *Come play!*

Jacob stopped several feet from his daughter. "Isla? What is it?"

"I don't know," she muttered. "I thought . . . I thought I heard something." She looked at her father. "Do you hear it?"

Jacob came to Isla's side. He squinted at the treeline not far from them. After a moment, he shook his head.

"Can't say I do. Must be the wind." He looped his arm through hers, leading her away from the woods.

"That place has always left me unsettled, myself. Never feels right going by it," said Jacob. "Don't tell your mama this, but whenever we went to visit your grandfather there, which wasn't often – you know how your mother feels about the woods – I always felt as if I was being watched." He shook his head. "I still find it hard to believe your mother and uncle were lost there. I never would have found my way out."

Isla remembered the scant details her mother had shared with her about getting lost in the woods when Greta and Hans were little. She had tried to ask her mother about it a few years ago, but was met with a glare so dark Isla never asked again.

She looked behind them, staring at the trees that seemed to call her.

"I suppose their guardian angel was watching over them," she said quietly.

Jacob nodded. "Must have been. Come along, we'll be there soon. Maybe you can make your famous stew for supper. Lukas needs good home cooking right now."

Isla nodded, still focused on the voice. She shook her head a little then faced the path leading to Hans' farm.

I had a name, once.

No one remembers it now, but sometimes I can hear it whispered among the cinders in the oven that hasn't been lit in decades.

It taunts me.

Once upon a time, I had a life. These woods were my home; these villagers were my neighbours, my friends. They've forgotten now, but I don't. I can't forget.

Trapped in this house, surrounded by the memories, all I think about are them. A little boy and girl, lost in the woods. Searching for something. For food. For home.

For hope.

I took them in, made them think I was their saviour. A guardian angel.

They never knew they were walking into the devil's house until it was too late.

Then again, I hadn't either.

Hans and Greta. Gretel and Hansel. Pushed the witch into the oven. Ran away. End scene.

But that's not the end. It wasn't thirty years ago, and it isn't now. They think they're safe from me, from what I can do. But they'll find out how wrong they are.

I haven't forgotten the promise of their flesh, baked in a pie, or stuffed like a turkey. I haven't forgotten what I am owed. And soon, they'll remember. Soon, they'll come to play.

I'll make sure of it.

~ 5 ~

LUKAS

Lukas sat on his front porch, an untouched block of wood in hand. He gripped his carving knife loosely in the other. He had grabbed the wood from the scrap pile with every intention of losing himself in his favourite pastime until it was time for evening chores, but now that he was here, all Lukas could think about was the bear he had been working on the day his mother died.

Inside the house was a mess of dirty dishes, piles of sweaty clothes, and the faint aroma of burnt bread. Lukas had tried to make a loaf, but he got distracted by memories and almost set the house on fire. He had left the house soon after, and now he was here, on the porch, wondering how it all could have gone so horribly wrong. One minute, he had a mother, a father, and a baby brother on the way. Now, he was alone on the farm, the animals and Isla as his only company. Some days he wished Isla wasn't there. She meant well, but she fussed almost as badly as Greta did. It was another reason he was on the porch. At least out here, he wouldn't bother her as she tidied up Lukas' mess.

Lukas ran a hand over his face, forcing himself to take a deep breath. He stared at the horizon, wishing for the two hundredth time that Hans would appear over the crest of the hill. Hans would be able to keep his sister from selling the farm. He would put to rights what had been left in chaos after Sarah's death.

But he isn't here. It's just me. Lukas had to figure something out. He just wasn't sure how to make things right.

Lukas glanced behind him at the kitchen window. Isla breezed past the window, her hair held back by a kerchief. He could just catch a glimpse of the handle of Sarah's woven laundry basket as Isla carried it. His heart clenched. So many pieces of his mother were hidden in the house. He could barely stand to spend any time inside.

He forced his gaze away from the farmhouse across the field towards his closest neighbours, Miriam's aunt and uncle. Lukas could faintly make out the people working the field. He wondered if Miriam was there, or if she was inside with her aunt preparing a late meal for the farmhands. Hans had only ever had help during harvest, but Lukas knew from what he overheard on market days that Miriam's uncle could afford to keep workers year-round to help manage his large cattle herd, his flock of sheep, and the various crops planted on his property. Lukas envied his neighbours.

What I wouldn't give for a few extra pairs of hands.

Lukas looked away from his neighbours and stared at the horizon. He wondered where Hans was sleeping that night. Lukas swallowed. He still couldn't believe his father hadn't come to the funeral. What would Sarah have said? Lukas shook his head.

He must come home sometime. He can't stay away forever.

If Hans didn't return, Lukas knew he couldn't hold Greta off. Part of him wanted to let Greta take over; that would teach Hans not to run away. But Lukas knew who Hans would blame if there was no farm to come home to. He had left Lukas in charge for a reason.

The front door slammed shut behind him. Lukas startled, dropping the block of wood as Isla's light steps came up to him. She settled beside him on the front step, her arms wrapped around her knees to keep the light breeze from blowing her skirt. She followed his gaze.

"Watching for him?" she asked.

Lukas sighed. "I keep thinking if I stare a little harder, he'll show up."

"He'll come back, Lukas." She placed her hand on his arm and squeezed. "We'll figure something out until then."

"I don't know what I'm going to do if he doesn't show up for the harvest. It's already starting to get colder."

"I could stay longer."

Lukas shook his head. "Constance wouldn't like it, and neither would Aunt Greta."

Isla smirked. "Since when do I care if my mother approves of something?"

"Well, in this case you should care. I don't want to burden you with all this," he said, waving his hands around the farm.

"You shouldn't be burdened with this either," she pointed out.

Lukas shook his head. "I don't want to talk about this right now." He got to his feet and put his knife in its sheath that hung from his belt. "I'm going to put the animals in for the night." He left before Isla had a chance to reply.

It didn't take long to get the horses and cow settled for the night. The chickens were a bit rowdier, but he managed to lure them in with feed. He dawdled longer than he needed to, mostly to avoid Isla, but also because the night air helped calm him. Since Sarah's death, he'd had trouble sleeping. If nightmares didn't wake him up, he couldn't fall asleep at all. He could tell Isla and she would make up a tonic for him, but he didn't want to become reliant on herbs to sleep. It didn't sit well with him. Yet he knew it was going to start affecting him soon. It was taking all his strength to put one foot in front of the other.

The sun had just finished setting when Lukas went inside. He found Isla finishing the last of the dishes. He grabbed a towel and picked up one of the clean plates from supper.

"You could have left those for me," he said quietly.

"I don't mind. I think I found all your hiding places for your dirty clothes. I've got the basket ready to do tomorrow."

Lukas nodded. "The clothing line is still outside. It should still be hot enough to dry them. I can bring in some water to boil, too."

"Thanks, I wasn't looking forward to hauling it in myself," she said with a chuckle.

They finished washing and drying the dishes in silence. Isla dumped the dirty water out the window, leaving the empty bucket to dry inside. Lukas hung the damp towel to dry. Before Isla could walk around him, he hugged her tight.

"I'm sorry for earlier. It's just . . . a lot right now."

Isla gave him a squeeze before stepping back. "I'm sorry, too. I shouldn't push."

"We can talk about it tomorrow. Maybe I'll have a clearer head then." He doubted he would, but he knew it made Isla feel better to have a plan of attack. "Goodnight, Isla," he said as he went to the ladder that led to his bed.

"Goodnight, Lukas. Sleep well."

He didn't light the candle beside his bed. He tossed his shirt and trousers across the loft and heard them hit the wooden floor. Isla had indeed found one of his stashes of dirty clothes. He fumbled in the dark for his longer sleeping shirt and softer trousers. Once dressed in his night clothes, he settled on his mattress, the divots familiar to him after years of sleeping upstairs. Exhaustion caught up to him, for he was asleep even before memories of his mother could crowd his thoughts.

A pounding on the front door woke Lukas from his dead sleep. He bolted up, his heart pounding. He glanced across the loft and saw the fireplace was still lit. It couldn't have been that long since he and Isla had gone to bed. He heard Isla get up from her cot to answer whoever was calling so late.

Could it be Papa? Lukas shook his head. Hans wouldn't have knocked to come into his own house.

Lukas sighed as he rolled out of bed, careful not to wander over the edge of the loft. He had almost done that quite a few times growing up. Lukas ran a hand through his messy curls then climbed down the ladder.

". . . missing since midday. We need everyone we can get to find them," a man, whose voice Lukas didn't recognize, said.

"Of course. Their parents must be terrified. I'll grab my coat," said Isla.

When she turned from the front door, she met Lukas' gaze.

"What's happened?" he asked, his voice still groggy with sleep.

Isla went to the peg on the wall where she had hung her coat earlier. "Hans and Frida Szabó are missing."

Lukas vaguely recognized the names. The Szabó family ran the mill not far from the village. At eight, Frida was the elder of the two siblings. Hans, called Hansel by everyone like Lukas' father once was, was five and notoriously afraid of the dark. Lukas couldn't imagine the two children would willingly stay out past sunset. Nor, he imagined, did their parents.

"I'll come," Lukas said. "They can't be far."

"No, Lukas. You should stay. You need to rest."

Lukas stepped off the last rung of the ladder, wondering where he left his coat. "You do, too."

Isla went to her cousin, shaking her head. She placed her hands on his shoulders. "You're exhausted, Lukas. I can't let you go wandering around in the woods. Mama would kill me if something happened to you."

Lukas glared at her. "Greta would kill *you* if she found out you were in there, too," he pointed out. After staring at each other for a moment, Lukas gave up with a sigh. "Fine. But if you're not back in a few hours, I'm coming to help."

Isla nodded then gently shoved him back towards the ladder. "I'll be back before you know it." She followed the man, who Lukas now saw was the children's uncle Uram Balog, out into the night.

Lukas glanced back at his loft then to the kitchen. He didn't want to climb up there again, only to toss and turn until Isla returned. He went to the couch, grabbed a quilt Sarah had made a decade ago, and laid on his back, staring at the ceiling.

He had almost dozed off when another knock at the door drew Lukas from his sleep. He got up and went to see who it was. He expected to see another relative of the Szabós asking for help with the search, not Szilvia and Erik on his porch. His eyes widened.

"What are you two doing out this late?"

"Is Isla here?" Szilvia asked. "She wasn't home."

"She's staying for a few days, but right now she's helping search for the Szabó children." Lukas then looked to Erik. "When did you get back?"

"Around suppertime," Erik replied, his chocolate brown corkscrew curls tucked underneath his cap. His dark, almost black skin, glistened with sweat, as if he had been running. "Isla wasn't at home, and she wasn't at Szilvia's, so we thought she might be here. What's this about the Szabó family? Little Frida and Hansel?"

"They're missing. Isla went to help when their uncle came here to ask for help searching." He glanced at the clock. It was after two o'clock in the morning. "I thought she would be back by now."

Szilvia stepped around Lukas and hung her cloak on the nearest peg. "I'll stay here and wait in case she comes back. You two should go look for her, and the children. Isla shouldn't have left. The woods aren't safe this late."

"What about Constance? Won't she worry?" Lukas asked, already getting his coat and a lantern.

"I told her we would spend the night here if we didn't find Isla," Szilvia said.

Erik raised his already lit lantern. "Let's go, then. They have to be out there somewhere."

The two men left the farmhouse and headed into the woods in silence. Besides the occasional snapping of twigs, the night was eerily quiet. They had just reached the edge of the treeline when Erik placed his hand on Lukas' shoulder.

"I'm sorry about your mother and brother. She was a wonderful woman." He shook his head. "And I'm sorry I missed the funeral. Isaiah was hosting dignitaries sent over by his father and—"

Lukas shook his head. The last person he wanted to think about right now was Isaiah. "Thanks, Erik. And don't worry about the funeral. I know you're busy."

"Isaiah passes along his condolences as well," Erik added.

Lukas glared at the ground, sidestepping a large rock in his way. "I'm surprised the young lord remembered her."

Erik sighed. "Don't be like that. You know Sarah was like a mother to all of us." He shook his head. "Isaiah may act like he didn't spend his childhood with us, but he does care. It's complicated."

Lukas snorted. "Someday I'll have to remind myself to care enough to ask him for an explanation." He would have said more, but something felt . . . off. He glanced around him, scanning the trees and brush for anything unusual, but found nothing to explain the shiver running down his spine.

Erik gave himself a shake, the lamplight flickering against the leaves. "I hate this place. I always hated when you and Isla used to try to drag us here to play."

"It wasn't so scary back then." Until that night, Lukas had never been afraid to go into the woods. His grandfather lived there, and in his mind, his grandfather was the wisest person Lukas knew, so if he wasn't scared, why should Lukas be?

Although right now, I'm beginning to understand what Erik and the other villagers mean. Lukas couldn't shake the feeling that someone was watching him.

Erik pointed ahead. "I see lanterns. Maybe they found the children."

Lukas and Erik picked up the pace, jogging down the path and avoiding as many branches as possible. By the time they caught up with the lanterns, the men were in a small clearing in the woods. It was only large enough for a handful of people to fit, but it was packed with villagers all talking at once.

". . . are they dead?"

"I swear I checked here."

"Me, too."

"Magic, perhaps."

"Sorcery, more like it." Lukas heard the wet splat of spit hitting the ground.

Lukas and Erik pushed their way forward until they found what everyone was staring at.

Amongst the grass lay Frida and her brother Hansel, still and silent as statues. Lukas' stomach dropped, fearing the worst, but then he saw Frida's chest rise and fall.

"Are they . . . asleep?" Erik whispered.

Lukas shrugged. "A deep sleep." He almost envied them.

"Let go of me! I've done nothing wrong!"

Lukas looked to where the shout came from and saw Isla kneeling by the children. Two men had one of her arms and were trying to pull her up.

"I told you, I just found them. Let go!" she said.

"What's the meaning of this?" Erik exclaimed. He tried to get between Isla and the men, but a few others from the village kept him back. He glared at the men, his gaze sharp as a knife. "What's she done?"

"We checked this area half a dozen times and the children weren't here. She comes strolling by and suddenly they're here, but no one can wake them," said Graham Molnár, a member of the village Council and owner of the local tavern. He had Isla's left arm in his grip. "I have questions, as will the rest of the Council, no doubt."

"It's dark enough to miss your hand in front of your face. Perhaps you walked by them," Lukas said as he joined Erik and Isla.

"Even if that were the case, why won't they wake up?" Baldwin Varga, another councillor, asked.

"Perhaps they're sick," said Erik. "They could have fallen ill and that's why they didn't return home."

"That's what I was trying to check before *you* all arrived," Isla said as she glared at the two councillors.

"Be that as it may, I'd like for you to come with us to answer some questions," said Councillor Molnár.

"Do I have a choice?"

Councillor Varga tightened his grip on Isla's arm, causing her to wince.

"You can't hold a meeting without representation from the Chief Steward," Erik pointed out. "His household must be notified."

Councillor Molnár nodded. "Rest assured, a messenger will be sent."

Lukas inwardly groaned. The last thing they needed was Isaiah stepping in.

He was sure Erik would have punched the Councillor had Lukas not grabbed Erik by the arm, forcing him to stay put. "Is she under arrest?" Lukas asked.

"No," Councillor Varga admitted. "Just questioning."

Lukas looked to Isla then went to her side. He leaned close to her ear. "Go with them. Erik and I will follow," he whispered.

Isla huffed then agreed. "I'll come. But I don't need to be walked out like a prisoner."

The councillors let go of her arms then called forward volunteers to bring the children with them. As the group made their way out of the woods, Lukas and Erik were forced further and further away from Isla. Lukas fell behind, sleep deprivation catching up with him. Erik urged Lukas to go home.

"I'll stay with her. When she's released, we'll come to the farmhouse."

Lukas nodded. "Send word to her parents."

Erik winced. "Greta will be furious when she finds out."

Lukas turned left when the others turned right. He watched for a moment, keeping a steady gaze on Isla's blonde head as she left the woods surrounded by councillors and other villagers. His stomach twisted into a knot.

Stay safe, Isla.

Lukas turned away from the villagers and headed for home, his heart ramming against his ribs.

~ 6 ~

ISLA

The quiet of the woods settled into Isla's bones, forcing her to take deep breaths to steady her pounding heart. As she heard the villagers calling out for the Szabó children, she wondered what had drawn them to this area shrouded in folklore and fables, a place that few outside of Isla's family dared to enter. For a moment, she wondered if Frida and her brother had heard the same voice calling them to play, as Isla had only hours ago. She shook her head. She wasn't even sure if there really *was* a voice.

Isla lifted her lantern higher, calling out for the children again. She had been searching with the others for over an hour. Her boots pinched her toes, and she was beginning to wish for the toasty fireplace waiting for her at Lukas' farm.

Perhaps I should have let Lukas come in my place. He likely needs the distraction.

No, it was best that she had come. Lukas looked like he could have fallen asleep standing up. The last thing she wanted to do was explain to Hans and her mother how she lost Lukas to exhaustion and whatever nocturnal creature stumbled upon him.

"Hansel! Frida!" Isla called again as she reached the edge of what looked to be a clearing. She stepped onto the trampled grass and was thrust back to her childhood. She remembered playing tag with Lukas here. Greta hadn't been pleased when Isla came home with grass stains on her new dress, but that wasn't the first time Isla had ruined an outfit, and as Greta would come to dread, it wouldn't be the last.

Isla opened her mouth to call for the children again when she paused. The hair on the back of her neck stood on end. The wind picked up, blowing her skirts from side to side. Isla turned her head, looking around the clearing.

Someone's watching. And it wasn't someone from the search party.

"Hello! Hansel? Frida? Is that you?"

Isla took a step forward.

Come play, come play!

She paused mid-step; her breath caught in her throat. The voice was just as clear and haunting as before. Isla couldn't tell where it was coming from. She moved further into the clearing, and gasped when her foot landed not on grass, but on fabric. She looked down and saw the missing children lying on the forest floor. Their hands were clasped over their chests, their hair neatly arranged so not a lock was out of place. Their clothes looked freshly washed and their shoes weren't even scuffed.

Isla got down on her hands and knees. "Hansel! Frida! Wake up. It's time to go home." She shook their bodies as gently as she could, but they didn't stir. She shook them harder; still nothing.

Perhaps they're ill. Maybe they have a fever and collapsed. That's why they didn't go home.

Isla felt their foreheads, but she found no trace of a fever. She examined their arms and legs, hands and feet. Nothing seemed injured or out of place. She would have done a further examination, had the villagers not arrived. She tried to explain what she was doing, but the men wouldn't listen, least of all Councillors Varga and Molnár.

"We checked this area already. How did you find them?" Molnár asked.

"I used to play here as a child. I know the area well enough to think of where children would like to hide."

Varga narrowed his eyes. "You're coming back to the village with us. The other Councillors will have questions, as do I."

He reached down and grabbed her arm.

"Let go of me! I've done nothing wrong!"

If Isla hadn't spotted Lukas and Erik, she wasn't sure what she would have done. She knew Lukas was right when he told her to go with them, but she hated being carted out of the woods like a prisoner. She had grown up around most of the men in the search party. They seemed like decent folk on the surface, but as they muttered under their breath about witchcraft and magic, she wasn't sure what awaited her in the village.

She felt Erik's gaze on her as she left the woods with the others. This certainly wasn't how she had wanted to greet him after their time apart, but she didn't have much of a choice.

Come play, come play!

Isla nearly tripped. She looked to the men closest to her, but neither of them reacted to the voice. Isla gulped.

Am I going mad?

She stuck closer to the men, wiping her clammy palms on her skirt. Isla hoped these "questions" were quick. She could certainly use a warm drink to calm her nerves.

~*~

"Did you see anything strange where the children were found?" Councillor Tóth asked, his glasses perched on his wide nose.

"No, but I didn't have time to look before the others arrived. I had only been there a few minutes."

"And you say you just stumbled upon them? By chance?"

"Yes, I used to play in the woods when I was a child. I didn't know if they would be there, but I thought I should check."

"No one told you it had already been searched?" Tóth asked.

"No, but even if they had, I still would have looked. The children could have gone there when the others left."

Councillor Varga cleared his throat. It echoed in the council room, its arched ceilings catching the sound and spreading it to each corner. Isla fidgeted in her seat in the centre of the chilly room. The councillors were behind a massive wooden table facing her.

"You say you played in the woods when you were little. Do you go there often now?" Varga asked.

Isla shook her head. "I'm kept busy with my work as a healer. I'm still training. I don't have time for play." *And even if I did go there, I wouldn't tell you.* Varga hadn't stopped staring at her since he put her in this chair an hour ago. The representative from the Chief Steward's house had yet to arrive. She wished the council would just let her leave.

"But to get to the healer's you have to go past the woods, don't you?" Varga asked.

"I can, but I often don't. It's the long way, and I'm usually in a hurry."

"When you have gone past the woods, have you seen or heard anything strange?" Councillor Molnár asked.

Isla narrowed her eyes. "What does this have to do with the Szabó children?"

"Merely curious, young lady. Merely curious. You are the daughter of Greta Kis, aren't you?" Councillor Horváth said.

"Yes, but—"

"She certainly is, and I can't imagine you don't already know that, Petr, since you were at her christening," Greta said as she flung open the council room doors. Her hair was pinned back in a messy bun and as she marched towards the men, Isla could see the shadows under Greta's eyes.

Greta glared at the councillors. "Just what are you doing questioning my daughter at three o'clock in the morning without a parent present? Has she committed some sort of crime?"

Councillor Horváth blushed. "No, she's not under arrest. She found the Szabó children and we just had some questions—"

"A fine way to thank the girl who did what you couldn't do!" Greta interrupted. "You should be thanking her instead of interrogating her."

Greta took Isla's arm in hand and pulled her up. "Come along, dear. We're leaving."

Councillor Varga stood. "Just a moment, ladies. I still have questions—"

"You can ask them tomorrow. I'm taking my daughter home."

"But the Chief Steward—" Councillor Horáth protested.

As if on cue, Isaiah entered the council room from the back entrance, where the servants usually brought refreshments. There were no servants awake at this hour, despite all the noise the councillors were making. Isla met Isaiah's cold gaze and frowned. He hadn't changed much in the last year since she last had the misfortune of speaking to him. She hadn't spoken to Erik for two days after he had arranged *that* meeting.

Isaiah stood with his hands clasped behind his back, helping to broaden his slender shoulders and make him appear taller than he really was. He had the disadvantage of inheriting his mother's short height and his father's large ears. She noticed he still kept his light brown curls loose to hide his ears. As much as they could be hidden. His grey eyes left Isla and he stared at the councillors, all men twice his age.

"Whatever did you have me dragged out of bed for at this time of night?" His crisp voice rang out in the large room, causing Isla to wince. She wished she could just leave.

The councillors began to explain all at once, but he ignored them. He went over to Isla and her mother. Greta bobbed a quick curtsey. Isla did not. She met her once-best friend's stare and tilted her chin down. He did the same.

"What did you do now, Isla?" he asked, quieter than before.

"Rescued some children lost in the woods. The usual," she said lightly, trying to keep the venom from her words. Once, it would have been so easy to slide back into their regular conversations. Once, she would have missed those days.

Isaiah smirked. "Ah, the Szabó children. I heard they were missing." He looked over his shoulder at the councillors, his dark cape rustling as he did so. "Go home. The children have been found. That's what matters."

"But my lord—" Councillor Varga started but was silenced when Isaiah raised his hand.

Goodness, he has gotten good at being a little lordling, hasn't he?

The councillors began to leave. Greta curtseyed again. "Thank you, my lord. May I take my daughter home now?"

"Of course. That order was for you, too." He smiled at Greta, and she smiled back. Isla remembered how polite Isaiah always was to her mother, and how much Greta appreciated his manners. She often complained about Isla's lacking in that area.

Just as Greta and Isla reached the front door, Isaiah's voice made Isla pause.

"Try to stay out of trouble, Isla. I don't like rescuing damsels in distress before dawn."

Isla's face flushed as she felt her body grow hot with rage. Before she could deliver a scathing retort, Greta grabbed her arm and practically dragged her out the door. It slammed shut behind them.

Once outside, Greta let out a deep sigh, her shoulders sagging. The early morning air bit into Isla's skin. She glanced up at her mother, who was staring down at her.

"Let's get you home. We'll talk once it's safe."

Isla wanted to ask so many things, but she was so angry and tired, she didn't know where to start. She followed Greta home, trying not to think about Isaiah and his stupid comments. Only once the front door was locked behind them and they were alone in the kitchen did Isla turn to Greta.

"How did you know I was there?"

Greta put the kettle on the stove and grabbed two cups for tea. She waved a hand towards the couch. "Your friend told me."

Isla raised an eyebrow. She turned to face the couch and saw Erik asleep on it. She smiled, her heart swelling with pride. She dashed over and gave him a quick kiss on the cheek before Greta could call her back. She sat down at the kitchen table as Greta prepared their tea. She propped her head up with one hand, blinking to stay awake. She had watched Greta prepare tea so many times, she could follow her mother's movements in her sleep. Greta was quite particular about her blends, making her own herself. There was always a hint of something Isla could never quite name. *Jasmine? Hazel?* It was on the tip of her tongue every time, but it changed ever so slightly with each cup that she was never sure.

"Why were they asking if I was your daughter? Most of them have known me since I was a baby."

Greta viciously stirred honey into her tea, the spoon threatening to crack the cup in half. "They were hoping you would say something incriminating, like you dance with demons and conspire with witches, or whatever nonsense men believe when they don't trust a woman." Greta went to the table and slid Isla's cup to her. She sat down across from her daughter and stared at her cup.

"Ever since Hans and I came back from the woods, no one has really trusted us. I had hoped people, least of all the councillors we trust to run our village, would see that nothing bad had followed us out of the woods. But that's wishful thinking, I suppose," she said then took a sip of her tea. Greta looked at Isla. "If they come tomorrow, I'll go with you. I don't want you talking to them alone."

"But I didn't do anything wrong!"

Greta shook her head. "You daft girl, don't you see? It doesn't matter if you *did* anything, it only matters if they *think* you did. I'm sure they're already thinking of people they can convince to say they saw you place the children in that clearing."

Isla's eyes widened. "You mean they want to blame me for the Szabó children disappearing? But they just wandered off and are sick! I'm sure in a few days they'll be fine."

Greta stared at Isla. "Do you really believe that?"

Isla thought of the voice in the woods, the eeriness of the clearing, and the sleeping children.

"What do *you* think happened to them?" Isla asked.

Greta finished her tea. "It's none of my concern what happened to them, only what happens to you." She met her daughter's gaze. "We were lucky this time. I know Isaiah's father has his opinions of you, but the councillors listen to him. The least you could do is write him a thank you note."

Isla snorted. "The least I could do is not throttle him the next time I see him."

Greta got up and took Isla's empty cup. "Time for bed. If I know Petr Horváth, he'll have the rest of those old men up at the crack of dawn, just waiting to talk to you."

"But what about Lukas? I should go back to the farmhouse. He may need me."

"Szilvia is with him. He'll be fine until tomorrow."

Isla raised an eyebrow. Greta pointed to the couch again where Erik slept. "He had a wealth of information to share."

Isla smiled. "Sounds like you two actually got along for a few minutes."

"Don't push your luck, Isla. Off to bed with you, I mean it."

Isla went to her door then turned back to Greta, who was still at the kitchen table. "Can Erik stay for breakfast?"

Greta sighed. "I suppose he's earned it."

Isla went over and kissed Greta on the cheek. "Thank you, Mama. And not just about breakfast."

Greta surprised Isla with a hug. It was almost too tight of an embrace, but Isla didn't mind. "You're my daughter. I would do anything to protect you."

A few minutes later, Isla was in her room, curled up under the covers. As she closed her eyes, she thought of that voice again. Whose was it? Where was it coming from? And what, if anything, did it have to do with the Szabó children?

Isla buried her head against the pillow. As she drifted off to sleep, she could have sworn she heard the voice again, asking her to play.

Men rarely change; men with power never do.

Looking at these councillors, remembering their predecessors, makes me cackle as they scramble to figure out who to blame. Who can they find to take the fall for these sleeping children, so innocent, lost to the world of the living? At least temporarily.

I wanted Isla. I almost had her. I'll have to take comfort in the chaos the sleeping children have caused, for now.

Soon, she'll come knocking on my door, ready to avenge her mother, her mentor, herself. It doesn't matter. She'll be drawn to me like her mother was. Greta may deny it, but she would have made the perfect apprentice. A good little witch to carry on my legacy.

A legacy I will still have if I can get her to my cottage.

I wonder what kind of life I would have lived if the Council in my day hadn't knocked on the door of my village home, accusing me of poison, of conspiring with the devil, of being a heathen, of simply being a woman they couldn't control. Driven from my home in the dead of night, forced to carve a new life for myself in the woods, something inside me shifted. The magic I always felt underneath the surface, the thing that made my potions more potent, my remedies stronger, changed that night. It no longer wanted to help.

It wanted to destroy.

So these powerful men may have congratulated themselves on ridding themselves of me, but instead all they did was create a bigger problem. And they'll pay for it.

Soon.

~ 7 ~

LUKAS

Lukas carefully put one foot after the other on each rung of the ladder, his mind still blurry from sleep. The rooster's crows woke him from a dreamless sleep. At first, Lukas tried to go back to sleep, but the nagging thoughts of all the chores he had to get done kept him awake. That was when Lukas remembered Szilvia had spent the night on Isla's cot. He wondered if his cousin and Erik had returned as promised, or if she was still with the councillors. He couldn't imagine what questions they had that would take so long.

As he entered the kitchen, Lukas was greeted by the bright afternoon sunshine nearly blinding him through the window. He squinted, turning away from the light, and searched for something resembling food. Apparently the rooster had slept in, too.

"How long was I asleep?" he asked, covering his mouth as he yawned.

Szilvia turned away from the stove. "A while. You didn't miss lunch, though," she said with a grin. "I let the horses out to pasture. The cow I left in her pen."

"The chickens?" Lukas as he blinked.

"Fed and watered. And complaining about their lack of freedom. I didn't think it a good idea to let them out of their coop."

"I'll do that before I get started on my chores. Thank you for all this," he said, gesturing to the rabbit stew in the pot. His stomach rumbled in appreciation. He went to Szilvia and hugged her. "I really appreciate it."

When they were younger and Isaiah was still allowed to play with them, Isaiah used to tease Lukas about having a crush on Szilvia. He didn't know how to tell Isaiah that while Lukas may like Szilvia, Szilvia didn't like boys. Any boys, not just farm boys who smelt like sheep and cows.

That was years ago, though. Childhood crushes had long since been forgotten, placed on a shelf too high for Lukas to reach. He had other troubles on his mind, anyhow. Like where Isla was.

Szilvia smiled. "It's no trouble." She glanced at the door, her smile fading. "I only worry what is keeping them so long. Erik should have brought her back by now."

Lukas grabbed a ladle and served himself a large bowl of soup. He grabbed the loaf of bread from the counter. It was still warm. He raised an eyebrow. *Just how long has she been up?*

"I'm sure they'll be back soon. If you need to leave, though—"

Szilvia shook her head. "Mama said she would be fine without me for the day. She was worried, too." She grabbed one of Sarah's laundry hampers that Isla had filled with dirty clothes the day before. "Besides, I can get started on this laundry. Did your mother usually do it inside?"

Lukas ignored how his heart twisted in his chest. "Usually, but the clothesline is outside. It should be warm enough for you to set up in the yard. I can bring the water to wherever you want."

"Outside sounds lovely. A bit of fresh air would be wonderful." She picked up the hamper then headed for the front door. "I'll let you eat in peace. It'll take me a bit to find a good spot. Do you want me to let the chickens out?"

"Actually, if you don't mind . . ."

Szilvia nodded then left, closing the front door softly behind her. After consuming another bowl of soup and two slices of bread, Lukas tidied up after himself and gave the floor a good sweep before he went outside to see where Szilvia was. He found her kneeling on the grass near the greenhouse. The dirty clothes were stacked in piles: darks and lights. There weren't many dyed clothes of bright colours in Lukas' wardrobe. Szivlia had the tin pot in front of her, its large opening ready for water. A bar of lavender scented soap rested on the overturned laundry hamper. He smiled as he came upon her and she grinned in reply.

"Ready for water?"

"Ready and waiting." Just as Lukas turned around to head to the outdoor pump, she called him back. "If I find anything that needs mending, do you want me to take it home with me?"

Lukas shook his head. "Mother taught me a little. Isla and I should be able to manage. I try to be careful with my clothes." Not that he was often successful.

Szilvia smirked. "Look at you, sewing your own clothes! I'm hardly needed at all," she teased.

It took about twenty minutes to fill enough buckets with water, then another twenty to heat them to be useful for washing the stains out. He and Szilvia carted bucket after bucket back and forth. By the time the washing tub was full, Lukas needed a nap. Instead of heading inside to his bed, he headed off to make sure his Uncle Jacob had found the right post to fix the previous night. Jacob had refused to leave until the fence post was fixed.

Lukas stopped by his father's tool shed to grab a hammer and nails, just in case. He swallowed thickly as he looked at the rows and rows of tools on the narrow shed's shelves. He grabbed the first hammer he found, shoved some nails in his pocket, then headed to the pasture.

Jacob had found the right fence post, but his fix hadn't lasted the night. His uncle wasn't known to be much of a handyman. Lukas easily pulled the wooden board from the post and set it on the ground. He knelt to inspect the post. He suspected it was rotting and that was why the board wouldn't stay in place, but as he crouched he heard a nearby board groan as if someone was leaning on it. He looked up and saw a young boy, no older than eight, a few feet from him. His dark curls were long, almost covering his brown eyes, and he had his feet on one board and rested his arms and chin on the next one up. He watched Lukas from his vantage point.

"What're you doing?" the boy asked.

Lukas blinked. He had never seen this boy before. "Fixing my fence. What are you doing?"

"Trying to catch that rabbit." The boy pointed behind Lukas into the field where his horses were grazing. "I almost had him, but then he got under this fence." He sighed. "Maybe next time."

Lukas shook his head, fighting back a smile. "You'll never catch him by chasing him. Rabbits are fast. It's better to trap them."

"I don't want to eat him! I just wanted to see where his burrow was. I like watching the babies." The boy stared wistfully at the field. "I like when they jump around."

Lukas scraped at the post with his nail and didn't see any rot. He would try nailing the board one more time, but if it came off again, he decided he would replace the post and hope that solved the problem. "You've missed the babies. They'll be big and leaving their burrows to find their own homes for the winter."

The boy scrambled off the post and knelt on the other side of the fence beside Lukas. "Can I help?"

Part of Lukas wanted to tell the boy to go home, but part of him desperately wanted the company. Better than being left alone with his thoughts. Lukas motioned for him to hold the board in place. "Hold it steady while I nail it in."

The boy did as he was told, careful to keep his fingers away from the hammer as Lukas nailed the board in. Lukas gave it a strong pull and was satisfied when it didn't pop back out. Perhaps it would yet hold. Lukas got up off the ground, as did the boy.

"Thank you for your help. My name is Lukas." He stuck out his hand for the boy to shake.

The boy had dirt under his fingernails, and he had calluses on his palm. "I'm Tobias. I live over there." Tobias motioned with his head back towards Mordecai's - Miriam's uncle's - farm.

Lukas was going to ask if he was one of Miriam's many brothers, for she had no shortage of those, when Szilvia called.

"Lukas! It's Isla!"

Lukas grabbed his hammer and said goodbye to the boy. He was on his way before Tobias could reply. By the time he put away the hammer and made it to the farmhouse, Szilvia and Isla, along with Erik, were already inside. Szilvia still had Isla in a tight embrace when Lukas tried to get inside.

"You had us so worried! What were you thinking?" Szilvia chastised.

"I promise I'll explain everything. But first I could use a cup of tea."

"I'll get it," Lukas said, gently squeezing Isla's shoulder as he stepped around the women. Erik offered to help, but Lukas insisted he join the women on the couch. "You look exhausted."

"It was a long night," Erik said with a sigh.

"Tell us everything," Szilvia insisted.

Isla waited until Lukas brought in a tray with four cups of tea. He handed them out then stood by the mantle, knowing if he sat down he wouldn't get back up.

"I would have liked to come back as soon as they were found, but the Council had other ideas," Isla said with a sigh. "They had more questions this morning. It was all Mama could do to kick them out by lunch."

"I would have thrown them out myself if your mother would have let me," Erik grumbled.

Between sips of tea, Isla told the group how she had come across the Szabó children. Unlike with the councillors, she left nothing out, including the voice. Lukas wasn't sure what to make of that, but he didn't interrupt as Isla explained what kind of questions the councillors wanted to ask. He forced himself not to laugh as he imagined Greta barging in on the meeting and freeing Isla from the interrogation. But what truly surprised him was Isaiah's assistance.

He hadn't expected him to actually go to the meeting, let alone end it and free Isla, at least for the night.

I may have to thank him next time I see him. He hoped it wouldn't be for a while, though.

"And now I'm here. It's all so strange. I don't know what to make of it." She looked at Erik then Lukas. "Did you two hear anything like a voice?"

Erik squinted. "No, but we weren't there long before we found you. What did it sound like? A woman, you said?"

"Yes, and she sounded young. A little older than us, maybe, but not by much."

"And you didn't recognize it?" Lukas asked.

"No, I don't think so. It's not someone from the village." She shook her head. "I don't know what to think."

"How are Hansel and Frida?" Szilvia asked as she sipped from her teacup. "Have they woken up yet?"

"I went by the Szabó's house after breakfast," Erik said. "There was a crowd outside their door. I couldn't get close, but I did hear they're still asleep. The doctor has been by, as has the preacher. I'm sure they'll be calling on your mother soon."

Szilvia shook her head. "Poor dears. I've never heard of anything like a sleeping sickness before."

Isla cradled her teacup in her hands, the steam wafting to her face. "I just hope they wake soon. Then things will get back to normal." She glanced at Lukas. "Any word from Hans?"

Lukas shook his head. "Nothing." He glanced out the window, his mind wandering. "He'll be back soon."

The others said nothing, the silence sinking in until Lukas couldn't stand it anymore. He could tell the others were holding back. "What?"

Szilvia was the one to crack. "Nothing. It's just . . . What if Hans doesn't come back? Or at least not for a long time?"

Lukas pressed his lips together. He wished she hadn't said what he had been worrying about aloud. "Why wouldn't he come back? The farm needs him. *I* need him."

"I know, and I'm not saying he won't, I just mean you should be prepared for anything." Szilvia stared at the clock on the fireplace's mantle, one his grandfather carved a year before he died. "I just remember how it was when Papa died. I was so consumed by grief, if I could have walked into the woods and just kept walking, I may have. I just wanted the pain to go away." She looked at Lukas. "I only wonder if Hans feels the same."

Lukas remembered when Constance's husband died. He was attacked in the woods by a boar, its tusks gouging his abdomen to the point where even Constance's skills couldn't repair the damage. He hadn't suffered long, but the unexpected loss had deeply impacted his family, especially twelve-year-old Szilvia.

He met Szilvia's gaze. "He'll return," he said, with more confidence than he felt. "Until then, I'll make it work."

A knock sounded at the door. Lukas had never been so grateful for an interruption.

Szilvia put down her tea. "I'll get it."

Lukas finished his tea, hoping it wasn't his aunt Greta come to check in on her daughter and nephew. He had seen most of the villagers at the funeral yesterday, so he didn't think there was anyone left to pay their respects. Jacob had managed to find a place for the baskets of food and other condolence gifts.

"Miriam, what a surprise! What brings you out here on such a lovely day?" Szilvia asked.

Lukas' eyes widened. He put his cup down and turned to see Miriam at his front door with Tobias at his side. The boy was holding a basket overflowing with gifts. Lukas hadn't seen her since the day Sarah died. She hadn't been at the funeral, but he knew Mordecai kept his helpers busy at the farm. He didn't blame her for missing it.

"I just wanted to stop by and speak to—Lukas!" She looked behind Szilvia where Lukas stood. Miriam blushed. "I'm sorry to bother you. I didn't realize you had company."

Szilvia stepped back with a smile. "Would you like to join us for tea? Isla and Erik just arrived. There's still bread from this morning if you're hungry."

Miriam's blush deepened. "That's very kind, but no, I can't stay, I'm afraid. I just wanted to give Lukas this." She motioned for Tobias to put down the basket. "I'm sorry we missed the funeral. We just got started making cheese and—"

Lukas waved away her apology. "It's fine, Miriam, really. I know how much work it takes to run a farm." He sighed. "Especially this time of year."

Miriam pulled back the cover from the basket. "Aunt Tanya and I put this together. Just a little something to let you know if you need anything, we're here."

The basket had a few jars of strawberry jam, fresh butter, a chunk of cheese as big as Lukas' head, freshly ground flour for bread, and an assortment of other treats Lukas couldn't make out. He met Miriam's gaze and returned her smile.

"You can see why I needed Tobias to help me carry it," she said.

Lukas turned his stare to the young boy he had met just a short time ago and grinned. "We met before."

Miriam gave the young boy a curious stare, but Tobias avoided her gaze, keeping his eyes on the floorboards as he smiled to himself.

Miriam looked back at Lukas. "He's staying at my uncle's right now. His parents passed away a few months ago. They were good friends of my uncle's," she explained.

Lukas' heart leapt to his throat. He smiled despite it, hoping neither of them saw the pain on his face. He couldn't imagine how lost and alone Tobias must have felt. *Actually, I can.* Lukas felt like an orphan himself at the moment.

"It was nice of Mordecai to take him in," Lukas said.

"He's a big help, aren't you Tobias?"

"When you aren't looking for rabbits, right?" Lukas said with a wink.

Tobias met Lukas' gaze and blushed.

Miriam laughed. She placed her hand on his shoulder. "Well, we should be heading back. There's still some cheese left to make."

Lukas nodded. "Please thank your aunt and uncle for me. I really appreciate it."

"Of course! We have to help each other, don't we? Come on Tobias, perhaps we'll see a rabbit on the way home."

As she and Tobias turned to leave, she paused and looked back at Lukas. "But Lukas, if you do need anything, anything at all, please come by. Aunt Tanya would love to have you over for supper sometime." She smiled sadly. "She told me to tell you she will miss her teatime with Sarah. She always loved it when Sarah stopped by for a visit."

Lukas knew that while he and his father were busy on the farm, Sarah would sometimes get lonely. Although she had her fair share of work to do, Sarah made time for her neighbours and made a point of visiting with the closest ones as often as she could. She especially liked to spend time with Miriam's Aunt Tanya.

"I'll do that, Miriam. I will," he promised.

He watched her and Tobias head down the lane back to Mordecai's farm. The sunlight caught her curls as they bounced loose of her ponytail. He smiled as Tobias took her hand as they walked down the lane. He hoped to see the little boy again.

Lukas closed the door then turned around to see Szilvia, Isla, and Erik grinning like fools.

"What?" he said, placing the basket on the table.

Isla smirked. "Nothing."

Erik shook his head, his arm around Isla's shoulders.

Lukas looked at Szilvia. "What's going on?"

"Nothing! She's just sweet on you, that's all."

Lukas snorted. "Being nice doesn't mean she likes me."

Isla rolled her eyes, the grin still on her face. "She's more than nice. Did you see how she was looking at you?"

Lukas fought off a blush. "Obviously I'm seeing something different." He went back to the basket, turning his back to the others. "Don't you all have anything better to do than tease me?"

Erik chuckled as he stood up. "I noticed a few fence posts were down in the far field. Jacob must have missed them. I'll get those done before supper."

"Wait, I didn't actually mean you had to work! Don't you have to head home?" Lukas said. *Or to Isaiah's?*

"Isaiah doesn't need me for a few days, and I told my parents I would be out here to help during that time."

Szilvia nodded. "I'll have to go home after supper, but until then Isla and I can set the house to rights. Maybe we'll even have time to weed the garden."

"Challenge accepted! I think I left Mama in a good enough mood where she won't be upset if my dresses are dirty when I go home in a few days."

It felt like Lukas' chest was going to burst, he felt such an abundance of love. "Thank you, all of you." He picked up the basket. "I suppose that leaves me with this. And the animals. They'll need to be let in and fed soon." He looked to Erik. "I'll meet you in the field after I'm done here. Do you still remember where the tools are?"

"So long as your father hasn't built a new tool shed since I was last out, I should be fine."

Lukas chuckled. "I think if he could have one as large as the barn, he still wouldn't have enough room for everything."

The four went their separate ways, the strange voice and sleeping Szabó children temporarily forgotten.

~ 8 ~

ISLA

Greta stood beside the main fireplace in Lukas' home, staring at her daughter and nephew. "Well?"

Isla sighed as she reached towards the table that separated her and Lukas from her mother. She grabbed her teacup. Greta had insisted on making a pot as soon as she arrived that afternoon. "I can stay longer. There's no need to rush." She glanced at Lukas, whose arms were crossed. He hadn't met Greta's stare since he let her in the front door several minutes ago.

Greta shook her head. "You've already stayed longer than we initially agreed. A week is long enough."

"Wouldn't it be easier if I just stayed here? You said yourself it was best if I stayed out of the Council's way."

"It is, but we need a long-term plan. You hiding here isn't good enough. I'd rather send you to Budapest with my second cousin's family, but since you're keen on becoming a healer, you can't afford to miss many more days. I'm sure Constance said as much the last time she stopped by."

Isla blushed. This wasn't the first time her mother had mentioned Budapest and all its opportunities for a girl like Isla, but Greta had never gone into more detail than that. And yes, Isla *was* serious about her training, but family came first. She had told Constance that, and while the midwife had agreed, she had reminded Isla of her talents.

"I don't want you to forget your dreams. There's so much left to teach you," Constance had said.

"And I don't want you to keep meeting up with Erik here. It isn't proper without a chaperone," Greta added.

Isla's blush deepened. It seemed her mother knew all her secrets. Erik had left a few days ago to return to work for Isaiah, but he would be back in a week. Isla had liked working with him on Lukas' farm.

Greta turned to Lukas. "I know my brother. If he was going to return, he would have done so already. Whatever field he's taken the sheep to, wherever he's hiding, let him. Right now, I want you taken care of."

"I'm managing well enough," Lukas said, his voice gruff and laden with sleepiness.

Isla had done her best to help, but there were too many tasks to complete and simply not enough hands. She could tell the pressure of keeping the farm going was wearing on Lukas.

"Well enough won't do. If you refuse to take on extra help, then at least come stay with me until your father returns," said Greta. Her hair was pulled back in a tight bun and her dark grey dress trailed the floor, catching the dust bunnies Isla had been sweeping up when her mother unexpectedly visited.

Lukas shook his head. "Who would manage the farm?"

"Oh, damn the farm! Damn it all!" Greta exclaimed. "What has this place ever done for any of you? Given your father a place to hide from the villagers' whispers, perhaps, but that's all. I won't let you waste away out here. What would Sarah say?"

A hush fell over the room.

Lukas ran a hand through his tangled curls. He stared at the embers in the fireplace. It was still too hot to keep an afternoon fire going, but soon that would change. Summer was quickly turning into autumn. Isla didn't want to think of Lukas trying to manage the harvest on his own. There was no way he could get it all done himself.

Isla stood. "If you won't let me stay, and if Lukas won't leave, why don't we ask Miriam to come? She's experienced, and she's already close by. I'm sure she can handle whatever this place can throw at her."

Isla ignored Lukas' blush and protests, focusing on Greta. She didn't care what Lukas thought about the arrangement. Anything was better than uprooting her cousin and forcing him into town.

Greta was quiet. She paced the length of the small living area twice before she stopped in front of her daughter. "Why her?"

"Why not? She's smart, capable, and hard working. With all her brothers and sisters, she certainly knows how to multitask, which is what this place needs."

"She's already helping her aunt and uncle," Lukas pointed out, his ears tinged red as his blush spread from his cheeks to his neck. "We can't ask her to leave her family. That wouldn't be fair to them."

"You know as well as I do her uncle has half a dozen farm hands helping him. Her aunt can spare her, at least in the afternoons." She met Greta's gaze, stretching out her hand for Greta to shake. "Let me talk to her. If she says no, we'll look at another option. Agreed?"

Greta stared at Isla then shook her hand. "Fine. We'll give it a try. But Lukas?" she said, staring at him.

Lukas looked at Greta, his blush fading.

"If I hear one word about you and Miriam doing *anything* improper, she goes back to her aunt and uncle. Understood?"

Lukas lowered his gaze as he nodded quickly. "Yes, Aunt."

Greta nodded as she let go of Isla's hand. "I'll see you for supper, Isla." She kissed the top of Lukas' head then hugged Isla quickly before leaving the farmhouse. As soon as she was gone, Lukas got to his feet, glaring at Isla.

"Why did you do that?"

Isla raised an eyebrow. "Save you from losing the farm? Because I knew you would hate it in the village, of course!"

Lukas shook his head. "I could have handled Greta."

"No one can handle my mother. At least I bought you time." She went to Lukas and stood in front of him, taking his hand in hers. "I know this isn't easy. I wish she would let it go, but she won't. My mother thinks she's doing what's best for you."

Lukas pulled his hand from Isla's. "So are you. You're shoving me and Miriam together to satisfy whatever silly romance you have going on in your head. The *last* thing on my mind right now is love."

"So what if I am playing Cupid? What does it matter? I wasn't wrong. Miriam *can* help here. She's the only one beside Szilvia I would trust. Let her come here and help."

Lukas shook his head and walked around the small table. "I don't need you meddling in my life, Isla. I wish everyone would just leave me alone!" He slammed the front door on his way outside.

Isla sighed, her shoulders sagging. *That didn't exactly go as planned.* She waited a moment then went outside, heading down the road that led to Mordecai's farm.

~*~

The steam from her cup of tea wafted up in front of Isla's face, warming her nose as she sat across from Miriam and her Aunt Tanya in their kitchen. It was much larger than Lukas', but just as cozy. Tanya had garlands of drying herbs hanging from the ceiling, and a row of sturdy shelves held her crockery.

Isla stared at the women, waiting for their response.

Tanya dried her hands on the nearest dishrag. She met her niece's gaze. "What do you think, my dear?"

Miriam chewed on her lower lip, her hands cupping the hot cup of tea before her. She held her aunt's stare for a moment longer then turned to Isla. "What did Lukas say when you suggested this?"

"He wasn't keen on it. He doesn't want to burden you."

Miriam took a sip of her tea. "For how long?"

Isla shrugged. "Weeks, maybe. Possibly longer. I don't know when Hans will return."

Tanya shook her head. "To leave his own son like that." She spat into the fireplace. "I could never."

"Aunt," Miriam said, her voice holding a warning that spoke of past conversations on this very topic. She looked to Isla again. "Just the afternoons, then?"

"You can stay for supper if you like. Lukas will need help most in the afternoons."

Miriam opened her mouth to say something when a young boy about eight years old came into the kitchen. "May I come?"

It was the same boy she had seen with Miriam when she delivered the basket of goodies. She hadn't gotten a good look at him then. She smiled as he came further inside. Dust lingered on his dark trousers and his hands were grubby from working outside. Tanya pointed to the basin of water.

"Wash your hands, Tobias. You know the rules."

Tobias dashed over to the basin and gave his hands a quick wash. Isla could still see the dirt on his hands from her seat. He turned around and faced Tanya and Miriam. "Can I go with Miriam? Please?"

Tanya raised an eyebrow. "And why do you wish to go to Lukas' farm? It'll be just as much hard work there, likely more."

"He has more rabbits. And chickens!" Tobias grinned. "I like the chickens."

Isla smothered her laugh. She liked this boy.

Miriam shook her head as she smiled. "If you come with me, you can't just play with the animals. You'll have to help Lukas outside. Do whatever he asks. He doesn't have lots of help like Uncle Mordecai does."

"I can help! I'm strong." Tobias flexed his arms, showing off his "muscles." Isla widened her eyes, pretending to be impressed.

Tanya sighed, putting the dish rag down. "Fine, but only for a little while. And make sure you listen to Miriam and Lukas when you're there! I don't want to hear a word about you running off."

Tobias beamed as he went over and hugged Tanya. "Thank you!" He ran from the room before Isla could say a word.

Miriam looked over at Isla. "I hope that was alright. Tobias is a good boy."

"One more pair of hands certainly can't hurt. Is he a cousin of yours?" she asked as she finished her cup of tea.

Miriam shook her head. "An orphan. His parents died a few months ago from a fever. Tobias went to get help, but when he came back with the doctor, it was too late."

Isla's chest tightened as she fought off tears. *How awful.*

Tanya refilled her own cup of tea. "I grew up with his mother. She came during the fall to help with canning our vegetables. I told her if anything happened to her and her husband, I would look after Tobias."

"He has no living family, then?" Isla asked.

"None Maria told me about," Tanya replied. "He's a good boy. Likes to make people laugh." She smiled, briefly lost to memories. "He smiled so much as a baby." Tanya shook her head then looked at Miriam. "Will you start tomorrow, then?"

Miriam glanced at Isla. "If that works for Lukas."

"It will. He'll be ready for you."

Isla thanked Tanya for the tea as she stood. She explained she had to make it home before nightfall. Miriam walked her to the door. When the two girls were alone, Miriam placed her hand gently on Isla's arm, causing the girl to pause in the doorway.

"Why me?" she whispered.

Isla contemplated telling Miriam the truth, that she saw the love in Miriam's eyes, even though Lukas claimed not to. But she knew if this was to work, she had to let Miriam and Lukas discover their feelings for each other in their own time. She couldn't rush it.

Instead, she smiled and gave her the same answer she had given to her mother just an hour ago. "Why not you?"

With that, she left Mordecai's farm and headed for home. The air started to grow crisp, causing a chill to run down Isla's spine. Her stomach growled, demanding supper. As she passed the woods, something glinted at her from the bushes. Isla slowed her pace, squinting. She tilted her head to the side and the fading sun caught whatever it was, making it sparkle. Isla took a step forward. She felt pulled towards whatever it was. Her feet carried her closer and closer until she was practically on top of the sparkling object. She stared down at it, her eyes wide.

A crystal necklace tied to a chain lay on the ground. It was a pale purple colour. She looked around for footprints but found none. It was as if the jewel had dropped from the sky.

Perhaps a raven found it and dropped it. Ravens and crows were known for their love of shiny things.

Isla picked it up and settled it in the palm of her hand. The weight felt familiar to her, like she had held the jewel before. She ran her thumb over its smoothed edges, the motion calming her racing heart. Without thinking she looped the chain around her neck. The jewel settled on her breastbone, immediately warming her skin. She placed her hand over top it, and stilled as the wind picked up around her.

Come play!

That voice.

Isla looked around but saw no one.

Come play! Come!

Isla took a deep breath, clasping the jewel tighter. She headed away from the woods and back towards the path. She thought of the Szabó children, still in their sickening sleep. Her heart raced. She hoped the voice meant nothing, just that she was tired, but she couldn't believe that, not when the voice was following her as she left the woods behind. She started to run for the village, her bag smacking her back as it hit again and again. The jewel bumped against her chest, warm and reassuring as Isla left the woods behind.

She found it, finally.

It was a risk to cut that chunk out of the crystal. I wasn't even sure if it would let me. It must have craved a new person's power as much as I do.

I knew it would call to her. But would she hear it? Would she answer?

Greta didn't. Not at first. It took many days in her cage before she listened to its instructions on how to break free. I almost fainted when I saw her in the attic, reaching out to touch the crystal. She was drawn to it, just as I was all those years ago when my mother first showed it to me.

It was my great-great-great-grandmother's. Mama never told me where she found it, and the crystal hasn't shown me how it came to be. It has its own secrets.

Mama passed it on to me the day before she died, and I've had it ever since. I'm sure it's one of the many reasons the villagers thought I was tainted. It came with me bundled up under my cloak when I ran from the village that night so many years ago. It helped me find this place to create my gingerbread house. It gave me the spells I needed to build my sanctuary.

I wonder what it will give Isla. Or what she will take from it.

$$\sim 9 \sim$$

LUKAS

Lukas had avoided going inside all afternoon.

He sat on the porch railing, balancing precariously as he tried to catch the last of the late afternoon sunlight. He held a hastily carved block of wood in hand. It felt familiar, like coming back to an old friend's house and sitting by their fire. He figured Miriam was as good of an excuse as any to start carving again. If everyone insisted he have her around, he might as well let her work. Not that Lukas hadn't spent most of the day outside, tending to the animals and garden. Tobias was inside helping Miriam, but he had helped Lukas in the garden before the heat became too much for him. The peas and carrots had been in desperate need of harvesting, and Bella had missed Lukas. She hadn't calved yet, as if she was waiting for Hans to come back.

Aren't we all, Lukas thought as he glared at the wooden block. It had turned from a bird into a bear, and now Lukas wasn't sure what the wood wanted to be. Lukas kept carving, his fingers beginning to cramp. He could smell supper inside, but he was holding out until the last minute. Miriam and Tobias had walked up the driveway just after lunch. Lukas had done his best to offer a welcoming smile, but all he had wanted was to find a private corner of the farm and work in silence. Miriam's presence sent his heart fluttering in his chest.

Since then, he had kept out of her way. Tobias stuck to Lukas' side like sticky molasses, asking repeatedly what he could do. Lukas came up with mundane work, but it kept the boy busy. He seemed to enjoy tending to the chickens, which was nice since Lukas wasn't fond of getting pecked as he collected eggs.

Lukas wasn't sure what Miriam had done before preparing supper, but he assumed she had found enough work to keep busy.

"I'll call you when supper's ready," she had said, shutting the door in Lukas' face hours ago.

Lukas had looked at Tobias, who simply shrugged. Since then, the two had worked outside, taking advantage of the nice weather. Lukas had settled on the porch an hour ago, soon after he sent Tobias inside to help Miriam.

Lukas sighed, adjusting his shoulders as they began to stiffen. He hoped Miriam wasn't reorganizing his house, taking away any trace of Sarah. Lukas swallowed, blinking away tears. He wished he could talk to his mother one more time, just to tell her he loved her. He felt he hadn't done that enough when she was alive.

Inside, Tobias and Miriam sang a song Lukas didn't recognize. The kitchen window was open, letting the sounds and smells from the kitchen entice him. The clanging of pots and pans became the harmony to their melody, relaxing Lukas' shoulders as he continued to carve.

He hadn't heard anyone sing on the farm since before Sarah died.

When Hans came home late from tending the sheep, he and Sarah would sit before the fire, Sarah sewing and Hans sharpening his knives, and the two would sing together. Quietly, so as not to wake their son. Lukas would listen from his loft where he was supposed to be sleeping; the music often put him to sleep before his parents finished their duet.

Lukas blinked, forcing the thought aside as he carved another sliver of wood out of the bird-bear. He dragged the knife over the edge just as the front door banged open.

"Supper's ready!" Miriam announced.

Lukas yelped as the knife caught his thumb. He winced as blood squirted onto the railing.

Miriam gasped. Her curly hair was piled atop her head in a bun, and her cream sleeves were rolled up past her elbows. The apron covering her dark brown skirt was spotted with stains.

"I didn't think you would be so close!" She ran inside and came back out with a damp cloth and bowl of water. She marched over and took his bleeding thumb in her hand. Lukas blushed at how warm her skin was. She dabbed the wet cloth against his thumb, clearing away the blood so she could get a better look at the cut.

"Not deep. It'll need a bandage, though," she muttered to herself. She wrapped the cloth around his thumb. "Hold that, and make sure to keep your hand above your heart until I get back." She was gone before Lukas could reply.

Lukas stared at his thumb, then looked to the grass below where his carving had fallen. Perhaps it was best to let that go the way of firewood. The large chunk now missing would be too big to work around.

Miriam came back outside with a clean linen bandage and a vial filled with something green the consistency of mashed potatoes. She sat across from Lukas on the railing and uncorked the vial. She gestured for him to hand her his thumb. Lukas extended it to her then watched as she unwrapped the cloth once again. She shook out a glob of whatever was in the vial and smeared some of it over the cut. It stung, causing Lukas to pull back. Miriam kept a firm grip on his thumb.

"It's just calendula. It'll keep out infection."

"Still hurts," he muttered.

"You're as bad as Tobias," she said with a smirk. She wrapped the clean bandage around the cut. "At least it's just a cut. You should have heard my brother Thomas wailing when I pulled a sliver from his foot. You would think he had been impaled by a tree."

Lukas smiled, momentarily forgetting the cut. As she tied off the bandage, Lukas cleared his throat. "Listen, I'm sorry about all this. About me. I'm trying my best, but I don't know what I'm doing out here." He looked over her head at the farm, his breath catching in his throat. "I know this likely isn't how you want to spend your time."

Miriam kept hold of Lukas' thumb, giving it a squeeze so he would look at her. When he met her stare, her cheeks were flushed. "What do you know about how I want to spend my time?"

"N-Nothing I just—" He sighed. "That came out wrong."

"Want to try again?"

"Very much so," Lukas said, a blush lighting up his cheeks. "I *am* glad you're here."

"But?"

"But I know your aunt and uncle need you. Please promise me that if you're needed there, you'll help them."

Miriam squeezed his injured hand. "So long as you promise me that, if I do, you'll come with me. My aunt likes company."

"I can't promise that. I can't abandon my home. My mother—"

"Isn't here anymore. She would want you to be safe and cared for. You can't do everything here by yourself, Lukas. Even with Tobias and I here, it's going to be hard." She smiled at him. "But I'll be here as long as you need me. Tobias and I aren't going anywhere."

Lukas cleared his throat, trying to get rid of the thick coating of tears. "If you're sure."

She let go of Lukas' hand then got to her feet. "Supper's ready. I hope you like roasted potatoes and turnips with your chicken."

Lukas' stomach gurgled in response. He followed her inside, leaving the carving outside in the grass.

He paused in the front doorway. "You certainly kept busy this afternoon."

Miriam had cleaned every square inch of Lukas' house, or so it seemed. There was a pile of blankets, clothes, and other pieces ready for the laundry by the door. Lukas stepped around it as he went towards the kitchen cupboards. She hadn't reorganized it exactly, but it was a lot easier to find what one was looking for now.

Tobias sat by the fire, nursing a cup of tea. Lukas ruffled his hair affectionately, earning a smile from the boy.

"How did you like your first day here?" Lukas asked.

"It was great! I like the chickens best. Can I find their eggs tomorrow?"

"Of course, I'm sure they'd be happy to see you again." Lukas grabbed a mug off the table and poured tea from the pot for himself. "Did you help Miriam like I asked?"

"Oh yes, we made quite the team." She untied her apron and hung it on a peg on the wall. "Come along, Tobi. We should head back. It'll get dark soon."

Tobias whined, and as he dragged his feet, Lukas insisted they stay for supper.

"You went to all this work to make such a delicious meal, I can't possibly enjoy it alone."

Tobias stared at Miriam, his eyes wide like a puppy's. "Please Miriam, can we?"

Miriam was silent for a moment, then sighed. "Fine, but as soon as we're done, we must go home. Uncle Mordecai doesn't want us outside after dark."

"I'll walk you home," Lukas promised.

Miriam sat across from him, grabbing the pitcher and filling both their glasses with milk. "What did you get up to while we were inside?" she asked.

The trio fell into easy conversation between bites of roast chicken and steaming potatoes. Lukas ate his fill and then some. Miriam helped him clean up, and, seeing the sun hadn't quite set yet, she offered to help him with the dishes. Tobias was careful not to drop the dishes as he dried while Miriam washed and Lukas put them away. Once done, Lukas tied Tobias' cloak around his shoulders then opened the door for a waiting Miriam.

"Come along Tobi, we can't have you late for Uncle Mordecai," Lukas said.

The crisp evening air made Lukas smile. He tried to keep up with Tobias, but the young boy had a burst of energy that kept him jogging farther up the lane, then racing back to a slower Lukas and Miriam. She shook her head with a smile as she watched him run back and forth.

"I don't know how he's this fast! Clearly we need to work him harder tomorrow," she teased.

"Clearly," Lukas said with a chuckle. "He really was a big help, though. As were you, of course. I don't think my house has looked that clean in years."

Miriam shrugged, hiding her blush. "I don't like to be idle."

The pair walked further down the lane as the sun began to set. Lukas shoved his hands in the pockets of his trousers. He'd have to bring out his gloves soon.

"I love autumn. It's my favourite time of year," he said quietly, almost to himself.

"Mine as well. I love the colours of the leaves on the trees," Miriam replied, wrapping her arms around her waist.

"Are you cold?"

Miriam shook her head. "I'll be fine. We're almost there."

Lukas took off his wool jacket and placed it over her shoulders. She looked up at him, an eyebrow raised. He shrugged. "I was getting warm anyway."

Miriam slipped her arms into the oversized sleeves. The cuffs of the jacket fell just past her fingers. "I'll have to bring my coat next time."

"Does this mean you'll stay for supper again?"

"If you don't mind the company."

Lukas wanted to tell Miriam her company was easily becoming the best part of his day. He most certainly didn't want to tell Isla that. She would only gloat.

"If you cook like that every night, I won't complain," he teased, hoping she understood what he hadn't said.

As they rounded the corner, Uncle Mordecai's farm came into view. Lukas marveled at the large farmhouse to his left, with a separate house for the farm hands several feet away. The barn was twice the size of Hans', and Lukas could hear the cows inside demanding their supper. Lukas took a deep breath and caught the scent of fresh bread on the wind. Miriam's aunt had been busy in the kitchen as well.

Tobias ran up the staircase to the front door and flung it open, shouting happily at whoever was inside. Lukas took his time, not wanting to leave Miriam just yet.

They paused at the bottom of the steps. Miriam began to take off the jacket, thanking Lukas for letting her borrow it. He placed a hand on her shoulder, stopping her from removing the jacket completely.

"You can bring it back tomorrow. I'll be fine for the walk home."

Miriam blushed. "Are you sure?"

He grinned. "Completely. I'll see you tomorrow." He took a step back but then Tanya came to the doorway.

"Lukas, would you like to come in for some tea?"

Part of him desperately wanted to say yes, but he knew he should get home. Miriam stared at him, waiting. Lukas swallowed his yearning and shook his head. "Thank you, but I should head home. I don't want to be caught in the woods."

Tanya nodded. "Perhaps tomorrow."

He bobbed his head. "Perhaps. Goodnight Tanya. Miriam." He turned around and headed back the way he came. His neck prickled as if someone was watching him. He turned his head once to look back. Miriam stood at the bottom of the staircase, watching him go. He waved goodbye. She did, too, then headed inside, his jacket still on her.

By the time Lukas got home, the sun was almost completely set. Instead of heading inside, he went to the barn. He wanted to make sure the animals were settled before turning in himself. He stopped mid-step as he caught a glimpse of his father's toolshed from the corner of his eye.

The door was open.

Lukas squinted as he stared at the wooden door. He hadn't been in there at all that day, and it was normally kept locked if not in use. Lukas glanced around for a weapon and spotted a long stick. He grimaced. It would have to do.

Stick in hand, Lukas made his way slowly to the toolshed. He took a deep breath then came around the corner, facing the open door.

Hans turned around, meeting his son's gaze.

"Papa!" Lukas tossed the stick to the ground. He stepped inside the large shed and hugged Hans, unaware of the tools in his father's hands. Hans dropped them on the ground as he embraced his son.

"I was hoping you would be out for a while longer," Hans said with a sigh. He released Lukas, taking a step back to gather his tools. "I needed to grab some things."

Lukas raised an eyebrow. "For what? Aren't you staying?"

Hans shook his head, his cap hiding his scraggly salt and pepper hair. His beard was longer, too. "Not yet. I'm taking the sheep further south to better pasture. Then on to Budapest to market. I should be back in a month, maybe two."

"*Two months?*" Lukas exclaimed. "Mama's dead and you're leaving me here alone for two months?" He shook his head. "The sheep don't need another pasture. *I* need you here!"

Hans shoved the tools in a satchel then slung it over his back. "You're managing fine on your own. I knew I could trust you." He straightened, avoiding Lukas' glare. "I can't come home. Not yet. There are too many memories here."

"You can't run away just because you're sad, Papa! I miss her too," he said, his voice cracking at the end.

Hans sighed, running a weary hand over his face. "I know, Lukas. I know you do. Please, I promise I'll be back in a few months. But I must leave. Now."

"But—"

"Lukas!" Isla's yell made both men pause. *What's she doing here?*

Hans took the opportunity and side-stepped around his son, getting out of the toolshed. "Go to your cousin, Lukas. I'll see you in a few months."

"Papa, wait!"

"Lukas!" Isla called again, more insistent this time.

Hans was halfway across the yard. Lukas let out a sigh, but it came out as a growl. He marched away from the shed, his anger coiling in his belly. When he got to the house, he saw Isla, Erik, and Szilvia at the bottom of the front stairs, lanterns in hand.

"What happened?"

Isla pulled her cloak tighter around her thin shoulders. "It's the Farkas children. They're missing."

Lukas' eyes widened. "Which ones?" The Farkas family had eight living children; Lukas had lost track of the number they had buried over the years.

"Rosemary and Todd," Szilvia answered. "No one can find them."

Lukas glanced at the woods. "Let me grab my lantern." He hurried inside, found one of his father's old coats, grabbed the lantern, then joined the others. He hoped the Farkas children were found in better condition than the Szabó children, but after seeing Hans, Lukas couldn't muster the courage for false hope.

Mama had many rules when I was growing up, but the most important one was to never tell the villagers what I thought about God. Even in church, as we sat in the pews beside the faithful Catholics of our village. I could bow my head and pretend to pray, and I must take the sacrament, even if I didn't believe it was truly Jesus' body and blood, but if anyone asked me what I thought, I had to lie.

I didn't understand until Mama received letters from my aunt and uncle. They lived in Budapest and the stories they shared with Mama . . . they haunt me still. Burned homes. Families thrown in jail, forced to convert or face the fires themselves. Children separated from their parents.

I asked her, once, why we didn't leave when Auntie and Uncle fled from persecution (I didn't even know what that word meant, but I saw it in the letter from Auntie). I was barely ten years old, still learning to read, and she was angrier that I read the letter than the question itself. She shook her head, her headscarf shifting to reveal her grey hairs, then burned the letter.

"We're needed here, Angel. We'll go when it's time."

But by the time we had to flee, it was too late. Mama was too sick, and I wasn't strong enough to heal her. The crystal barely spoke to me, and no matter how many herbs I crushed, they didn't get rid of the fever burning my mama from the inside out.

I risked asking a neighbour for help, but when she came inside and saw no crucifix on the wall and a Bible not in Latin, but translated to Hungarian, she knew what we were.

I've always suspected it was her who told the council we were heathens.

Thankfully, Mama died before the council came to our door. I don't know what they did with her body, for she had barely taken her last breath before they came knocking.

I know they didn't bury her in the churchyard. I checked.

Perhaps when my work with Isla is done, I can find Mama and put her to rest.

$$\sim 10 \sim$$

ISLA

Isla's boots sunk into the damp earth as she followed Erik and the others further into the woods. The fallen leaves crunched softly underfoot, but otherwise the woods were eerily quiet. Again.

"Where were the Szabós children?" Szilvia asked, her voice hushed as she kept pace with Isla. Lukas walked beside Erik, their lanterns leading the way.

"Further in," Isla said, her hand clutching the crystal as it hung around her neck. "In a clearing."

"I hope they're awake," Szilvia said.

Me too.

Isla hoped she didn't find them. Or if she did, she prayed the councillors were not part of the search party. Greta would throw a fit if Isla was dragged before the council again. Worse yet, what if Isaiah joined the meeting, and asked questions? Isla shuddered.

Szilvia looped her arm through Isla's. The sun was almost fully set, and although Szilvia wasn't afraid of the dark, she had grown up hearing the same stories as Isla, ones that told of creatures who stalked the woods when the moon was high, ones that preyed on naughty children. Despite the ridiculousness of it, Isla couldn't shake the feeling she was being watched, again.

The crystal warmed in her hand as they passed a fork in the road. She paused mid-step and stared at the path leading left, the opposite one Erik and Lukas had chosen. Szilvia tried to tug her along, but Isla's feet wouldn't move. The crystal grew hotter, almost burning.

"Wait," she called.

Erik and Lukas turned around. "What is it, Isla? We really should carry on. It's getting dark," said Erik. The news had reached the Chief Steward's castle, and although Isaiah had been off hunting, Erik had heard the news. For once, Erik hadn't been out with Isaiah, and he ran straight to Constance's to get the girls. It was his idea to ask Lukas to join their search party. Isla could see the bags under Erik's eyes and wished he had stayed at the castle and taken advantage of his rare time off to rest.

"You're going the wrong way," she said.

"How can you tell?" Szilvia asked. She glanced at the glow emulating from the crystal. "Is it speaking to you?"

Isla had shown the gem to Constance just that afternoon. The old woman claimed she didn't recognize it. She had fetched her book on crystals and handed it to Isla before leaving to go check on a woman who had just given birth.

"Perhaps it's hiding in here. Tell me what you find," Constance had said.

In the woods, Isla withdrew her hand from the crystal and watched as it shifted on her chest, pointing towards the left path. Erik and Lukas came over and looked at what the crystal was doing. Lukas paled, taking a step back. Erik gulped.

"I still say you should get rid of it. No good can come from it," Erik said.

Isla shook her head, unwilling to get into an argument with him for the second time that night about the crystal. "Let's see where it leads. If I'm wrong, we'll come back the way we came."

"Fine, but we're only going down the path half a mile. If there's nothing there, we turn around," Erik said.

Isla nodded. The four headed down the left path and were soon directed off the dirt lane into the woods. Isla led the way, borrowing

Lukas' lantern so he could fall back with Szilvia. She wasn't sure what they were discussing, she was so focused on the crystal. They walked for another twenty minutes before the heat abruptly left the crystal. Isla stumbled, not used to walking without the tug at her chest, and looked around. They weren't in a clearing like last time, but the tall grass had been flattened down in a circle. Isla lifted the lantern higher and swallowed, dread curling in her belly.

Rosemary Farkas was curled up against her older brother's chest, asleep like the Szabós. Todd was almost ten and tall for his age. He slept on his side, his long blonde hair falling over his forehead, as if someone had stroked it. They seemed unharmed, just like the other children.

Szilvia shook her head, crossing her arms against her chest. "They look so peaceful."

"In a creepy sort of way," Erik added. He went closer and knelt. He felt for a pulse, just to be sure, and nodded to the others. "Steady. They're asleep."

Isla handed the lantern back to Lukas and crouched down beside Rosemary. She brushed away the six-year-old's blonde curls and felt for a fever. She ran through a list of possible symptoms but found none. Lukas and Erik kept watch for other searchers as Szilvia helped Isla check the children over.

"I just don't understand. Two sets of children in just over a week with the exact same symptoms. And the Szabós children haven't woken up yet, so who's to say when these two will either? What's going on?" Isla murmured to Szilvia.

Szilvia shook her head. "I don't know, but I don't like it." She motioned to the crystal. "Anything?" Although Szilvia didn't understand the crystal, she was curious about it and its powers. Growing up, she had loved the stories about girls with magic in their bones, while Isla always favoured the ones where knights went on epic quests and came home heroes. Until she learned she could never *be* a knight.

Isla glanced at the crystal, but it wasn't glowing like before. It was, however, growing warmer. She leaned over Rosemary and the crystal grew hotter. Isla unhooked the chain from the back of her neck and held it above the children. It slowly started to spin in a circle, but Isla had no idea what that meant.

Shouts echoed in the woods. Isla looked up, the crystal forgotten. Erik cursed.

"They must be from the village. Szilvia, take her back to the farm. We'll meet you there."

"But what about you and Lukas?" Isla asked as she got to her feet, hurriedly clipping the crystal back around her neck.

"We'll follow, once the others get here."

"We should stay. I can tell them—"

"Your mother would kill me if I let those men see you with that crystal." Erik kissed her forehead. "Go. I promise we won't be long."

Isla sighed, hating that he was right, and kissed him quickly. "We'll wait up. Be safe."

"You too."

She waved goodbye to Lukas then took off down the makeshift path, Szilvia right beside her. Once they were far enough away from the sleeping children, Isla clasped her friend's hand.

"First the Szabó children, now the Farkas family. Who's next?" Isla whispered.

"No one, I hope," Szilvia said with a sigh. She squeezed Isla's hand. "Does Erik have to go back to the castle tonight?"

Isla shrugged. In the rush to get to Lukas' she had forgotten to ask. "I assume so. Isaiah is probably back already and wondering where his servant is," she grumbled. "I wish Isaiah would just let him leave. He pays Erik well enough. Erik could stop working for him tomorrow if he wanted." But she knew that wouldn't happen. Despite how Isaiah had treated Isla and the others, Erik couldn't abandon the boy who had been like a brother to him for over a decade.

"What would he do if he didn't work for the Chief Steward, though? I know you think Erik stays out of loyalty, but a young man can't just lounge around all day. You said his father won't let him inherit the business."

As the second son, Erik wasn't likely to inherit his father's butcher shop, and he had said on numerous occasions how much he hated the stink. He liked being outdoors, which was one of the many reasons Isla loved him. They had talked countless times about Erik going to work for one of the local farmers, but the pay was better at the Chief Steward's. If they wanted to marry within the year, like Isla so desperately did, it was best to stay at the castle and keep saving up for their dream home. The more they had, the better.

"I don't know. All I can say is, I'm putting my foot down when we get married. No more having Isaiah call him away every other day to do Lord knows what." She stepped over a fallen log, clasping Szilvia's hand tighter. "I just want to marry him and live a happy life. Such a simple thing, and yet it seems so much to ask for."

"You'll find a way, Isla. You always do." She stared ahead, her gaze far away. "I just hope the Chief Steward lets Aliz come home soon. It's been four years since I last saw her," she said with a sigh.

Isla doubted their childhood friend would join Isaiah at the castle anytime soon, but she didn't want to discourage Szilvia. She squeezed her friend's hand as they continued.

"Now that Erik rescued you from the council, you may even get your mother's approval, instead of having to elope," Szilvia teased, drawing her thoughts away from Aliz.

Isla blushed as she chuckled. She had said frequently over the last year and a half that if Greta didn't approve of the match, Isla would just run away with Erik and elope. Now, though, Szilvia had a point. Now, Greta had been civil to Erik whenever they spoke, and she asked about him at dinner. Greta pretended not to show much interest, but Isla could read her mother well enough to know she was starting to see Erik how Isla always had.

The girls made it back to Lukas' farmhouse just as it grew fully dark. Isla went to the flowerpot and lifted it, revealing the spare key. Once inside, she went to the fireplace and stoked the coals. Szilvia grabbed a kettle and filled it with water. Isla was about to grab the tea leaves when there was a knock at the door. The girls exchanged a look. Who would be out this time of night?

Isla glanced at the counter and picked up one of the knives, just in case. She opened the door and upon seeing Miriam, nearly dropped the knife.

"Miriam! What are you doing here? Come in, come in, before you catch cold," Isla said, ushering the girl inside.

Miriam followed Isla. Szilvia grabbed another mug for tea. Miriam stood in the centre of the room, doing her best to stay out of the way.

"I heard about the Farkas children. Uncle and a few others went to help search. Lukas let me borrow his jacket earlier, and I thought he might need it." Her ears burned red. "I missed him, didn't I?"

Szilvia waved her hand dismissively as the kettle boiled. "He'll be back soon. Why don't you stay and wait with us?"

"Or does your aunt expect you home?" Isla didn't want Miriam to get in trouble.

Miriam shook her head. "She told me to stay here, as it wouldn't be safe to walk home so late." She hung the jacket up on the nearby peg and smoothed her skirts. "She didn't want me to go in the first place, but when Uncle offered to walk me there on his way to the woods, she let it go."

Isla smiled. "We're glad for the company. Would you like some tea?"

The three girls brought their chairs close to the fireplace as they sipped on the hot beverage. They chatted about the crops, the flocks, Miriam's first day, anything but the sleeping children. The conversation didn't turn to the Farkas family until the girls were on their second cups of tea.

"So you found them, then?" Miriam asked.

Isla nodded. "Lukas and Erik stayed behind to show the others where they are."

Szilvia sighed. "I hope they get here soon. It's getting late."

Miriam placed a hand over her heart, shaking her head. "The poor things. Their parents must be terrified."

"I just wish there was an explanation. It can't just be a coincidence," said Szilvia.

"Perhaps it's a new sickness we've never had before. Uncle says there are many travelers coming from or heading to Budapest who pass through the village market. It wouldn't be the first time someone sick passed through and children caught it," Miriam suggested.

"But to *only* affect the children, and so soon? It seems strange," Szilvia said, shaking her head.

As Miriam and Szilvia theorized, Isla thought of her mother and uncle, trapped by a witch in the woods. Two children, a boy and a girl, lost in the woods . . . Isla bit her lip. *Impossible.*

"Isla, are you listening? Isla?"

Isla blinked and realized the girls were staring at her. She blushed. "I'm sorry, I must be more tired than I thought. What were you saying?"

Szilvia smirked. "Actually, we were just talking about sleeping arrangements. Do you know where Lukas keeps the spare cots?"

"I couldn't find them today when I was taking an inventory of the house," Miriam explained.

Isla finished her tea and stood. "Uncle Hans keeps them in the barn. I'll go fetch them."

"Do you need help carrying them?" Miriam asked.

"No, they're quite light. You two can find us some blankets. Aunt Sarah had a special spot for them."

"I found some today. There should be enough for all of us." Miriam got up and led Szilvia to Hans and Sarah's room.

Isla went back outside, shutting the door firmly behind her. Inside the barn, it was warm thanks to the animals. She went to the back wall where Hans had hammered nails into the wall to keep certain items off the ground, away from the mice. She spotted four cots and fetched a stool to get them off their nails.

As she was heading back inside with the cots, the crystal warmed.

Come play, come play!

Isla whipped her head around, nearly dropping the cots. Her heart hammered against her ribs.

Come play, come play!

She broke out in a cold sweat. "Who's there?" she called. No one answered.

Isla ran the rest of the way to the front door, the cots banging against her shins, leaving bruises. She slammed the door behind her and locked it.

Szilvia and Miriam turned away from the pile of blankets to see Isla shaking, her face flush.

"Isla? What happened?" Szilvia asked.

Before she could reply, the door unlocked behind her. Isla scrambled out of the way just as Lukas and Erik opened the door.

Lukas eyes widened to find his cousin clutching the cots and Szilvia and Miriam rifling through Sarah's quilts. "What's going on here?"

Isla let Szilvia explain. Erik side-stepped Lukas and took the cots from her. His eyes narrowed when he saw her hands shaking. "What's wrong?" he murmured.

"I heard it," she whispered. "The voice." She clutched Erik's hand around the cots. "I thought it was coming for me." Silly to say out loud, but her heart still beat furiously in her chest as she thought of how close that mysterious voice was.

Erik lent the cots against the nearest wall and wrapped Isla in his arms. She buried her face against his chest, willing herself to stop shaking. *Get it together, Isla. It was just a voice. Voices can't hurt you.* But with this voice, she wasn't so sure.

A moment passed and she was able to take a deep breath without trembling again. Isla looked to see Miriam had taken charge of the arrangement of the cots. Lukas stood nearby, a frown on his face.

"I told you, you can have the bed. It's much more comfortable," Lukas said.

"And I told *you* that I'm perfectly fine on the cot! I appreciate the offer, but sleeping in your parents' bed isn't necessary. We'll be fine on the cots, won't we Szilvia?"

Szilvia held up her hands, a grin on her lips. "Don't involve me in this. I just want to sleep!"

"What's going on?" Isla asked.

Miriam sighed. "Oh good, perhaps you can convince your cousin."

"Convince him of what?"

"I'm merely being a good host. There's a perfectly good bed in there, and I don't see why you all should sleep on these old cots," said Lukas.

Isla and Erik exchanged a look. A bed sounded much better than a cot, especially separate cots, when all Isla wanted was to curl up in Erik's arms and rest.

"We'll take the bed," Erik said.

"But don't tell Mother!" Isla added, her cheeks red.

Szilvia laughed as Lukas grinned in victory and Miriam merely rolled her eyes. "Well, now that that's settled, would anyone like more tea?"

Isla bit the inside of her cheek to keep from laughing at how Miriam took control of Lukas' house. He didn't seem to mind, though. He sat on what was Isla's chair, but Isla let him have it. She held Erik's hand as she led him to another empty chair. She stood by him, weaving her fingers through his hair. It calmed not only Erik, but it worked wonders on her own anxiety.

Miriam came back with two fresh mugs of tea and handed them to the boys. Szilvia sat cross-legged on her cot and Miriam took the other empty chair. She had refilled her mug as well.

"How did it go?" Isla asked.

"About the same as last time, except they didn't threaten to drag us to the village," Lukas said then shook his head, rubbing his hands together. "We didn't mention you two had been with us."

"What do you make of it?" Szilvia asked.

"It's strange, certainly. And unsettling. But the woods have always been a mysterious place, even when we were children," said Lukas.

"Children didn't disappear back then, though. Not like this," Szilvia pointed out.

"Not that we know of, anyway," Lukas said. "None except our parents," he added quietly.

Isla thought of the voice. She met Lukas' stare and licked her lips. "Do you think this has something to do with the witch?"

"But I thought the witch was thrown into the oven? She's been dead for over thirty years," said Szilvia as she curled her stocking feet up underneath her.

"That's what our parents have always told us. Not that they've shared many details. But you must admit, it is quite similar. A brother and sister go missing in the woods and something happens to them."

"Our parents made it out alive. Healthy and whole," Lukas pointed out.

Isla shook her head. "Healthy, perhaps, but I've always suspected the woods took something from our parents. To remember them by. I don't know. You may be right, but I'm sure I'm not the only one in the village thinking it right now." She thought of the councillors, especially the ones eager to hear about her parentage.

They'll start looking for reasons to blame Hans and Greta.

"People should be focusing on those poor children, not finding someone to blame for all this," said Miriam.

Szilvia was about to say something, but a yawn came out instead. "On that note, I think it's time for bed."

Lukas got up and stretched his arms. "I couldn't agree more." He glanced at Miriam. "You're sure?"

"Completely. Sarah's quilts will make it feel like a feather-filled mattress," she said with a grin.

Lukas said his goodnights then climbed up to his bedroom loft. Szilvia and Miriam angled their cots so they were close to the fire for warmth, but wouldn't risk setting the wooden frames on fire. Erik and Isla wished them a good sleep then went inside Hans' bedroom. She shut the door behind them and sighed, her shoulders dropping. It was dark inside, no candle to guide the way, so Isla and Erik had to feel their way to the bed. She giggled when Erik muttered a curse after stubbing his toe on the bedframe. She fumbled with the ties of her dress and had to get Erik to help.

"I should be warm enough in my chemise," she said, mostly to herself. She had to fight to keep her eyes open.

Erik's fingers were gentle as he tugged the strings loose. He helped her step out of the dress and placed it on a chair in the far corner of the room. "I'll just sleep in my clothes. I'll keep us both warm," he said, the moonlight catching his smile.

Isla wrapped him in a hug and squeezed him tight. "I'm scared, Erik."

Erik kissed the crown of her head. "We'll figure it out. I won't let anything happen to you, I promise."

She hugged him tight a minute longer, then the pair climbed into bed. Isla had never shared a bed with a man before, but she had always imagined it would be easier to fall asleep with someone else's deep breathing lulling her to sleep. She usually slept on her stomach, but inside the dark room, she kept her back to the wall and curled up against Erik's chest. Erik slid his arm underneath the pillows so Isla could curl up closer, while his other arm rested atop her waist.

"Comfy?" she whispered.

"Very." A pause. "You sure you're okay with this?"

Isla nodded, placing a kiss on her chest. "I didn't expect to share a bed with you until we were married, but I've never been one for tradition."

Erik chuckled. "No, you certainly aren't. Goodnight, Isla."

"Goodnight, Erik." She laid her head against his chest, listening to his heartbeat slow as he fell asleep. She thought of the sleeping Farkas children and sent a prayer to whatever god was listening to wake them.

Why can't I get closer to that farmhouse?

A barrier, icy cold to the touch. Or what remains of my ability to touch. It reminds me of the chill that always pervaded my mother's workroom.

Although we say we're Christians, I know our healing ability comes from some deeper power. Some Other source. Mama never agreed, claiming God blessed us with this gift, and it was our right to use it to help others. While I did want to help, I knew if I told anyone about the powders, books, and incantations we used, our patients may not find our help very godly.

Looking back, Mama was partially right. God did want us to help, but His help wasn't enough to stave off the illnesses invading our community. Starving children, men with lost limbs, women dying in childbirth – it was too much for God to handle. He had so many more important households to watch over. Why shouldn't we have taken some of the burden off him with our gifts? Especially if they came from a source other than Him.

Even now, I don't know where the magic comes from. The crystal's origins are still unknown to me, as are the books. Mama had them since I could remember, and now they sit in my house, gathering dust.

Perhaps Isla will be able to make more sense of them than I ever did.

One can hope.

~ 11 ~

LUKAS

Lukas wiped the sweat from his brow, pushing back his curls. He stood up, stretching his back with a groan, and propped himself up against the railing by the front door. A pile of withered flowers laid at his feet. He took a deep breath, inhaling the crisp fall air. Before he left for Isaiah's, Erik chopped wood so Lukas could focus on Sarah's neglected flower garden. He hadn't touched it since her funeral. He had gotten lost in the acts of dead-heading the flowers that had withered and pruning back the ones still alive. It had taken far longer than expected, but it was good work, forcing him to sit in a place his mother loved and not run from the memories.

A breeze picked up, cooling the back of his neck. Lukas glanced at the house, the quiet unsettling him. Miriam had gotten up before the others and prepared breakfast. After Isla, Erik, and Szilvia left, she went to the cellar, and he hadn't seen her since. Part of him suspected she was avoiding him because of the cot incident the night before, but he had too much to do to dwell on it. Over breakfast, she had asked what Sarah had preserved, but he couldn't remember much other than strawberries for jam. Although Tobias would have much rather been outside with Lukas, once the chickens were tended to, he sent the young lad downstairs to help Miriam.

Lukas caught the whiff of fresh bread in the oven and soup boiling on the stove. With the extra set of hands, she must have found time to make lunch, too. His stomach rumbled.

He picked up the pile of dead flowers and tossed them in the compost box on his way to the water pump. The box was almost full, just waiting for whatever they couldn't salvage from Sarah's vegetable garden. That was on Lukas' to-do list for the afternoon. As Erik had chopped wood nearby, he had commented on the bite in the air.

"It'll be an early winter," Erik had grumbled in agreement.

If Lukas wasn't careful, he would wake up to snow one day, his fall chore list only half done.

The water was cold, sending a shiver through Lukas as he washed his hands. He glanced over his shoulder towards the field where he last saw Hans. At the memory of his encounter with his father the day before, Lukas swallowed bile. He had managed to avoid thinking of Hans as he searched for the Farkas children, but as soon as he went to bed, he tossed and turned most of the night, his thoughts occupied by his father's retreating frame. He wanted to say he understood what Hans was doing, but he just couldn't. Lukas was barely holding it together as it was. With winter baring down, missing children in the woods, and so much left to do, Lukas felt himself being stretched thinner and thinner everyday. He glanced at the house.

At least Miriam is here. Tobias, too. He wouldn't admit it to Isla, who would only gloat, but he *was* glad she had asked Miriam to help. At least Lukas could hold his head above water with them here.

On his way back to the house, Lukas heard Bella bellowing from the barn. He paused and listened as the pregnant cow shuffled in her stall. Lukas bit his lip and took a detour. When he arrived at Bella's stall, he saw mucus coming out of her back end. Her labour had finally started.

"Did you sense him, then, old girl?" Lukas murmured. He stood behind the stall door, watching as she paced the length of her stall.

She contracted, the muscles working to push the calf out, but after half an hour, there was no progress. Lukas bit the inside of his cheek. He had never helped with any of her labours in the past; Hans was always home. He had watched, however, and he knew it was going to be messy if he had to get in there and get the calf out. But what other choice did he have? Hans had made it clear yesterday Lukas was on his own.

Lukas grabbed two pails off the floor, shook out the bits of hay, and ran to the pump. Bella's baying followed him there and grew louder when Lukas returned. He went into her stall, setting the pails far from her in case she decided to kick. He spoke in low, soothing tones like Hans did, and unbuttoned his shirt. He couldn't roll the sleeves up far enough to stick his arm inside Bella without making a mess, so he decided to go without. The fall air chilled him immediately, but Lukas ignored the cold. He rubbed Bella's sides, letting her know he was there to help. He looped a rope around her neck and tied her as close as he could to one of the stall walls. She was forced to stop pacing. He took a deep breath and pushed his arm inside her. It was oddly warm, unsettlingly so, but he kept going until he felt something inside. Something that he hoped was a calf. He felt around, accidentally poking one of its eyes, and winced as he pulled back. He noticed one of the front legs was hooked underneath its body, making it impossible for Bella to push it out. Lukas tried to maneuver the leg into the right spot, but Bella didn't like that. She mooed and shifted, forcing Lukas to pull back. He stumbled backward and fell on his rump. He sat there, staring at Bella's rear end, but he couldn't move. Lukas kept hearing Sarah's voice, telling him to fetch the midwife. To save her.

Lukas tried to take a deep breath, but it came out in short rasps. He felt like he couldn't get enough air in.

"Lukas!"

Miriam found Lukas still on the ground. "Lunch is—" She paused when she saw exactly what was going on. "Heavens, is it time already?" She rolled up her sleeves as she went over to Bella's stall.

She pulled her hair back into a bun then felt Bella's sides, inspecting her much like Lukas had.

"How long has she been in labour?"

Her question jostled Lukas enough to get him back on his feet. He hid his shaking hands from her sight. "At least a half hour. I think a foot is caught."

Miriam gently nudged Lukas out of the way and stuck her arm up inside the cow. Lukas stared at Miriam in surprise but let her do as she pleased. After a moment, she nodded.

"Front left. If you distract her, I think I can move it."

"Distract her with what?"

Miriam smirked. "She's a cow. I'm sure hay will work, and it'll give her strength. Birthing takes a lot out of you, doesn't it, Bella?" she cooed to the cow, who mooed in response.

Lukas used one of the buckets to wash his arm off then he went to grab some hay. He was glad Miriam had arrived when she did. Bella's situation reminded Lukas too much of Sarah's, and he wasn't sure what he could do that would help any more than he had with his mother's birth.

Soon enough, Bella was munching on the hay in Lukas' hand as Miriam worked the calf's leg free.

"Come on, girl, push!" Miriam grunted. "You've no excuse now."

Lukas watched as Bella's muscles contracted again. Miriam kept her arm inside, bracing herself as she helped guide the calf out. A minute later, the calf was free and Miriam's skirt was covered in blood and mucus. The afterbirth came out soon after, narrowly missing Miriam as she took the other bucket and splashed half of it on the calf, clearing most of the mucus out of its mouth and nose.

Lukas freed Bella from the rope and he watched with pride as the cow cleaned off her baby. Miriam used the rest of the bucket to clean her arm. He stood beside her as they both watched Belle tend to her baby. The calf was a decent size and dark grey.

"How did you know how to do that?" Lukas asked.

Miriam smiled up at him. "Uncle Mordecai never neglected my education when it came to running a dairy farm," she said simply.

Lukas nodded, running a hand through his hair. "Well, Bella and I are sure glad you were here to help. Papa usually does this but—"

Miriam waved away the thanks. "It's no trouble. I'm just glad we got the calf out." She knelt and patted the calf's head. "She'll be a great milker like her mama."

"It's a girl, then?"

Miriam nodded. Lukas grinned. Hans would be pleased.

"You said something about lunch?" Lukas said as his stomach grumbled.

Miriam laughed. "Yes, and I'd say we both earned it. We'll be lucky if Tobias hasn't eaten most of it already." She got up and brushed the hay from her ruined skirt. "Although I definitely need to change first. You go ahead and dig in. Tobias will be glad for the company. He's been stuck inside doing 'women's work' all day," she said as she rolled her eyes.

Lukas smirked. "I'm sure he'll be glad he missed this once he smells us." He tossed his shirt over his shoulder then left the barn. Outside, he gave himself a shake, flexing his hands to get them to stop trembling. He blinked away images of Sarah and Bella, both playing on a loop in his head. He headed inside and found Tobias digging into a bowl of lentil soup. He ruffled the boy's hair in passing, placing his ruined shirt by the fireplace to burn later. There would be no getting those stains out, even if Miriam was a meticulous laundress. He went to his loft and grabbed another shirt from his stack.

"How was the cellar?" he called down.

"Boring. I've never counted so many jars in my life!" Tobias whined between slurps of soup.

Lukas chuckled. "You're lucky you know how to count. Most farmhands can barely write their own name." He exited the loft and headed to the cauldron of soup, grabbing a bowl along the way.

"Aunt Tanya makes me sit down and do my numbers and letters before bed every night. At least when I'm here she gives me a break!"

Lukas shook his head but said nothing. Tobias didn't realize how lucky he was to have *an aunt* who also knew arithmetic. His aunt Greta knew more than most village women, only because of their father. Sarah had known how to spell her name, but that was it. He knew more households were starting to invest in their daughters' education, but it would take time – and money – to educate so many people, boys included. Lukas barely remembered his time at the village church where he learned how to count and write. As soon as he could be of use at the farm, the lessons stopped.

The front door banged shut as Miriam came inside, just in her shift. Although her shift was thin, the pale blue fabric kept her covered. Lukas put his bowl down.

"Would you like to borrow one of Mama's dresses?"

Miriam turned to face him, her arms crossed across her chest. Blushing, she met his gaze. "Are you sure?"

"I was going to ask you to take them with you to Aunt Tanya's. Perhaps she knows of some families who could use them." He had thought of asking Isla if she wanted to save any, but Isla wasn't much for new clothes. She had, however, taken Sarah's brush when Lukas offered it. Hans had gifted it to her for a wedding anniversary years ago. It was from Budapest, carved with intricate vines and flowers in the handle. The wood was smooth with age. Isla had teared up when he gave it to her.

Now, Lukas watched as Miriam looked through Sarah's trunk in his parents' room. He went back to his soup and was halfway through his first bowl when Miriam came back in a dark brown dress. Sarah had stitched red flowers along the bottom of the skirt. It was Lukas' turn to blush. He had never seen Miriam look as lovely as she did then.

When she walked past on her way to the soup, Tobias' nose wrinkled. "You stink! What did you do?"

"Birthed a calf," she said as she filled her bowl. "I don't smell half as bad as you," she teased, tweaking his ear before she sat down at the table. "How are the flowers?" she asked as she tore a chunk of bread and dipped it into the soup.

"Not as bad as I feared. I think I can check that off my list. How about the cellar?"

"Not as empty as I expected." Miriam took a sip of the soup then shook her head. "Too hot. There are enough jars of preserves to get us through the winter, but I'd like to get more wheat and oats stored. Fresh bread on a cold day is something one can't do without, especially *our* winters."

Lukas nodded. "We've got at least two fields that need to be harvested. I can show you this afternoon. There should be enough if we can get it harvested in time."

Tobias finished his soup. "Can I have another?"

Miriam nodded. Lukas held out his bowl and Tobias took it without complaint. Lukas smiled his thanks.

"What do you normally do for meat during the winter?" Miriam asked as she cut herself another slice of bread.

"We just cull the old chickens. There's usually a handful who won't last the winter and are done laying. And I'll go hunting for a deer. That usually gets us through. Why?"

"I was thinking I could ask my aunt and uncle if they have an old cow to send to the butcher. If salted and stored properly, you could make do with that. Saves you from having to go hunting."

Lukas thought for a moment, considering the offer. Hans would hate to accept charity, but he had left Lukas with few options. If he was going to get the harvest done in time, clear out the vegetable garden, and get the animals ready for winter, something would have to give. He nodded. "If they have one they don't need, I think that's a great idea. When our cow herd was bigger, Papa used to take a cow to the butcher in late fall. But that was years ago."

"Why don't you have more cows?" Tobias asked as he grabbed a slice of bread, dunking it into his soup.

Miriam glared at him. Tobias blushed. "Just curious," he muttered before stuffing his face with bread.

Lukas smiled. "It's fine, he can ask." He shrugged. "I'm not sure. One year, Papa just decided he didn't want to deal with cattle anymore. He kept Bella and a bull, but the bull died a month after he impregnated Bella. I think Papa just likes his sheep more and decided it was easier to manage them than a herd of sixty cattle. Costs less, too."

Miriam nodded. "They can be a handful. And it makes your job easier, I suppose. Imagine trying to feed that many cattle this winter. You'd probably have to sell half the herd just so they wouldn't starve."

The three sat around the table, enjoying the good food and company, for another half hour, before they cleared the table and got back to work. Lukas asked Tobias to go check on Bella, then he could put the cots from last night's unexpected sleepover back in the barn. When Tobias was done with that, he was to come find Lukas to see if there was anything else he could do before it was time to go home.

Meanwhile, Lukas took Miriam to the fields that needed to be harvested. They stood before the acres of wheat, oats, and barley. Lukas felt her warmth as she stood beside him, barely an inch separating them. Lukas pointed to the far right corner, trying not to think about how close she was. "It's about fifty acres total. Usually Papa would ask the neighbours, but I'm not sure if he offered any services in return, or how he did it." Lukas sighed. "I should have asked him yesterday."

"Yesterday?"

Lukas lowered his gaze, crossing his arms against his chest. "He was in the tool shed. Grabbing some things for a trip. He won't be back for a few months." Lukas sighed heavily. "It's up to me to make sure everything doesn't fall apart until then."

"Us," Miriam said, placing a hand on Lukas' arm. "It's up to us. You, me, and Tobias. We'll manage."

Lukas met her gaze and nodded slowly. He unfolded his arms and clasped one of her hands in his, holding tightly. He looked back at the field, taking slow, deep breaths.

"I'm really glad you're here, Miriam," he said quietly.

Miriam squeezed his hand, running her thumb over the back of his hand. "Me too, Lukas."

They stood watching the wind blow through the fields for some time. The silence calmed Lukas' pounding heart. Memories of Sarah's labour and Bella's weren't quite as prominent as before.

"I'll talk to Aunt Tanya and Uncle Mordecai tonight. My brothers might be free, too. I'm sure they'd love any excuse to get out of the house."

"My uncle could come, too. Maybe Erik, if Isaiah doesn't need him for anything." Which was unlikely, but one could hope.

"We'll get it done." She tugged on his hand. "Come on. Let's go see Bella's baby. Perhaps Tobias is still there." She gasped. "You didn't name the calf before! You have to do that, too!"

Lukas chuckled. "I'm awful with names."

As they walked back to the barn, Lukas didn't let go of her hand. Miriam glanced up at him. "What about Sarah?"

Lukas smiled. "I think Mama would get a kick out of a cow named after her. She was quite fond of Bella." He nodded. "Sarah it is."

They headed back to the barn, thoughts of harvest and winter swirling in Lukas' mind.

~ 12 ~

ISLA

Isla set the cup of tea down on the side table beside her father as he smoked his pipe in his favourite chair. His feet rested on the stool in front of the fire, angled so his sore feet got most of the heat. She kissed his forehead, causing him to open his eyes.

"Tea's ready," she said with a smile.

Jacob gave his head a little shake, blinking as he came out of his nap. "Thank you, my dear. Are you going to join me?"

She shook her head. "Mama's still putting away supper."

"Best help her, then. Do you need another set of hands?"

"No, you rest. I can handle her."

Jacob sighed as he tilted his head back. "I thought mining was hard. Dealing with demanding customers isn't easy."

Isla handed him his tea. "Yes, but at least there's less chance of a cave-in."

"Some days, I'd take the cave-in. But don't tell your mother," he whispered with a wink.

"I heard that!" Greta called from the kitchen.

Isla chuckled then headed back to the sink, leaving her father to his tea. She rolled up her sleeves and grabbed the nearest dish towel. She picked up the first dish in the growing pile and got to work. Truth be told, she would much rather be in front of the fire with her papa, but since finding the Farkas children, questions kept

119

nagging at her. It was easier to ask Greta about her childhood when she was preoccupied with work, and when Jacob slept.

"Mama," Isla began, putting away the stack of soup bowls.

"Hm?" Greta worked a particularly tough stain out of her favourite pot.

"What was it like at the witch's cottage?"

Greta paused mid-scrub. "Why in heaven's name do you want to know about my time in that wretched place?"

Isla focused on the dishes, refusing to meet her mother's gaze. "It's just with the children. It seems odd that it's a boy and a girl going missing. In the same woods, too."

"Children go missing all the time."

Isla looked over at Greta. "They don't come back in a deep sleep like that."

Greta shrugged. "Children also get sick."

"Mama, I really think there's a connection—"

Greta slammed the pot onto the kitchen counter. "The witch is dead, Isla. I pushed her in the oven myself. I will *never* forget that creature's screams. She has nothing to do with the Szabós or Farkas children. Let it go." She slid the pot towards Isla on the counter then went back to washing, her back to her daughter.

"Were you scared?" she asked softly.

Greta didn't answer for several seconds, long enough that Isla thought her mother was ignoring her.

"Terrified. Hans was, too. But he hid it better," Greta said as she let the sink drain. Greta pushed back the hair that had come loose from her bun. "He's always hidden how he really feels. That's why he moved to that damn farm. It's easier to hide when there's no one around." Greta sighed. "Perhaps he was right, though. Maybe we should have moved away too, away from the woods and all the memories there." She glanced at her daughter. "The opportunities in Budapest..." she trailed off. Greta shook her head, drying her hands on a towel. "It doesn't matter if those children were lured into the woods by some wicked witch, or if they just got lost and sick on their own. It's none of our business. I don't want you going to look for them anymore. Do you understand, Isla?"

Isla's hand went to the crystal she kept tucked underneath her dress. She laid her palm flat against it. She hadn't told Greta about it. She wasn't honestly sure if she ever would. Greta had little faith in magic, for good reason. Isla wasn't sure if the crystal was magical, but it certainly was strange. Strange enough that Greta may get rid of it if she knew how it had helped Isla find the Farkas children.

"But Mama, they're children. They needed help and—"

"And that's what the Councillors and their men are for. If you keep showing up with those children, do you know what they'll say, what they'll think? That you caused it. You're a witch, or consorting with a demon, or a woman that's just cleverer than they are. They hate that. Any of those options puts you in harm's way, and I won't have it, Isla. I won't lose you." Greta roughly wiped her eyes, the tears glistening on the back of her hand.

Isla took a step to her mother, closing the gap between them. She hugged Greta, surprising them both. "You won't lose me, Mama. I'll be safe."

Greta shook her head, squeezing Isla tight. "Promise me, Isla. Promise me you won't go into the woods."

"I promise," Isla said, surprised at how easily the lie came out.

She helped Greta tidy the rest of the kitchen then grabbed her cloak by the front door. "I told Erik I would meet him in the village square. He has the night off, but he has to be back early tomorrow morning."

Greta nodded. "His parents are visiting a sick aunt, aren't they?"

Isla nodded. They had left just yesterday for Budapest.

"You may offer him the extra cot for the night, if you wish," said Greta.

Isla paused as she tied her dark brown cloak around her neck. "Really?" Since she began seeing Erik, Greta had *never* willingly invited Erik over for anything besides afternoon tea, and even that had taken weeks of pleading and Jacob stepping in to get it to happen.

Greta avoided Isla's gaze. "It's not safe to travel alone at night. Not in those woods."

Isla hid her smile. "I'll let him know, Mama." She looked over at her papa, but Jacob was still asleep. She headed outside, the crisp night air calming her racing heart. She made it to the square before Erik and decided to wait for him by the fountain. She sat on its edge, the sturdy rock worn smooth by so many people taking advantage of its peaceful atmosphere. She looked up at the sky, watching the sun as it began its slow descent.

"You're early," Erik said as he sat beside her. "Or am I just late?"

She smiled at him. "A little of both." She pecked his cheek. "How was your day?"

"Long, and I'm glad it's over." He kissed Isla. "Come, let's go to the tavern. I could use a drink."

Isla took his hand and followed Erik's lead. The Swan's Nest was one of the few places in the village open past sunset. It wasn't as rowdy as the tavern at the edge of Lobkovice, the one Isaiah and his young knights tended to frequent. Isla knew Erik went with him sometimes, but she didn't want to know what he got up to while there. It was best not to ask. The Swan's Nest was loud enough for Isla and Erik to have an excuse to sit close together to hear each other.

It was about half-full inside. The sconces on the wall were already lit, and the rough, wooden tables scattered around the large room were sticky with spilled ale. Erik went to the bar to get their drinks while Isla scouted out a secluded booth. Men back from the mines were drinking away the troubles of their day among good—if loud—company. A few women mingled about, but Isla avoided their gazes. Greta would throw enough of a fit if she knew she was at The Nest, least of all if Isla made friends with the women who frequented the place for more than just the food.

Isla found a booth near the back of the tavern and claimed it before another group could. The red cushion had a few rips in it, but the table was clean, and the back of the bench was comfortable. Isla relaxed into it as she watched Erik at the bar. He laughed at something the owner said then took the drinks. Isla waved and Erik spotted her. He slid over an apple cider for her as he settled beside her, their legs touching. His ale smelt strong, and Isla shook her head. She hated the taste even more than the smell. She took a sip of her cider. "So, that bad of a day, huh?"

Erik shrugged, staring at the rim of his mug. "Isaiah got a letter from his father."

Isla's eyes widened. When Erik didn't continue, she nudged his arm. "And?" she pressed.

"I really shouldn't tell you. He told me to keep it a secret."

Isla rolled her eyes. "I'm going to be your wife, Erik. There are no secrets between us."

"True." He took a sip of his ale. "The Chief is coming back to the castle, and he's bringing Aliz with him."

Isla nearly choked on her cider. "You're serious?"

"I read the letter myself."

"Isn't Isaiah happy to have his sister back?" From what she recalled, the two had been close as children. But perhaps living apart for so long had changed things. Worse yet, perhaps the Chief Steward had wanted to sever the ties between his children much like he had with Isla and Isaiah.

Erik shrugged. "From what I understood of his rant, it's complicated. I think Isaiah is worried his father's return means he plans to look for a bride for Isaiah."

Isla wrinkled her nose. "I thought the Chief was more worried about securing a marriage for Aliz?"

"That's what I thought too, but Isaiah made it sound like the Chief Steward is aiming for an important alliance for each of his children. I'm sure that means the castle will be bustling with prospective brides and bridegrooms." He sighed. "Which means I'll be busier than usual in the stables attending to their horses."

"You could just leave, you know. You don't *have* to work for Isaiah."

Erik ran a hand through his hair. "And leave him alone with his scheming father and those women vying for his inheritance? What kind of a friend would I be if I left?"

"One who values self-preservation, and the opinion of his soon-to-be bride?"

Erik placed his hand over Isla's. "You know I respect your opinion. And honestly, you're right. You have been for years. But you don't know Isaiah like I do. He'll be lost if left alone in that castle."

"The only reason I don't know him is because he acts as if he doesn't know *me*. Or Szilvia and Lukas. If he didn't want to be so alone, he could treat us like human beings."

"And defy his father?" Erik shook his head. "That man controls every minute of Isaiah's life, even from Budapest. If Isaiah even nodded to you in the market, one of his servants would report it to the Chief Steward immediately. He's always being watched."

Isla wanted to argue her point further, but she didn't want to spend the rest of her night with Erik fighting about Isaiah. He was too much a part of her relationship with Erik to begin with.

Erik squeezed her hand. "Let's see what this latest visit brings. If Isaiah is content, perhaps we can have that winter wedding you always wanted."

The couple spent the next hour enjoying each other's company and discussing wedding plans. Erik ordered a bowl of stew, as he hadn't had a chance to eat before leaving Isaiah's. Another group sat in the booth to their left. Isla couldn't see who they were; she hadn't caught much of their faces before the four men sat down, but she could hear them clearly.

"What did he say?"

"I caught Varga on his way out of the meeting. He said there will be a ban put out tomorrow. No children left unsupervised. No going into the woods."

One man snorted. "They expect that to fix the problem?"

"It's a start," the second man said.

"What of the children? Nothing?" the first man said.

"They're the same. Nothing wakes them. The doctor and preacher have tried everything," said the second man.

"Has anyone asked the healer, Constance?" the fourth man asked.

"No, and no one will, if what Varga said is true," said the second man.

"What do you mean?"

"The children have clearly been bewitched. Why ask the woman who probably did it to inspect her handiwork?" the second man said.

"Varga said that?"

"Not outright, but you could tell he was thinking it. I wouldn't be surprised if there was a warrant out for her arrest in the next few days."

Isla's hand was shaking so badly she spilt her cider. Erik grabbed her hands, ignoring the sticky cider, and squeezed them tight. She met his gaze, her breathing shaky. She thought of what Greta had said, about witches and powerful women and looking for someone to blame.

They can't arrest Constance. She hasn't done anything. She remembered the way Varga and his fellow councillors had looked at her that night they questioned her. They were looking for a way out, an explanation to the mystery of the sleeping children, and who better to blame than a widow who cured the sick in ways they couldn't understand?

Isla tried to focus on what the men said, but she couldn't shake the terror running through her veins. Erik took the lead and helped her from the booth. They kept their backs to the occupied booth and headed straight for the door. Isla clasped her cloak tightly around her body with one hand, the other holding Erik's. As soon as they were outside, Isla turned to the nearest road leading out of the village.

"I have to warn Constance," she whispered.

"Tomorrow. It's too dark to go over tonight."

"But what if the council arrests her tonight? Those cowards wouldn't hesitate to do it under the cover of darkness." Especially Varga.

"Your mother would have a fit if I let you go there."

"Who says anything about letting? I'm my own woman, Erik. I can do as I please."

Erik squeezed her hand. "I know, my love. I know." He kissed her forehead. "But think logically. It's cold, dark, and late. It'll take you twice as long to get there, and by then you'll be exhausted. If you wait until morning when you have a clear head, you'll stand a better chance."

Isla looked down the road then turned away, her mouth set in a grim line. "Fine. Tomorrow. But I'm going over as soon as dawn breaks."

"I wish I could help you, but Isaiah wants the stables completely cleaned and the horses gone over before his father returns. I have to supervise."

"Don't worry, I'll be fine."

The two walked on in silence until they reached Isla's front door.

"Oh, I almost forgot! Mama said you could stay over tonight, if you like. The spare cot isn't much, but it's better than walking home alone."

Erik's eyes widened. "What brought that on?"

Isla smirked. "She doesn't want you travelling alone."

Erik grinned. "Well, it would be rude to turn down a free cot, wouldn't it?"

"I should think so!"

Isla led Erik inside, mindful of her sleeping papa still in his chair.

~ 13 ~

LUKAS

A gust of wind whipped through the field, sending a chill down Lukas' spine. He straightened up, shielding his eyes from the bright sun. Or, it *was* bright. Somehow, between driving in fence posts, the sun went to hide behind the clouds. Lukas' shoulders slumped.

Tobias shifted from foot to foot, the most recent fence post tight in his grip. "Those clouds look scary."

Lukas stuffed the handful of nails he had left in the pocket of his coat. "Come on, we'd better head back to the farmhouse. I'll walk you and Miriam home once it clears up."

Tobias left the fence post on the ground and stuck close to Lukas' side as they made their way back. Lukas glanced down at Tobias, the little boy's face pale and his eyes wide.

"Not a fan of thunder?"

Tobias shook his head. Lukas grabbed Tobias' nearest hand and held it gently. "I didn't like it either when I was your age."

"Thunder's loud," Tobias murmured, gripping Lukas' hand tighter.

"It is, but I like to think it's the angels in heaven playing a game of chase. Their footsteps sound louder because they're running to catch each other."

"Wouldn't they fly?"

Lukas winked. "It's against the rules."

They were silent for a moment. "Do you think my mama and papa are playing chase?" Tobias asked quietly.

Lukas squeezed his hand tight. "Yes, I'm sure my mama is too. Perhaps they're on the same team."

Tobias smiled a little. "My papa's fast. He played chase with me all the time."

"My papa did, too." He sighed. "I miss him."

Tobias looked up at Lukas, meeting his gaze. "Do you get lonely?"

Lukas nodded. "That's why it's nice that you and Miriam come to visit. You're a big help."

Tobias' eyes widened. "I am?"

"I wouldn't have gotten as far as I did on the fence without you!" Lukas swung Tobias' arm. "I like having you here."

Tobias smiled. "I like being here, too. Your chickens are nicer than Aunt Tanya's. They peck me whenever I try to get the eggs."

Lukas laughed. "Well, I'm glad to hear I have nice chickens."

They fell into a peaceful silence as they made their way through the field. As they neared the gate to the fenced field where the horses were grazing, Tobias swallowed.

"Maybe, instead of going home with Miriam at night, I could stay out here with you. If you want. So you wouldn't be lonely."

Lukas paused, his hand hovering above the lock on the gate. He looked down at Tobias, their hands still laced together. "Tobias, I'm not sure—"

"I won't be any trouble! You know I work hard. I can help make food like Miriam does. Then she wouldn't have to come over. It would just be the two of us!"

Lukas sighed. "Tobias, I like having you here, but living with me . . . I can't take care of you. Not like Aunt Tanya does."

"Aunt Tanya isn't my mama. She doesn't understand what it's like! You do." Tobias let go of Lukas' hand. "You know what it's like to not have parents," he whispered.

Lukas' heart twisted in his chest. "I do understand, Tobi, I do, but it's not a good idea—"

Lukas wasn't sure what he would have said if the first crack of thunder hadn't shaken the fence. He glanced at the sky and saw the rain clouds had caught up with them. He swung the gate open and nudged Tobias. The boy was frozen, his wide eyes as he stared up at the darkening sky.

"Head for the farmhouse! I'll be right behind you," he shouted as the wind whipped through the field, threatening to steal the hat from his head. He nudged Tobias again, and this time the boy moved. Lukas followed his lead, pausing where the horses were grazing in the middle of the field.

"Rowan! Gerdie! Home time!" he shouted above the wind. Gerdie lifted her head at the sudden noise, but Rowan ignored Lukas, his nose to the ground as he munched away on the last of the season's grass.

Lukas grabbed the rope he left on one of the posts earlier that morning. He went over to Gerdie and gave her a light tap on the rump, sending her trotting towards the gate, and home. Lukas tried to get Rowan to follow Gerdie's lead, but Rowan refused to budge. The wind blew harder, sending Lukas' hat flying. He forgot it as he looped the rope around Rowan's reluctant neck. The horse snorted and planted his feet, refusing to budge.

"I'll give you an apple when we get home," Lukas said. "Get going, boy!"

Lukas wasn't sure how long the stand-off between horse and master would have lasted had it not been for the lightning. It was a sheet that painted the sky blinding white. Lukas had to cover his eyes, but Rowan wasn't as lucky. He whinnied and rose on his hind legs, sending Lukas to his knees as he tried to hold on. Rowan landed back down on all fours, his breathing frantic. He took off at a canter towards the gate. Lukas tried to keep up but gave up and let the rope go. He ran after Rowan, shutting the gate behind him once he was through. Gerdie was waiting in the next field, the barn in sight. Lukas gave her another light tap as Rowan breezed past her, heading straight for the safety of the barn.

Gerdie trotted on, keeping pace with Lukas, as if she didn't want to leave him behind. Lukas appreciated that, especially when the first drops of rain hit his face.

As the three passed through the last gate, the rain came down harder. By the time he got the horses in their stalls, he was soaked through. He gave Rowan the promised apple, giving Lukas a chance to wipe the rain from his face. Lukas noticed Bella's stall was empty. He left the barn door open as he ran out, trying to remember what field she and her calf was in.

Miriam came through the gate leading to the south field, Bella and her calf Sarah close behind. She, too, was drenched, her curly hair plastered to her face. Lukas nodded his thanks as he ushered Bella and Sarah inside.

"I got the horses," he shouted over the latest crack of thunder.

"Have you seen Tobias?"

"I sent him ahead of me. He should be inside."

Miriam nodded. "The chicken coop is shut. They should be fine."

Another peal of thunder, another sheet of lightning. The rain came down harder. "Let's get inside. We'll have to wait it out," Lukas said.

Although his jacket was soaked, he shrugged it off then lifted it over himself and Miriam's heads to keep the worst of the rain off them as they ran to the farmhouse. Lukas slammed the door shut behind him, his breath coming out in short pants.

Tobias stood in front of the fireplace, a puddle forming underneath his feet as his clothes drip-dried on him. It looked like he was adding a log to the embers from the morning fire. Lukas went over to him and put an arm on his shoulder. Tobias didn't turn to look at him.

"I'll find you something dry to wear." He glanced at Miriam who was at the kitchen table, slicing up a loaf of bread. "Both of you. You can borrow another of Mama's dresses. I don't think I gave all of them to Aunt Tanya."

Miriam blushed, her wet curls hanging limply around her face. "Lukas, you don't—"

"You'll freeze if you stay in that dress," Lukas pointed out. He went up to his loft to find some hand-me-downs for Tobias. By the time he came downstairs, Tobias was curled up in a blanket in front of the fire, his head on Miriam's lap. Her hand was woven between his curls, brushing them back. Lukas placed the clothes in a folded pile by Miriam. She smiled at him, and he nodded in reply.

Sarah's nightgowns were still neatly folded in her dresser in the bottom shelf. He forced himself to take deep breaths as he rummaged through the soft fabric. Her scent, lavender and mint, wafted up at him. He breathed Sarah in, and tears came to his eyes. He shook his head, grabbed the first one on the pile, then went back to the main room.

Tobias was fast asleep on Miriam's lap. Lukas knelt beside Miriam and gently cradled Tobias' head in his hands. He lifted the boy up and slowly slipped him over to his lap. Miriam mouthed the words "thank you" then went inside Sarah's room to change.

Alone now, Lukas let out a deep breath, the tension leaving his shoulders. His calloused fingers smoothed back Tobias' drying curls. Tobias' mouth was slightly open, his breath warming Lukas' knee as he breathed deeply. As Lukas stared at the sleeping boy, he felt guilty for saying no to Tobias' request. Would there really be any harm having Tobias stay with him?

At least I wouldn't have to spend my nights alone.

Lukas shook his head. But it wouldn't be fair to Tobias. He couldn't raise a child.

I'm barely managing as it is. I can't be responsible for him. Yet wasn't he already, at least during the day?

Miriam re-entered the main area, interrupting Lukas' thoughts. She brought a quilt with her from his parents' bed and wrapped it around their shoulders as she sat beside Lukas.

"Do you want me to take him back?" she whispered.

"No, I'm quite comfortable." He motioned to the nightgown. "Did I choose a decent one?"

Miriam grinned, her cheeks red. "Yes, it's very soft. Sarah always seemed to like soft fabric for her clothes."

"And her quilts. She made so many over the years." He glanced at the fire. "I don't know what to do with them all now."

"Perhaps you could give some away. There are many families in the village who would love a cozy blanket for the winter."

Lukas nodded. "You're right; I think she'd like to know her quilts were going to help others."

The two were quiet for a time, letting the crackling logs in the fireplace fill the silence.

"He asked if he could stay," Lukas whispered.

"What?"

Lukas motioned to Tobias. "He asked if he could stay with me. I told him no."

Miriam licked her lips. "Do you *want* him to stay?"

"Part of me does. The other part is terrified I'll get him killed or scar him for life."

Miriam smirked. "I think most parents are afraid of those things."

"But I'm not a parent. I'm just a kid."

"He could use a big brother."

"So you think I should do it?"

Miriam shrugged. "Give it time. He may change his mind by tomorrow. Children often do," she said with a grin.

Thunder shook the house and the rain started to fall harder. Lukas clucked his tongue as he stared at the ceiling. "I haven't heard a storm this violent in years. At least this time of year."

Miriam nodded. "I don't think it's going to let up soon."

"Guess you'll be spending the night in my parents' room again."

"I'm quite comfy right here, to be honest."

Lukas smiled, glancing at her from his peripheral vision. "Me too."

Miriam got up. "I'm going to brew some tea. Want a slice of bread?"

Lukas nodded. He watched the flames engulf the logs while Miriam made up a tray. When she came back, Lukas held the tray as she placed her half of the quilt back around her shoulders. Lukas placed the tray beside him, handing Miriam her cup and plate. She smiled her thanks then dug in. Lukas followed her lead. He was careful not to drop crumbs on Tobias. He wondered when the lad would wake up.

"I'm amazed he can sleep through all that racket outside," Miriam muttered.

Lukas took a sip of tea, nearly burning his tongue. "Whenever a big storm rolled through, Mama and I used to go out on the porch and watch." He glanced outside and saw the nearest tree's branches bending in the forceful wind. "Although right now, I'm much happier to be inside."

Miriam brushed the crumbs from her bread onto the floor. "Do you think the children will wake up?"

It took him a moment to realize she wasn't talking about Tobias. "I don't know. I hope so, if not for their sake, then for Isla's."

"It's ridiculous of the Council to suspect her, or any woman, without any proof," she said with a huff. "Stubborn old men," she grumbled.

Lukas stared into the fire. "They're afraid. I don't blame them for that, but I agree that they're jumping to conclusions."

Miriam snorted. "You're not the one who would be charged with witchcraft if they turned their suspicions away from Isla."

Lukas raised an eyebrow. "What do you mean?"

Miriam stared at her mug in her lap. "Any woman is in danger whenever something strange happens in the village. Any village really. If you don't act the way a woman is 'supposed to,' you're seen as strange. And being strange is dangerous."

Lukas was silent for a moment. "I never thought of it like that." He reached over and covered one of her hands with his. "I'm sorry, Miriam. You shouldn't have to be afraid like that. No one should."

"Thank you," Miriam whispered.

They drank their tea in silence for a few minutes, the pop and sizzle of the fire playing in time with the steady rainfall against the windows. The next crack of thunder made them both jump a little. Lukas wiped the droplets of tea off his tunic, then placed his mug back on the tray. Miriam handed him her mug and he did the same. He watched her cover her mouth as she yawned.

"You can go to sleep, if you'd like," Lukas said. "You've had a long day."

"As have you," she said with a chuckle as Lukas suppressed his own yawn. "I'll stay up until Tobias wakes up. He doesn't like to be alone when it's storming."

"Nightmares?"

Miriam nodded. "He used to get them every night when he first came to stay with Aunt Tanya. Now it's only occasionally. But usually if there's a storm, he gets one." Miriam leaned over and brushed back Tobias' curls. "I'd let him share my bed to help with the nightmares."

Lukas glanced at the door to his parents' room. "I could carry him in there and you could both get some sleep."

"What about you?"

Lukas shrugged. "I've got my loft. It's nice listening to the rain as I fall asleep up there."

Miriam got up. "Let's get him settled. If nothing else, it'll give you a chance to stretch your legs."

It was harder than Lukas expected to extract himself from underneath Tobias. He managed with Miriam's help, especially as she kept Tobias' head from hitting the floor as Lukas stood. He gave his legs a shake to get the blood flowing again. He bent down and lifted Tobias up, taking the blanket with him. Miriam opened his parents' bedroom door then pulled back the covers. Together they slid Tobias beneath the quilts, making sure he would be warm. They left the door propped open when they exited the room. Lukas hoped he slept for a while longer.

"Can I hear it?" Miriam asked.

Lukas raised an eyebrow. "Hear what?"

"The rain. In the loft. You made it sound quite peaceful."

Lukas blushed, thinking of how cluttered it was up there. "Are you sure? It's not exactly spacious . . ."

"All the better to stay warm up there, right?"

Lukas had no argument against that. He motioned towards the ladder. Miriam went up with Lukas following behind. When he got up there, he tried to kick his dirty clothes out of the way, but Miriam didn't seem to notice the mess. Lukas took his blankets off the pallet and pushed it to the side to make room for them both to lie on the floor. Miriam laid on her back and stared at the ceiling. Lukas laid beside her, not sure what to do. He glanced at her and saw her eyes were closed. Lukas swallowed, his cheeks aflame.

After a moment, Miriam grinned. "You're right, it is nice up here. I can see why you like it so much."

Lukas shrugged in the darkness. "It's quiet. Sometimes too quiet," he muttered.

Miriam shifted onto her side, staring at him. There was barely an inch between them. Lukas was glad the darkness hid his blushing cheeks. "Harder not to think of your mother when you're up here, I suspect."

"If I keep busy, it's not so bad."

"You can't avoid thinking of her forever. She's your mama."

Lukas' eyes pricked with tears. "I know. There's just too much to do. I don't feel like I have time to think, let alone grieve."

Miriam slid her hand into his. "Take the time. Tobias and I are here to help. Even if that means giving you time to find a deserted place in the woods to scream or cry or whatever you have to do."

Lukas didn't say anything for a moment. He swallowed down his tears and nodded. "Thank you," he whispered.

A few moments passed; Miriam rolled back onto her back. She kept a hold of Lukas' hand, though. "Do you think what Isla said is true about the witch? That she's the one taking the children?"

Isla had come over a few days ago for tea, and to bounce her idea off her cousin. Miriam, of course, had been over and listened, offering her own suggestions. At the time, Lukas wasn't sure what to make of Isla's theory. It was possible, but the idea of the witch still lurking in the woods, luring children and causing panic in the village, was unsettling. He wished Constance had found a logical reason for the sleeping sickness affecting the children, but so far Constance hadn't come across an explanation, and that put her in danger.

"I don't know, my parents never spoke much about their time in the woods. But I hope whatever is causing the children to wander off stops. It's been a week, so maybe whatever it is has passed," Lukas said.

"I hope so. I don't want to think about what will happen if more children go missing."

They'll go after Constance. He knew as soon as Isla told him about the conversation at the tavern that Constance and Szilvia were in danger. Isla had told the women what she heard, but they hadn't left their cottage. According to Isla, Constance refused to be driven from her home, and Szilvia wasn't going to leave her mother behind.

Lukas looked over at Miriam and saw her eyes were closed. Her breathing had evened out. For a moment, he thought she was asleep.

"I forgot to tell you, my uncle said he, my cousins, and some other farmers will come in two days to get the harvest off. I've sent a message to my brothers as well. I think we can count on them," Miriam said, her voice soft with sleep.

Lukas leaned over, emboldened by the darkness, and kissed Miriam's cheek. "Thank you."

Miriam's eyes opened wide. They stared at each other for a moment, then Miriam looked away. She curled up beside him, giving his hand a squeeze. Lukas used his free hand to drag a blanket overtop them. It didn't sound like the rain was going to let up anytime soon, and he was so tired. Lukas rolled onto his side facing Miriam. She moved closer until her head was nestled underneath his chin, their hearts beating in sync. He took a deep breath and as he exhaled, he rested his arm across her waist. As he started to fall asleep, he wasn't afraid of the thoughts that may creep in.

He just hoped word didn't reach Greta about this particular sleeping arrangement.

~ 14 ~

ISLA

Isla knelt amongst the flowers in Constance's garden, her hands clutching at roots as she pulled out the row of calendulas. Their orange and yellow petals fluttered in the cool breeze. Yesterday's storm had made the land smell clean, but it had also left behind a path of destruction. On her way over to Constance's earlier that morning, Isla saw fallen trees, some split at the trunk from lightning strikes. The wind had pulled fence posts out of the ground and flattened flowerbeds. Thankfully, Constance's were spared, for the most part. Since she had arrived, Isla had been in the garden, salvaging what she could for Constance's medicines.

Szilvia grunted to Isla's left as she pounded the latest fence post into the ground. Constance didn't like fences, but Szilvia had insisted that if they didn't put up some sort of barrier around the garden, the wild rabbits would get into it. Constance had left the girls to their work, too tired to argue. Although she hadn't admitted it in Isla's hearing, Isla suspected the stress of the Council's suspicion was wearing on Constance. Isla couldn't imagine what it would be like to have a village you spent your life healing turn on you.

Isla stared at her pile of flowers for a moment then added them to the others in her woven basket. She glanced at Szilvia. "Time for lunch?"

Szilvia wiped her sweaty hands on her apron as she nodded. "I'm starving."

The girls went inside, the basket bumping against Isla's leg. She put it on the floor then cleared off enough room on the kitchen table for a quick meal. Szilvia dug in the cupboards for jam and butter, bread and plates. Isla shoed Anna off one of the chairs. The calico yawned then curled up in front of the fire, ignoring the noise Szilvia made as she gathered the food.

Isla helped her carry the various jams to the table. Szilvia had found strawberry, raspberry, and peach jams from last season. As the girls grabbed their thick slices of bread and made their jam selection, Isla remembered it would soon be canning season. She wondered if Miriam had already gotten a head start at Lukas'. She had promised her mother she would go check on the two of them this week, but she hadn't had a chance to stop in yet. Personally, she didn't want to barge in on them. She knew Greta only wanted her to check on Lukas because she would rather Isla be safe on the farm then tempting fate by being at Constance's. Isla had made the mistake of sharing the tavern gossip with her mother. Greta had turned bright red with rage.

"Such men have no business discussing what they don't understand," she said, shaking her head. Greta may not enjoy Isla's training, but she respected the midwife. She admired any woman willing to make it on their own.

Greta had given Isla a stern warning. "Don't go over to Constance's as often, Isla. Especially not when other people would notice. I don't want you getting mixed up in this."

But I already am. Isla's crystal hadn't come alive again like it had the night of the Farkas children's disappearance, but she kept it on. And she couldn't deny what it had done. Without the crystal, Isla didn't think she would have located the children. There was some sort of connection, but she had no idea what it meant.

Szilvia bit into her bread, a satisfied smile spreading across her face as she chewed. "Good idea about lunch. I can't believe so much time has passed. I thought we had only been at it an hour."

Isla nodded as she coated her bread with a thick layer of strawberry jam. "I'm just glad you made bread before I got here. I love your fresh bread." She took a big bite, her teeth sinking into it.

"Where does Greta think you are today?"

"At Lukas' helping him and Miriam get ready for harvest tomorrow." She brushed the crumbs from her lap, a treat for Anna. "I *do* plan to go by. Just after the garden's done."

Szilvia shook her head. "It likely won't be done until late tonight."

Isla shrugged, already eyeing up another slice of bread. "Then I go tomorrow. Lukas will probably want another set of hands anyway. Mama won't mind."

"I don't like that you have to lie about coming here. It feels wrong."

"What else can I do? You know she worries. And she has a right to. For all we know, the Council—"

"Can go to Hell," Szilvia interrupted, her cheeks flush with rage. "Until they come with warrants, and proof, we're not leaving."

Isla sighed and focused on the meal. She and Szilvia had had this same fight several times already, and she really wasn't in the mood to have it again. Isla didn't blame her for wanting to stay in her home, but she was worried. What if the Council came when Isla wasn't there? How could she protect the girl she thought of as a sister? She had considered asking Erik if he could get some time off from Isaiah's, but she knew the answer before she even opened her mouth. With Aliz and the Chief Steward expected any day, Erik barely had time to sleep, let alone check in on Constance and Szilvia.

At least when she had shared Aliz's return with Szilvia, it seemed to lighten the mood. Szilvia had admitted she knew about the journey, but Aliz hadn't sent a letter since she left Budapest. For the last few days, Szilvia had jumped at every knock on the door, wondering if a messenger was on the other side with word from Aliz. Or better yet, Aliz herself.

With their bellies full, Isla and Szilvia put away the jams and slid their plates into the sink. As Isla stood in the doorway, tying her hair up into a ponytail, Szilvia came up behind her and hugged her.

"I'm sorry. I know you just want to help."

Isla leaned back against her friend's embrace, placing her hands overtop Szilvia's. "I'm sorry, too. I wish there was more I could do." If only she had a magic wand, or a spell to send the Council packing.

Szilvia let Isla go then stood beside her. They stared at the expanse of field opening before them. "No children have gone missing since the Farkas children. Perhaps whatever lured them away has left."

Wishful thinking. Something Isla had thought many times herself, but she couldn't fully believe it. It was too simple, too easy. Besides, the Szabós and Farkases were still asleep. No cure for them meant suspicion would still be cast upon Constance and Szilvia. Until they woke, Isla's best friend was in danger.

It was mid-afternoon when Constance rode up on her donkey, Millie. The old girl had been Constance's faithful steed for almost twelve years. Isla had asked Constance why she didn't have a horse like Lukas' family, and Constance had laughed.

"Have you seen Rowan lately? A horse is all well and good, but I need a stubborn donkey to get me to my patients."

Now, Constance got Millie settled in her stall before she came over to check on the girls. Her basket that she had left with that morning was empty. Isla could see the exhaustion in her eyes as Constance inspected Isla's work.

"Get the hawthorne before you go, please. I'll need it tonight."

Isla nodded and got to work. From the corner of her eye, she watched Szilvia finish the last fence post then follow her mother inside. When her basket was full, Isla headed inside, closing the new garden gate behind her. Inside, Constance was seated before the fire, Anna purring on her lap. Constance's hair had loosened from its practical bun and framed her face in auburn curtains, a streak or two of grey catching in the firelight. Her boots were by the door and her apron hung beside the stove. Szilvia was there, filling a pot with the vegetables she had already chopped.

"Are you staying for supper?" Szilvia asked as she added carrots.

"You should go home, Isla. Your mother will worry," said Constance.

Isla put the basket of hawthorne on the table. "I can stay. Here, let me help. Would you like tea, Constance?"

The older woman smiled, her eyes closed. "Tea would be delightful. I had such a long day." She explained the case to them: a man with a broken femur. Most of those in attendance at the sick man's bedside thought she would have to cut the leg off, but Constance was determined to save it.

"What would you recommend, Szilvia?" Constance asked.

"Splint the leg so the bone resets. Make it so he can't move," Szilvia replied.

"How many weeks on bedrest?"

"At least eight, if not more. But check it at six, then again at eight."

Constance nodded. "Good." She glanced at Isla. "What do we leave for pain management?"

Isla grabbed the boiling kettle and Constance's cup, a tall, beige mug that held almost a full kettle of tea. "Rosemary, willow bark, and turmeric."

Constance smiled. "You're getting better. Have you been reading that book I gave you?"

Isla nodded. She handed Constance the cup. "And the one about the crystals, although nothing matches. Not even a little." Isla slipped the crystal free from beneath her dress, letting Constance see the light catch it. "I don't know what to do with it."

The healer stared at the crystal as it spun on its chain. "It came into your life for a reason, Isla. Keep it close. As you said, it helped you with the children. We may need it again."

"Don't say that, Mama! No children have gone missing in a week. Whatever it was has passed," Szilvia said as she set the soup to boil.

Constance shook her head. "At the man's house, I heard talk. A new curfew has been issued in the village, and not just for the children. Parents are frightened and the Council is at a loss. *I'm* at a loss." She waved towards her bookcase full of texts. "If one of these damn books could tell me what was wrong with them, I'd sleep a lot better." She shook her head, staring at her tea. "That blasted witch is behind this, I'm sure. Torturing us from beyond the grave," she muttered.

Isla's eyes widened. "The witch?"

Constance met her gaze. "You think your family was the only one she cursed?"

"We're not cursed," Isla said, her eyes narrowed.

Constance smirked. "So says your mother." She shook her head. "I never met the woman, but my mother did. When she would go harvesting her plants, they would meet in the woods. Sometimes by mistake, sometimes planned, but only long enough to exchange knowledge. Which plants healed. Which poisoned. Which killed. She said the woman was odd, but intelligent."

"She lived in a house made of candy. I'd say she was more than odd," Isla said.

"That was later, after my mother died. Before then, I never knew her to live any differently than a normal person. Something happened, I'm not sure what; perhaps someone got sick and accused her. It was all the Council needed to force her out." Constance took a long sip of tea. She leaned back against her chair, one hand holding her cup as the other stroked Anna's soft fur.

"Why didn't you tell me you knew the witch?" Isla asked.

"What good would it do? And I didn't know her, not really. But I respected her. Living alone in the woods as she did, she had to be brave. And a bit stubborn. I can remember the Council of the day complaining about her, too, as much as they do about me now." Constance glanced out the window. "I just hope I don't meet the same fate," she whispered, so Szilvia wouldn't hear as she made the soup.

Supper was on the table when someone knocked at the door. The women froze in their seats, staring at the door. Isla gave herself a little shake and went to answer it. She had never been so relieved to see Erik's face. Except when she saw how pale it was.

"What happened? Is it Mama? Lukas?"

Erik shook his head. "Another boy and girl have gone missing."

"Who?" Constance croaked, her voice dry and brittle.

"The Papps."

Isla's heart sank. *No, not again.* She would have said more, but a familiar voice spoke up behind Erik.

"What a thing to come home to, right Isla?"

Isla's eyes widened when Aliz stepped out from behind Erik's shadow. She hadn't seen the girl in years. With her golden hair tied back in a braided bun and her brown eyes sparkling, Aliz looked like a picture of her mother that hung in the castle. Isla barely remembered the woman, but she knew the Chief Steward had grieved deeply for his wife. It was said among the local gossips it was why he sent his children away. They reminded him too much of her.

Isla dipped a quick curtsey. "My lady."

Aliz waved away the formality. "Please don't call me that. There's a reason I left Budapest, and it wasn't just the men," she said, wrinkling her nose.

"Aliz!" Szilvia exclaimed. She ran from the table and collided with the young lady. The two embraced for a long moment. When Szilvia pulled back, Isla noticed there were tears in her eyes. "When did you get back?"

"Just in time for supper. I was going to send word, but a messenger from the Council told Papa about the Papps children, and I insisted I join the search party."

Isla looked to Erik for confirmation.

"She wouldn't let me leave without her," he said with a smirk.

Aliz smiled at Erik. "I figured he would stop here before the woods. I couldn't miss the chance." She took Szilvia's hand in hers and squeezed tightly.

Constance got up from her chair and smiled at the Chief Steward's daughter. "Welcome back, my lady. We've missed you."

"And I you. Budapest is dull, lacking all colour and life. I wish Papa had let me come back sooner."

"What about Isaiah? Is he here, too?" Isla interrupted.

"He went with his own men. I suspect we'll see him later," Aliz said.

Isla let out the breath she'd been holding. *Thank goodness he didn't come.*

"I hear we're to fetch more people from our little childhood group before we're to rescue the Papps," said Aliz.

"Be careful," Constance warned. "All of you. I don't like what's going on in the woods."

"We'll be fine, Mama." Szilvia went over and kissed her mother's cheek before joining the rest outside. Isla heard Constance lock the door.

Now outside, Isla could see Aliz was still dressed in her court finery. A loose-fitting, pale pink blouse, its sleeves puffed out, was sure to stand out in the woods. Her matching skirt would catch on countless branches. She was about to suggest Aliz go home to change, but there was no time. She fell into step with Erik, leading the group of four – and giving Szilvia time to catch up with Aliz. They made their way to Lukas', hoping he wasn't far from home.

I watched Constance, even though her mother never let me near her. She must have sensed my magic.

Constance's mother wasn't magical. Hazel. I never felt it when we met in the woods. She had power though. Knowledge. Kindness, too.

Hazel never commented on my abilities, but she must have noticed how quickly the people who came to me were cured. Or cursed, after I went into the woods. And never left.

I found out about Constance when she was wandering in the woods looking for mushrooms. I felt the magic in me flare as I watched her look under bushes and push aside leaves. Like calls to like.

I asked about her, once. Hazel said she was none of my concern. I wasn't offended, as by then the Council had begun to spread lies about me. I thought she was falling into their trap, but she had her own reasons to keep Constance from me.

Constance should have followed her example with Szilvia.

The girl is much stronger than her mother, although I'm not sure how or why. Perhaps the father had some magic of his own.

I will do anything to get my revenge, but I do have one regret. Constance doesn't deserve to be blamed for the children. It can't be helped, though. What has started must be finished.

Perhaps she'll forgive me. Someday.

~ 15 ~

LUKAS

Lukas stood in front of the barn, assessing the storm's damage. A few shingles littered the ground, but the door was still sealed shut, and for that Lukas was thankful. He had spent most of the day inspecting the fields and fixing downed fence posts.

So much for all that work I did yesterday.

He tested every gate leading to and from the fields. Some were loose, but they all held. He walked the perimeter, keeping his back to the house. Tobias had been avoiding Lukas all day, sticking close to the chickens and the wild rabbits. By the time the rain let up, it was already close to dawn. Lukas hadn't walked them home; instead, Miriam got up from Lukas' loft floor and made breakfast. It had been hard to meet Miriam's gaze that morning, but he held her stare over fresh bread, his cheeks on fire.

Tobias hadn't noticed. He hadn't said a word since he got up. Lukas hadn't given him a list of chores like he normally did. He got the feeling Tobias needed to be alone.

That had been several hours ago. Despite Miriam's shouting, Tobias hadn't come inside for lunch. Lukas had offered to take a sandwich to him, but Miriam shook her head.

"I'll talk to him. He can't pout all day."

Now, with suppertime creeping up, Lukas put his hands on his hips and sighed in dismay as he stared at what remained of Sarah's garden. The worst of the damage had been there. Any remaining flowers were uprooted by the violent wind. The vegetable patch had been mostly cleared away before the storm, but the stalks Lukas would have used to feed the horses as a treat were too mangled to use. He shook his head and left the garden for another day. His stomach rioted. It was time to face Tobias.

He made sure to make a lot of noise on his way up the front stairs, warning the boy of his approach. Lukas took off his muddy boots at the door then headed inside. He hung up his thick wool sweater then looked around. He paused at the table, his eyes wide.

The table was set with the finest dishes Lukas' family owned. Sarah had brought them with her as part of her dowry. He could only remember the white plates with red roses along the border coming out twice in the last eighteen years.

Two candles were lit in the centre of the table, their warm glow falling onto the feast Miriam had prepared. Somehow, she had found time to roast a chicken, mash potatoes, roast a variety of root vegetables, and bake a fresh loaf of bread with garlic and other spices added. Lukas' stomach growled with pleasure. He looked from the table to Miriam, and then saw Tobias standing beside her. She nudged the boy closer. Tobias stumbled forward. Lukas noticed he was wearing the hand-me-down clothes from the night before. He had been so tired that morning, he hadn't noticed the outfit change. Tobias came to a stop right in front of Lukas, his hands folded behind him.

"What's all this?" Lukas asked.

Tobias ducked his head. "I wanted to say thank you."

Lukas knelt, forcing Tobias to meet his gaze. "For what?"

"For letting me help on the farm. And I'm sorry." He wiped his nose with the back of his hand. "I shouldn't have asked you if I could stay here. I just love being here. I feel safe."

Lukas put a hand on Tobias' shoulder and squeezed. "I'm glad you do, Tobi. And there's nothing to apologize for. I'm sorry we didn't have time to talk about it. I've been thinking. While I know

Aunt Tanya loves you, and she does a wonderful job taking care of you, perhaps I can ask her if you could stay one night a week. Would you like that?"

Tobias' head shot up and he met Lukas' gaze. "Really? You mean it?"

Lukas nodded as he smiled. "Really. We'll give it a try and see how it goes. Okay?"

Tobias launched himself at Lukas, giving him a tight hug. "Okay," he whispered.

After a moment, the two stood. Lukas noticed Miriam discreetly wiping a tear from her cheek. "Are you hungry? Tobi and I were busy today in the kitchen."

"I can see that! My stomach and I are starving."

Suppertime flew by. Tobias' excitement at the invitation to stay over was palpable. Miriam and Lukas insisted that they inform Aunt Tanya of the arrangement first, before having Tobias stay overnight. That meant after supper, Miriam and Tobias would head back to her uncle's farm. Although Tobias understood, the disappearance of his smile almost made Lukas have the boy stay overnight anyway. That, and he didn't want Miriam to leave, either. Thinking of the night before, he hid his blush behind his mug of tea. He certainly wouldn't mind a repeat of that peaceful sleep.

As the cooks, Miriam and Tobias were kicked out of the dining area. Lukas insisted on cleaning up after the delicious meal.

"Don't go yet! I'll walk you home," he said as they went to wait on the porch.

As he stacked the dirty dishes for later, he wondered how Isla was doing. He hadn't seen her since she had brought the disturbing news of the Council moving against Constance a few days ago. He hoped she was sticking close to home. Lukas gave the kitchen table a quick wipe-down with a damp cloth, blew out the candles, then headed outside.

Miriam greeted him with a smile. "Ready?"

"Reluctantly," he said with a grimace. "I quite liked last night's sleepover."

"Me too!" Tobias said as he skipped down the steps and headed down the lane. Miriam and Lukas fell into step, their fingers brushing. Lukas took a deep breath and was about to reach out for her hand when Miriam beat him to it. She intertwined their fingers, staring straight ahead down the lane.

"Do you play cards?" Lukas asked, saying the first thing that popped into his head.

Miriam raised an eyebrow as she looked up at him. "Why?"

Lukas ran his thumb idly across her knuckles. "I was thinking after the harvest, we could take a break from work and play a game of Noddy. We could use a rest."

Miriam smirked. "Are you asking me on a date, Lukas?"

"No! Yes? Do you want it to be?" He certainly did. Not that he had much experience with dates. He hadn't said so much as hello to another woman outside his family, besides Miriam and her aunt Tanya.

Miriam squeezed his hand. "I've been waiting for you to ask me for years."

Lukas wasn't sure what to say to that. He opened his mouth, hoping something witty would come out, when down the road he saw a group coming towards them. Tobias had somehow gotten turned around and appeared to be leading the group back towards Lukas and Miriam.

"Lukas!"

Lukas squinted and saw Isla, Erik, Szilvia, and a grown-up Aliz running down the lane. Isla's cloak blew behind her and her hair had fallen out of its ponytail. He and Miriam jogged ahead and met the group partway. He stared at Aliz a moment, surprised to see her after so long. Lukas remembered himself and bowed. "My lady." Miriam curtseyed at the same time.

Aliz smirked. "You and your cousin are nothing if not polite." She shook her head. "Just Aliz, please."

"What are you all doing here?" Miriam asked.

"More children are missing. The Papps this time," Erik said. "Isaiah and some of the Chief's men are already searching. We wanted to get you."

Lukas swore. Rosie and Marcus Papp were twins. At seven years old, they were charming children.

"I was just taking Miriam and Tobias home," he said with a sigh.

"We can manage the rest of the way," Miriam said. She looped her arm through Tobias'. "You should go and help. I'll tell Uncle Mordecai."

Lukas' heart sank. He missed Miriam's hand in his.

"Does Greta know you're here?" he asked Isla.

"She technically told me to be here this afternoon. I got tied up."

Lukas rolled his eyes. "I wish I brought a lantern." He noticed what Aliz was wearing. "Would you like me to head back to the farm and fetch a thicker cloak for you, Aliz? Or a change of clothing?"

"It's too far to backtrack, Lukas. We need to hurry," Isla said.

"We could go to my uncle's. Aunt Tanya will help," said Miriam.

Aliz shivered. "Now that you mention it, this dress was a poor choice for an adventure. Do we have time for a detour?"

Isla sighed. "I suppose."

The group hurried to Mordecai's farm, kicking up dust behind them as they ran the rest of the way. Miriam went inside and explained the situation, taking Aliz with her.

Isla grinned at Lukas as soon as Miriam and Aliz were gone. "I saw you holding hands. I *knew* you liked her."

Lukas ran a hand through his hair. "Now is *not* the time, Isla."

"I think now is a perfectly good time to ask about—"

The door opened again and Uncle Mordecai stood in the doorway. "More children?" he asked, his voice gruff from his evening nap.

Lukas nodded. "The Papps twins."

Mordecai swore. "I'll round up some men. Aliz will be out in a moment." He disappeared inside.

Miriam came out soon after, Aliz close behind. In one of Miriam's thicker, more plain dresses, and a cloak with a hood, she was much more prepared. Aliz went down to where the others waited. Lukas met Miriam on the porch.

"Thank you for helping Aliz. I'll see you tomorrow?"

"Bright and early as always." She took his hand and gave it a squeeze. "Be careful, Lukas." Before he could say anything, she kissed his cheek like he had done to her the night before.

"Miriam, come inside! I need your help," Aunt Tanya shouted.

Miriam pulled back, a smile still on her face but her cheeks were on fire. "Goodnight, Lukas." She looked behind him. "Good luck!" She waved then went inside, shutting the door behind her.

As soon as he rejoined the others, Isla noticed his flushed cheeks. "I told you," she said in a sing-song voice.

"Told him what?" Aliz asked.

Szilvia tugged Aliz along. "I'll explain along the way. We'd better get going before Mordecai's men decide to join us."

"The crystal is pulling fiercely. They mustn't be that far," said Isla.

Lukas glanced at Aliz.

"She already knows. I couldn't *not* tell her," Isla said.

"You would be surprised how many court ladies believe in crystals and magic," Aliz added with a wink.

The five headed into the forest.

~ 16 ~

ISLA

Isla and the others found the Papps much faster than the other children.

Lukas stood back as Isla knelt beside Rosie. Her dark brown curls framed her face as she appeared to sleep in the secluded grove of the woods. The group had only walked for about fifteen minutes before the crystal pointed Isla right towards the children. Aliz had stared at the jewel but made no comment.

Isla didn't bother to check the children's vitals; she knew the results would be the same as the Szabós and Farkas children. She unclasped the crystal from her neck and pressed it against Rosie's heart. The crystal's glow intensified.

"What are you doing?" Erik asked.

"Trying to see if this crystal will heal her. It led us to her. Perhaps it knows what's wrong."

"You're acting as if it's magic," said Lukas

She gestured to the glow. "I'd call that magical, wouldn't you?"

Lukas shook his head. "I don't know what to call it, but I do know you shouldn't be here. Other villagers are bound to be here soon." He glanced at the woods ahead of them. "I'm a little shocked they aren't already."

Isla looked back at the crystal and the child it rested upon. "I'll leave soon, but I can't miss this chance. What if this is the way to prove to the Council it's not Constance's doing?"

Lukas snorted. "All you'll do is turn their malice from Constance to you, which isn't what anyone wants, least of all her."

"I have to try *something*," she snapped at her cousin. "We all can't just hide on our farm and pretend something isn't happening to the children of the village."

Lukas narrowed his eyes. "What happens in the village isn't my responsibility, nor is it yours."

Isla shook her head. "But it is, if it's to do with our parents."

"You don't know that for sure," said Szilvia.

"And *you* don't know for sure it isn't," Isla said, glaring at Lukas. "None of us do. But maybe this crystal has the answer. Now stop arguing with me and let me see what happens." She turned her back to Lukas, ignoring his muttered curses.

Isla closed her eyes and focused on the heat and the glow pulsating from the crystal. She covered it with her hand, pressing it harder against Rosie's chest. The child didn't stir. Isla took deep, calming breaths. The heat from the crystal travelled from her palm and seemed to make a pathway inside the child, leading Isla from Rosie's heart to her lungs, up her throat, past her nose and into her brain. There, something lurked. It appeared to Isla like a dark cloud had descended over the child's mind, holding her someplace Isla couldn't reach. When she tried to poke the dark cloud with an invisible finger, a shock of electricity leapt out and sent Isla back onto the forest floor, staring up at the branches overhead.

Erik was beside her instantly, his hand cradling her head. She couldn't hear what he was saying; she could only make out his mouth moving frantically. She shook her head and suddenly the sounds of the woods rushed in.

"Are you alright?" Erik asked.

Isla met Erik's concerned gaze and nodded. She sat up with his help. She saw the crystal was still on Rosie's chest. She tentatively reached out and, when it didn't shock her, put it back around her neck.

"What happened?" Aliz asked.

"Something is wrong with their mind. It's keeping them prisoner. I can't wake them. No one can. Not until this . . . this *cloud* leaves them."

Aliz left Szilvia's side and knelt beside Rosie. She reached out a hand, placing it on the child's head. "What a pity," she muttered. "Sleeping Beauty, reincarnated." She shook her head then stood. "It's like a story coming to life."

"More like a nightmare," said Szilvia.

Aliz shrugged. "What now?"

Before anyone could answer, they heard rustling in the nearby bushes. Erik helped Isla up then nudged her to Szilvia. "You need to leave. If the councillors see you here—"

"You'll become another problem for me," Isaiah said as he stepped into the glade. He was dressed in a dark blue tunic with matching trousers. Isla suspected he hadn't changed from his dining clothes before heading into the woods. She looked around him, but saw no guards or servants attending him. He met her searching gaze.

"I told my men to head for the village to rally more searchers. Seems we won't need them anymore, though."

Isaiah knelt and stared at the children. He didn't touch either of them. From his position, he stared at Isla. "Why is it you who finds them, I wonder," he mused.

Aliz stepped between Isla and Isaiah. "Dumb luck, brother. You know we used to play in the woods as children."

Isaiah stood up, refusing to take his eyes off Isla. "Luck, perhaps. Magic, more likely. Is that what those old councillors are so afraid of? Some magic hiding inside the daughter of the woman who was captured by a witch?"

"Enough, Isaiah," Erik said, his voice crisp and ice cold.

Isaiah smirked. "I knew you would side with her eventually. It was only a matter of time before she convinced you—" Isaiah stopped mid-sentence. He looked behind him, eyes wide. "Do you hear that?"

For a moment, Isla thought he was playing a trick on her.

"Hear what?" Lukas asked.

Isaiah took a step away from the group and the sleeping children, back the way he came. "That voice . . ." he muttered.

"I don't hear anything," said Szilvia as she went to Aliz's side. But before Szilvia could take Aliz's hand, Aliz tilted her head to the side, listening.

"I hear it, too," Aliz said.

Without warning, Isaiah ran back into the woods, away from the glade.

"Isaiah, wait!" Erik cried out.

The young man didn't turn back.

"I'm coming!" Aliz said before taking off after him, her skirts clutched in her hands so they wouldn't snag on any branches.

"Aliz!" Szilvia shouted but like her brother, Aliz didn't stop. Szilvia turned to the others, a frantic look in her eyes. "We have to go after them."

Lukas volunteered to stay behind with the children. Isla, Erik, and Szilvia followed the Chief Steward's children deeper and deeper into the woods. The crystal warmed against Isla's skin. She wondered at the connection but didn't have time to think about it for long. The trio slid down a bank and waded through a shallow river, trying to keep Isaiah and Aliz in sight.

"She sure can move fast," Erik said, trying an attempt at humour as they ran faster and faster through the woods.

"Never underestimate a determined woman," Szilvia grumbled as she sped past Isla, leading the group now.

They finally caught up with Isaiah and Aliz, but what they found made Isla's heart stop mid-beat.

Isaiah and Aliz were laid out on the forest floor, just like the three sets of children from the past few weeks. Isaiah's hair covered his eyes and he looked oddly peaceful as he laid on a bed of moss, fast asleep. Aliz's dress was spread out around her, her hair loose, taking the form of a halo around her head. Her hands were folded across her chest.

"Aliz!" Szilvia screamed. She launched herself at the young woman, dragging her onto her lap and holding her tightly to her chest. Isla had never heard Szilvia sob so wretchedly before, not since her father's death.

Isla glanced at Erik. His face was pale in the moonlight as he stared at Isaiah on the forest floor. Isla took his hand and squeezed. Erik shook his head then stared at her. "How is this possible?" he whispered.

"They heard a voice, right? Perhaps it was the same voice that led the children astray," Isla said.

Szilvia sniffed, wiping her eyes with one hand as her other kept Aliz propped against her chest. "You mean she's enchanted? She won't wake up?"

Isla shrugged, exhaustion setting in after such a long time running. "I don't know, Szilvia. I could be wrong, but—"

Szilvia smoothed Aliz's hair away from her face. "Sleeping Beauty," she muttered. She kissed Aliz's forehead. "We'll find a way to wake you," she promised.

Isla nodded. They had to. It was clear this *being* that was enchanting people was no longer content with only children. She met Erik's gaze. "Go back to Lukas and lead the men here. Someone has to tell the Chief Steward."

"Are you sure you'll be safe?"

Szilvia gently laid Aliz back down on the ground. She took Isla's free hand. "We'll be safe."

Erik kissed Isla's cheek then headed back the way they had come. Isla took one last look at the sleeping siblings before leading Szilvia back towards her cottage. *Perhaps Constance can explain what that cloud in Rosie's mind means.* It was the best option they had.

As they left the woods behind, Isla glanced at Szilvia from the corner of her eye. "You love her, don't you?"

Szilvia smiled sadly. "Since we were children. I'm not a fool. I know her father will marry her off sooner or later, but until then . . ." she trailed off.

Isla squeezed Szilvia's hand. "We'll wake her up. I know we will."

Szilvia didn't say anything.

By the time the girls reached Constance's cottage, the moon had fully risen. They trotted up to the front door and Isla was going to knock when she noticed the broken hinges. The door was hanging on by one tiny bolt. Isla's blood hummed in her veins. She gently pushed against it, her hand shaking, and Szilvia's screams echoed in the cottage.

The kitchen table was overturned, the herbs and flowers from the day's work scattered across the floor. Bags of powder had been upended, their contents crushed under careless feet. She didn't see any blood, but she didn't hear anyone inside, either. Not even Anna the cat.

"Mama!" Szilvia called. Nothing. Szilvia searched the back room but came out alone. They left the destruction of the cottage behind and ran outside to the tiny barn where Constance kept her donkey. The donkey was there, but no Constance.

"What happened to her?" Isla muttered to herself.

Szilvia kicked the barn door shut. "You know what happened. The Council must have taken her!" Szilvia went back to the cottage and grabbed a thicker cloak. "We have to find her."

Isla went inside as well and snatched a blank scrap of parchment. She scribbled out a note to whoever came to find them, and explained they were going to the village to find Constance. She hoped they had at least taken the woman somewhere warm. The night was growing colder with every passing hour.

It took another hour to reach the village. Upon entering the main square, Isla could sense something was off. No music poured from The Swan's Nest. Everyone appeared to be inside their houses. Shutters were shut, and the doors closed. The only sounds the girls could hear were the nocturnal animals scrounging for scraps under the cover of moonlight. Isla pulled her cloak tighter around herself and clasped Szilvia's hand.

"Let's head to the council building. Maybe they're holding her there for the night," Isla suggested.

When they reached the building, two men guarded the door. Isla knew them from church and suspected she would get nothing from them besides dark looks and orders to leave. They went around the back alley, avoiding the guards, and peered into a window that hadn't been closed for the night. Isla saw the councillors seated at their table like they had been when they interrogated her, but she didn't see Constance. Isla's eyes widened when she saw the Chief Steward was with the councillors. She shuddered and took a step back.

Isla and Szilvia left the councillors and Chief Steward behind then wandered further into the village. As they passed the church, Isla narrowed her eyes. It was one of the oldest buildings in the village, but besides being a place of worship, she had heard her father mention there were storage rooms in the cellar.

Big enough to serve as a jail cell, I wonder?

Isla tugged on Szilvia's hand and led her to the church's back door.

"What makes you think she's here?" Szilvia whispered. "They could have taken her anywhere."

"A feeling. A bad one," she said then knocked on the door.

A minute passed, then they heard the lock click and the door opened. The village preacher was an overweight man of middle age; his beard was sparse, but he had a full head of thick, brown hair that he kept neatly trimmed. Although he wore a robe overtop, Isla could see sleeping trousers peeking out underneath the pale fabric.

"Yes? How can I help you?"

Isla considered lying, but she was too tired to come up with a convincing story. Bluffing would have to do.

"We need to speak to the prisoner being kept in your cellar. It's urgent."

Father Timmons raised an eyebrow. "She's been charged with witchcraft and consorting with the devil. Whatever could you want with her?"

"She's my mother," Szilvia said, tears in her eyes. "And she hasn't done anything wrong, except heal people that others can't."

Father Timmons had the sense to look ashamed. "Be that as it may, I'm afraid she's not allowed visitors. The council gave me strict orders to let no one in."

Isla reached out and took Father Timmons' hand in hers. "Father, please, you must know this woman is innocent. Constance is a healer and a midwife. She cares for the sick and those in need, much like you do, except where you heal their souls, she heals their bodies. The Council is looking for someone to blame for the tragedy that has struck our village. But all they're doing is blaming an innocent woman with no proof. It won't wake the sleeping children."

"And what will?"

"I don't know, but I plan to find out. I just need to talk to her first."

Father Timmons didn't say anything for a long time. Finally, he sighed. "I didn't want them to bring her here. I told them a church was not a prison, but they wouldn't listen." Father Timmons took a step back and let them in. "Five minutes. That's all I can give you. Then you must leave."

The girls promised they would and Father Timmons led them downstairs. It was clean and warm. *Thank goodness* Isla thought, appreciating the warmth. Father Timmons unlocked Constance's cell door and locked it behind them once they were inside.

"Mama!" Szilvia cried out.

Constance sat cross-legged in the middle of her cell. There was a bed against the back wall, but she seemed content to sit on the hardwood floor.

Szilvia embraced Constance, shocking her out of a trance she seemed to have been in. "Szilvia! What in heaven's name—?" She wrapped her arms around her daughter then looked up at Isla. "What are you doing here?

"We saw the cottage," Isla replied.

Constance patted Szilvia's back as her daughter cried on her shoulder. "There, there now. Calm yourself, my dear. No more tears."

Isla knelt beside Szilvia, in front of Constance. "I found the Papps."

"The Chief Steward's children were enchanted, too. We lost them soon after we found the Papps," added Szilvia.

Constance narrowed her eyes. "They're hardly children. That makes no sense."

"That's why we're here," said Isla.

"What did your crystal show you?"

"A dark cloud has a hold of their minds. They can't wake up until whoever put it there releases them."

Constance sighed. "Of course, she would make it complicated."

"Who?" Szilvia asked.

"How do you plan to find her?" Constance asked, ignoring her daughter.

"So it is her, then? The witch?" Isla said.

"Do I have to spell it out for you?"

Isla shook her head. "Do you know where her cottage is?"

"I never went there. Only your mother and uncle have ever entered and lived to talk about it."

Isla's stomach dropped. She had hoped to avoid that conversation with Greta.

The preacher tapped on the door, clearing his throat. "Only one minute more!" he warned.

Isla took one of Constance's hands. "Is there anything else you can tell me about her?"

Constance closed her eyes. "She's waited all these years to come back. Beware, my girl. She won't be easy to defeat."

Isla kissed her cheek. "I'll do whatever it takes to prove your innocence."

The preacher unlocked the door and Isla had to pry Szilvia off her mother. Father Timmons locked the door and led them out the way they came. Neither said anything until they were outside the church.

"What do we do now?" Szilvia asked.

"I'm going to find the witch's cottage. It's the only way to prove Constance is innocent."

"Alone? You'll get lost!" Szilvia said.

"That's how Mama and Uncle Hans found it, by getting lost. Perhaps it'll work for me."

"I'm coming with you."

"It won't be safe, and I have no idea how long it will take to find the cottage," Isla warned.

"And staying here is safe? You and I know the Council will come for me soon, especially once the Chief Steward finds out this curse has got his children. If we don't stop her soon, I'll be joining Mama in her cell."

Isla hated to think of Szilvia locked up. She hoped Erik would be the one to break the news to the Chief Steward about Isaiah and Aliz. The girls headed to Isla's home for supplies and refreshments, both of which Isla desperately needed. That, and a nap.

This is taking too long.

Why is it so hard to put the pieces together that are perfectly laid out in front of you? It shouldn't be this difficult. I thought Isla was smarter than this.

Of course, she would befriend the Chief Steward's children. And bring them right to me. I couldn't have asked for a better opportunity.

I don't remember much about the Chief. His father kept him in Budapest for years, and when he took his father's seat, he didn't seem interested in stopping by our little village often. I wonder if the Council would have harassed me as much as they did if he had supervised them better.

I doubt it. Men tend to stick together.

His son will take after him, no doubt. He's hiding something, that much I know, but who isn't? And his sister is a beauty, so she's sure to cause trouble wherever she goes. Perhaps that's why her father keeps her in Budapest. Best to secure her a husband before she uses that mind of hers to get out from under her father's thumb.

Or to join Szilvia in her cottage in the woods.

They're not children, but there's no way Isla can ignore me now. The Chief Steward won't let his children suffer, at least not with everyone watching.

Come to me, Isla. I'm waiting.

~ 17 ~

LUKAS

Not long after Isla left, the first group from the village arrived. The three men who made up the trio included the children's father. Lukas had met Uram Papp on a few occasions, mostly during his trips to the market for Hans. Uram Papp often went there with his children, letting them help him sell his wood carvings. He had been close to Lukas' grandfather – as close as anyone from the village could be – and he had always given Lukas a smile and waved whenever they passed in the market. Tonight, there was no smile on Uram Papp's face.

Uram Papp knelt before his twins and sobbed, his hands trembling as he grasped one of Rosie's and Marcus' hands.

Councillor Varga stared at Lukas, refusing to look at the children. "When did you find them?"

"Not long ago. I was just going to find someone to help me bring them in when you showed up," Lukas said.

"And your cousin? Where's she?"

"She didn't come. I suspect she's at home."

Councillor Varga narrowed his eyes. "We both know you didn't find them on your own."

"Is it so hard to believe that I managed to get here before you did?"

"Enough," Uram Papp said, his voice gruff and low. "Help me take them home."

Lukas offered to help but Uram Papp shook his head. "Thank you, but you've done enough."

Lukas wasn't sure whether that was a thank-you or a dismissal. He grabbed his lantern and was about to leave when he heard footsteps steadily approaching. He paused just as Erik appeared in the clearing.

"What happened?" Lukas asked, fearing the worst.

"The Chief Steward's children. They're asleep like the others," Erik said, panting.

Councillor Varga's eyes widened. "Where?"

"This way," Erik said as he pointed behind him.

Councillor Varga directed the other men to take the children to the village. "I'll go with you, Erik." He looked to Lukas. "Since you're so eager to help, go tell the Chief Steward what has happened."

Lukas nodded then left for the castle. It had been many years since he last entered the Chief Steward's home. He worried he wouldn't remember the way, but his feet did. He reached the Chief Steward's door within an hour. He pounded on the door for a full minute before a disgruntled servant opened it.

"May I help you?" the older man asked, his wrinkles illuminated in the lamp light.

"I need to speak to the Chief Steward. It's urgent."

The servant glanced behind him, as if waiting for instruction, then opened the door wider. "You're in luck, he just returned. Follow me."

Lukas let out the breath he had been holding and followed. The carpets were just as plush under his feet as they were when he was a child running down the hall with Isaiah and Erik. The same paintings stared down at him as he headed upstairs to the Chief Steward's office. That particular door had always been locked, but now he saw it propped open, the fireplace aglow inside. Lukas tried not to stare at the wall-to-wall bookshelves, but it was hard not to be entranced by such a secluded place. He tore his gaze away from the books and looked to the Chief Steward. Krystof Popel had gotten greyer in his beard and his hair since the last time Lukas saw him, but his presence was still as commanding as Lukas remembered. Krystof wore a warm burgundy coat; he was staring at a book open on his desk when Lukas came in. He finished the page then looked up.

"Lukas Baláž, to what do I owe the pleasure?" he said, his voice as dry as tea leaves.

Lukas cleared his throat. He wished Varga had sent anyone but him. "Isaiah and Aliz are asleep in the woods."

The Chief Steward stared at him for a long moment. "The curse," he muttered. He glanced behind Lukas at the servant who had escorted Lukas. "Prepare their rooms and fetch my healer."

The servant bowed his head then left, leaving the door open behind him. Krystof got up from his desk and went over to stand face to face with Lukas. "I have a message for your cousin. I don't believe Constance is the cause of this curse, but until she brings proof, I can do nothing."

Lukas didn't believe that. He opened his mouth to say just that, yet the Chief Steward shook his head before Lukas could get a word out.

"I just spent the better part of my night arguing with the Council about their rash actions. I may be Chief, but they hold the majority. The best I can do is hold them off for a short time. Tell your cousin to be quick."

Lukas stared at the older man. He wanted to ask so many things. Why was it Isla's job to fix this problem? Why had he forbidden Isaiah and Aliz from befriending the villagers? Instead, too weary to argue, he merely nodded his head. He wasn't sure when he would see Isla next, but he would do as he was told.

Krystof held Lukas' gaze then went back to his desk. He picked up his book again. "You may go."

Lukas shut the door behind him and ran down the hallway, eager to leave a place full of bittersweet childhood memories. He couldn't understand how Erik could practically live in this place. As soon as he got outside, he took a deep breath of night air, hoping it would calm his nerves. On his way home, as he passed by the woods, he felt as if he was being watched. He tugged the collar of his sweater up and ran home, the wind pushing him further and further from the Papp twins and the Chief Steward's castle.

The farmhouse door was locked. Lukas pulled out his key and saw the fireplace only had coals in it, the flames long dead. The chill set into his bones. Alone, the place seemed so cheerless. He wished desperately that he'd insisted Miriam and Tobias spend the night. After what he had witnessed, he could use another comforting presence to help push the memories away.

Lukas stoked the coals and managed to get a decent fire going before exhaustion forced him to his ladder. As soon as he reached his loft, he fell onto his pallet face first, his head cradled by the soft pillow. He was asleep within seconds.

The smell of bacon frying on the stovetop awoke Lukas. He blinked and yawned, stretching out underneath his blanket. Sunlight coming in from the windows downstairs had made its way up to his loft. He swore underneath his breath.

How did I sleep so late?

The harvest workers would be arriving soon. Lukas got up and ran a hand through his knotted hair, doing his best to straighten out his sweater and pull up his socks while heading towards the ladder. Once safely on the ground, he shoved his feet into the closest pair of boots he could find. He wouldn't have time to change and get things ready for the harvesters, so he would have to sacrifice his looks.

When he glanced up, he was shocked to find Miriam had been cooking up a storm for what seemed like hours.

How long has she been here for? And where's Tobias?

She had already plucked two chickens clean, started chopping vegetables for a soup, and three loaves of bread were cooling on a rack. He blushed, feeling even more guilty for sleeping in.

Miriam turned away from the stove where she had been boiling a kettle. Tobias slammed open the front door and ran towards Miriam.

"Here are the eggs you wanted! Can I go let the cows out now?"

Miriam chuckled. "Go ahead. Just make sure you lock their gate."

Tobias nodded. He turned around and when he spotted Lukas, he grinned. "Good morning!"

"Morning," Lukas said with a smile. "Already starting your chores, I see."

Tobias nodded. "The horses are out in the field, and the chickens have been fed. What else can I do?"

Lukas went to the cupboard, his side pressed against Miriam's, and grabbed a plate. "Meet me back here and we'll get started preparing for the harvest. What time did Mordecai say he'd be here?" he asked as he glanced down at Miriam.

"You've got about an hour." Miriam's cheeks were flushed, but she didn't move away from him. "I can fry up an egg quickly if you'd like."

Lukas snagged two pieces of bacon from the pan. His fingertips burned, but the crisp bacon was worth it. He looked to Tobias who was bouncing on his heels. "What do you think, Tobi? Do I have time for an egg?"

"Make it two, you'll be busy today," Miriam said.

Tobias nodded. "I won't be long!" The boy left the kitchen as quickly as he had entered.

Lukas chuckled as he sat at the table while Miriam got to work on his eggs. "He certainly has a lot of energy today. I wish I could say the same," he said with a yawn.

"What time did you get in last night?"

Lukas squinted, trying to remember. "It was close to midnight, I think. Maybe later." He had forgotten his pocket watch. "When did you get here this morning?"

"A few hours ago. Tobias was up at dawn and Aunt Tanya begged me to take him over early." Miriam flipped the eggs. "What did you find in the forest?"

Between bites of bacon, Lukas relayed the events from the night before.

Miriam slid the eggs onto his plate with a shake of her head. "How awful. I don't remember Aliz much, and I can't say I care for Isaiah a great deal, but that's a horrible thing to happen to them. The Chief Steward must be devastated."

Lukas shrugged. "He keeps his emotions under lock and key. Growing up, I never once saw him smile."

"Probably because you were always getting into trouble with his children," she teased.

"You'd be surprised how little we saw of him in those days. I honestly don't think he knew we were as close to Isaiah and Aliz as we were until we were a little older. By then, he couldn't ignore us, or force his children's care on governesses."

The two chatted while Lukas finished his breakfast. He washed his plate then grabbed his sweater, ready to hunt down Tobias. "Do you need anything before I head off?"

Miriam shook her head. "I should have a feast ready for supper. I was thinking of just bringing sandwiches to the field for lunch. Will that do?"

"It's better than anything I could do! It smells delicious in here already."

She grinned. "Good. Well, you'd best be off before Tobias gets bored and finds his own trouble."

Lukas brushed back his tousled hair then went over to Miriam. He bent down and kissed her cheek, his mind still muddled enough from sleep to not worry about the consequences of this show of affection.

Miriam gazed up at him, an eyebrow raised. "What was that for?"

How to explain a growing affection that had been building for years, that suddenly came to a head now that everything was chaos? His mother was dead, his father missing, the forest was stealing children – and all he wanted to do was properly court Miriam.

Lukas forced his jumbled thoughts to the side and just smiled at Miriam. "I'm looking forward to cards."

As if that was a useful explanation.

Miriam seemed to accept it, though. Either that or she was already thinking of all the work she had ahead of her and was too busy to think about silly boys and their random kisses. He hoped it wasn't the latter.

She smiled and took his hand, squeezing it once. "I am, too. Which means you had better get that grain harvested or we'll never see who's the better Noddy player."

"Oh, that's definitely me. No questions asked."

Miriam laughed. "We'll see about that! Off with you." She playfully shoved him towards the door.

Lukas wanted more than anything to stay in that kitchen with Miriam. Yet with a sigh, he did as he was told and went out to get to work.

What he didn't expect to see was his cousin coming up the lane, Erik and Szilvia in tow.

Now what? Lukas thought with a groan. More children couldn't be missing already.

Tobias ran from the barn and skidded to a halt when he saw the company. Isla walked with determined purpose, which could only mean trouble.

"What's happened?" Tobias asked as he came to Lukas on the porch.

Lukas laid a reassuring hand on Tobias' shoulder. "I'll take care of it. Would you go to the shed and start getting the tools ready? I'll meet you there."

Tobias looked over at the group coming close to the farmhouse then back at Lukas. He nodded.

Once he was gone, Lukas left the porch and met Isla and the others near the barn. The three were outfitted for a hike of some kind, heavy bags on their backs and sturdy walking boots on their feet. He raised an eyebrow. "Going on an adventure?"

"Of a sort," said Erik.

"I wanted to come and tell you before we headed out. We're going to find the witch's cottage and prove Constance didn't curse those children," Isla said.

"You're *what?*" Lukas stared at his cousin then looked to Erik. "And you're supporting this? Both of you?"

"If it means Isaiah and Aliz will wake up, of course," said Erik. "After I brought them to the castle, I went to Isla's and she had already come up with the plan. I can't *not* go."

"There's no other way. The Council already arrested my mother. If we don't find proof, they'll kill her," said Szilvia. Her eyes were red from crying.

Lukas remembered the Chief Steward had mentioned Constance, but as the group filled him in on what had befallen her, it was much worse than Lukas expected. It was clear from Isla's pacing she was eager to get going, and her cousin couldn't blame her.

"Chief Steward had a message for you," Lukas said, once their tale was told.

Isla narrowed her eyes. "He gave it to Erik as well. Seems he didn't trust you would get it to me in time." She shook her head. "If he wants proof, I'll find it."

"What did Greta have to say about your plan?"

Erik winced. "I'm sure you can imagine Greta's opinion on the matter."

Oh, he could. Lukas wondered how long Greta had managed to deter the group from their quest before she gave up.

"Do you need anything? Supplies?"

Isla shook her head. "Papa gave us enough to last a week in the woods. We should be fine." She went over and kissed Lukas' cheek. "Stay safe, Lukas. We'll be back soon."

Lukas shook Erik's hand and hugged Szilvia. A part of him wanted to follow Isla into the woods and find the witch's cottage. He felt it was his duty as the son of Hans. He glanced towards the fields and shook his head a little. If Hans were here, it wouldn't even be a question if he would go or not.

He waved goodbye to the group of adventurers. Lukas stood by the barn for a moment, his heart pounding against his ribs. He cleared his throat then looked once more towards the woods.

Good luck, Isla. You're going to need it.

Lukas headed towards the shed, the sound of tools falling urging him to hurry up and help Tobias.

$$\sim 18 \sim$$

ISLA

Isla ducked under a low-hanging branch, a few leaves falling onto her shoulders in the process. Erik came up behind her and brushed them off. She smiled at him then continued, heading further and further into the woods.

"How far do you think we've walked today?" Szilvia asked. She came up from behind, her long skirt tied up to avoid getting wet in the puddles. Her thick stockings kept her legs warm, just as Isla's matching pair did. Szilvia had borrowed quite a few pieces of clothing from Isla's closet before they set out on their journey.

Erik glanced up at the sky, but the branches were so thickly intertwined, it was hard to see the sunlight peeking through. "It certainly feels long," he said with a sigh. He had insisted on taking Isla's pack an hour ago, which Isla still thought was silly, but she was too tired to argue about Erik's chivalry.

"We'll keep going for another hour then find a place to camp," Isla said, pushing back another branch.

Isla didn't know how far they would have to go to find the witch's cottage. Greta hadn't been forthcoming with details before the village children became sick. Now, she was even more tight-lipped. Early that morning, when Isla explained what she planned to do, Greta had gripped the kitchen chair in front of her, her knuckles white and face pale, as she stared at the stained table.

"You're going to *what?*" she had whispered. The faint traces of dawn had just started to pour in from the window behind her.

"It's the only way, Mama," Isla had said. "If we don't go, Constance will be killed."

A knock at the front door had interrupted them. Jacob, who had been roused from bed when Isla and Szilvia came in only a few minutes ago, had gone to the door. He came into the kitchen with Erik on his heels. Upon seeing Erik, Isla had rushed over and threw her arms around his neck, pulling him close.

"What are you doing here?" she had whispered.

Erik had held her tight, burying his face in her hair. "Isaiah and Aliz are at the castle. My place is here with you."

Greta had cleared her throat. "What's this about the Chief Steward's children?"

Isla had quickly explained what had happened to Isaiah and Aliz. Erik had sat at the table, a cup of tea in front of him. Isla had stood behind him, a hand on his shoulder.

"So you see Mama, we have to go. It's not just the children who are being cursed. Anyone could be next."

Greta had shaken her head. "The Chief Steward has men. Let him send them."

"He's trusting Isla with this," Erik had said. "Before I left, the Chief Steward told me if there is proof Constance is innocent, Isla has to bring it."

Isla wasn't sure what to make of that offer, but Greta had hissed in anger. She looked at Szilvia and Erik. "I need a word with my daughter. Alone."

Erik and Szilvia had gone to Isla's bedroom to wait, taking their tea with them.

Jacob stood beside his wife. "What's this about the witch?"

Isla had quickly explained what she had discovered. She took a deep breath and pulled out the crystal from underneath her dress. "This crystal led me to the children. I believe it knows what's going on. It's . . . connected somehow."

Upon seeing the crystal, Greta's eyes had widened, fear pulling her lips back in a snarl. "No!" She stepped away from Isla. "How did you find that cursed thing?"

Isla had raised an eyebrow. She had expected many different reactions to the crystal, but this wasn't one of them. "It was in the woods."

Greta had shaken her head, her eyes filling with tears. "I threw it away. You never should have found it."

"What are you talking about, Mama?"

"When you were little, you got lost in the woods. I found you, and you had that damned crystal on you." Greta's hands had trembled as she crossed her arms. "I got rid of it. You said a woman had given it to you."

Isla's eyes had widened. "The witch," she whispered.

"I don't know who it was, but that crystal can only lead to trouble. Give it to me, Isla."

Isla had tucked it under her dress. "No. I need it to find the witch and save Constance. Once this is over, I'll get rid of it."

"How do you know you'll find her? You don't even know where to go!"

"Then tell me! You must remember how to get there."

Greta had glared at Isla. "If you think I'm going to give you directions to the most cursed place of my childhood, you're more foolish than I thought."

"Of course, I'm desperate! My best friend's mother, my *mentor,* is on trial for a crime she didn't commit. These children are trapped in a cursed sleep! If we don't do something, more children will be hurt. Constance will die. The Council will come after us next. There'll be no mercy from the Chief Steward." She had returned her mother's glare. "You know as well as I do if we don't find out what's causing the children to get sick, they'll come after you or me next."

Neither of the women said anything for a time. Jacob sighed, his shoulders sagging. "She's right, my dear. If something doesn't change, it'll be you next. I can't let that happen." He had gone over to his daughter and placed a hand on her shoulder. "What do you need?"

Isla had explained her plan. Jacob had nodded and went to the cellar to gather the supplies needed for a week in the darkest part of the woods.

Greta had turned away from her daughter and busied herself tidying the kitchen. Isla had gone over to Greta and grabbed her hand. "Mama, please. Tell me how to find her cottage."

Greta had licked her lips, her cheeks pale as she refused to meet Isla's stare. "Get yourself as thoroughly lost as possible. That's what Hans and I did."

Isla's heart had sunk. "That's it? Get lost?"

"We were children, Isla. We didn't go searching for the cottage. We just wanted to go home. With the poor harvest, people were starving to death. After Stepmother convinced Papa to leave us in the woods, that was all we cared about. We were scared and hungry." Greta had stepped away from Isla then left the kitchen. Isla heard her slam her bedroom door shut.

Isla hadn't seen her mother since. Jacob saw the group off and wished them luck, but Greta didn't come to say goodbye. Isla wished she could have explained herself better, but she didn't have time to mend that particular bridge with her mother. She had to find the witch.

Now, as night was closing in on the group, Isla sighed, thinking of her mother and how she ventured into the woods at such a young age. She hadn't exactly been willing – Isla still couldn't believe Greta's stepmother had been cruel enough, and desperate enough, to send her young stepchildren into the woods to starve.

Just get lost. Should be simple enough. But how lost was lost, exactly? Isla sighed as they went further into the woods.

"I think we've gone far enough," said Szilvia. "My feet are killing me."

Erik came up beside Isla and pointed ahead. "There's a clearing over there. We should be able to set up camp for the night."

Isla agreed and the three entered the small clearing. It was large enough to fit three people, but they would have to share a tent, as three tents wouldn't fit in such a small place. Erik volunteered to go get firewood while the women set up camp. Szilvia unpacked their rations and began dividing out their supper for the night while Isla set up the largest tent they had. It would be tight, especially if Erik tried to stand up, but they would make do. Isla had hoped they would find the cottage that day, for Constance's sake. If the Chief Steward wanted proof, Isla couldn't waste any time.

Isla said a quick prayer to whichever god was listening. She hoped the preacher was being kind to Constance.

Erik appeared with the firewood and soon they had a warm fire going. Szilvia handed out the slices of bread, chunks of cheese, and strips of dried meat.

"I saw some berry bushes nearby," Erik said as he took a bite of cheese. "Tomorrow we can have those with breakfast."

"I saw some oats in one of the bags. Oatmeal for breakfast with fresh berries sounds delicious," Szilvia said.

Isla leaned back against a nearby tree trunk, her gaze focused on the woods, the branches waving at her in the wind. "I wish we had a better idea as to where we're going. I thought the crystal would be more helpful."

Szilvia shrugged as she tore off a piece of bread. "Perhaps it just needs to be closer to the cottage in order to guide us."

"Or maybe it's not connected to the cottage at all," Erik said.

Isla grimaced. She hoped he was wrong. Greta and Constance both had no leads for her; the crystal was her last option.

The three ate in silence for some time, listening to the woodland creatures begin to stir around them. Isla hoped nothing would be interested in the campsite and came to investigate the source of the fire.

"How much do you want to bet when we return, Lukas and Miriam are officially courting?" Szilvia asked as she sat cross-legged before the fire, feeding it kindling.

Erik smirked. "I think they already are, they just haven't told anyone."

Isla snorted. "Lukas is horrible at keeping secrets. If he's made a proposal, he'd have told me. Or you." *Or someone.* She dipped her head back and stared at the sky, spotting a few stars between the branches. "He used to talk about her all the time when we were children. Perhaps this was just the push they needed."

Szilvia crossed her arms as she stared at the fire. "Do you think Aliz is scared?" she asked quietly.

Isla opened her mouth, but nothing came out. She pressed her lips together then shook her head. "I don't know."

"I bet she's dreaming of adventures she wants to go on. Like she did when she was a girl. Remember the stories she would read to us when we visited? Pirates, sword-fighting—"

"Or giants and fairies, masked men and dangerous quests," Isla added.

Szilvia smiled. "She still reads those books. She's gotten me to smuggle her a few."

"I'm sure she'll have some new stories to tell us when she wakes up," Isla said.

"You really think this is going to work?" Szilvia asked.

"It has to," said Isla. *We don't have any other choice.*

The fire was getting low, and Isla couldn't stop yawning. Erik suggested they head to bed so they could start again early the next morning.

"I'll keep watch for the first few hours," he said.

"I can take the second shift," Isla offered.

No one changed out of their travelling clothes, the air too chilly to think of changing into cold clothes that had been squashed on the bottom of their bags. Erik fed the fire a few more logs and pulled out his knife, resting it on his lap. Szilvia went into the tent and Isla went over to Erik. She kissed him quickly.

"Stay safe. Shout if you need anything."

"Sleep well," Erik said with a smile.

Isla went into the tent and curled up under the blankets beside Szilvia. The girls clung to each other, sharing body heat to warm up the cold blankets.

~*~

Isla sat in front of the fire, watching the shadows play against the trees as she kept an eye out for anything suspicious. Her shift had barely started, and she already wished she was back in the tent. She covered her mouth, suppressing a yawn, and blinked rapidly, trying to stay awake.

The crystal around her neck suddenly grew warm. Isla glanced down at it and saw it was glowing. Her eyes widened as it lifted and hovered in the air, seeming to point left. Isla slowly got up and took a step to the left. The crystal pulled her further ahead. She looked behind her at the tent and grimaced. She should turn around and warn the others, but she didn't have control of her feet. They were following the crystal.

Isla walked for a few minutes then came to a stop at the edge of another clearing. This one, however, was large enough to fit a house. The crystal's glow grew brighter, lighting up the area. Isla gasped as the building came into view.

The gingerbread walls were lined with gumdrops and other candies. Isla's mouth watered at the delicious treats before her.

The witch's cottage hadn't been damaged by time or neglect. It looked as if it had waited for Isla all these years.

Isla shivered. She turned around and ran back to the campsite. She hoped Erik and Szilvia wouldn't mind an exceptionally early wake up call.

LUKAS

The last of the wheat waved at Lukas as he surveyed the final field after a long day of harvesting. He leaned heavily against the staff of his scythe, his heart swelling with gratitude towards his neighbours who had come to help him with the massive undertaking. The sun was beginning to set, but the farmers had insisted on finishing.

"This won't be the last time we harvest in the dark," Miriam's uncle Mordecai said.

"And it's certainly not the first," said Vlad, Lukas' neighbour to the east.

Lukas wanted to finish the work with them, but his lower back had started to complain a half hour ago. A day in the field meant turmeric tea before bed.

He glanced at the woods to his left and wondered how Isla was faring. He grimaced as he pictured her making her way towards the cottage and all the secrets it held. Lukas had kept himself busy in the field for two reasons: the wheat needed to be harvested, and it kept him too occupied to think about the danger his cousin could be in.

A half hour passed and the several men in the field stood up, their work now complete. Lukas went to them and shook each of their hands, thanking them again and again.

"If you ever need anything, just ask," he said.

Mordecai smiled, his salt and pepper mustache covering most of his lips. "No need, Lukas. We're neighbours. We help each other."

Miriam crested the little hill, Tobias at her side, and waved to the men. "Supper's ready! We're eating outside," she called.

Lukas' stomach gurgled. The men cheered. Mordecai, Miriam's brother Brandon, and the other men went as fast as their tired feet could carry them to the farmhouse's front yard. Lukas trailed behind. When he got close enough to Miriam, he extended his hand. She took it in hers and squeezed. Tobias joined Mordecai's side, somehow wrangling the older man into giving him a piggy-back ride. Lukas smiled as he shook his head at Mordecai as he ran ahead, Tobias' screeches carrying over the fields.

"All done?" Miriam asked.

Lukas nodded. "The scything at least. If it stays this dry, we could start bundling it tomorrow." He winced as he tweaked his back. "Or maybe not."

Miriam squeezed his hand. "I'll make tea instead of hot cocoa before I leave."

"Good call. I'll walk you home." Lukas motioned to Tobias. "Did he behave himself?"

"Doesn't he always?" She smirked. "Actually, he was quite happy to be in the kitchen with me. I think an hour in the field was more than enough for one day. If nothing else, it smelled tastier inside."

Lukas squeezed her hand. "Thank you, Miriam."

"For what?"

"For working so hard! I couldn't have done this without you."

He hadn't forgotten how he'd fumbled his explanation of his feelings that morning. They hadn't had a private moment since Isla, Erik, and Szilvia left. Lukas had barely gotten through his morning chores before Mordecai and the others arrived. Since then, he'd only seen Miriam when she brought lunch, and they hadn't exchanged more than a few words before the hungry men appeared for their midday meal. He wasn't sure what he would have said, though. He wasn't as eloquent as Sarah had been.

She would know what to do. If ever there was a moment Lukas wished he could go to his mother for advice, it would be now. It made his heart squeeze painfully in his chest.

Lukas raised an eyebrow when he saw the large table taking up most of his front yard. "Where did you find *that?*"

"It was hiding in your barn. The chairs were scattered here and there in the sheds. I hope you don't mind," said Miriam.

It reminded Lukas of when his grandfather was still alive. When they could convince him to leave the woods and share a meal with them, Greta and her family would join, and they would enjoy the last of the warm weather together just like this. Lukas rubbed at his eyes, willing the tears to disappear.

"It's wonderful," he said, flashing her a smile, before heading to the smaller buffet table Miriam had set out.

The roasted chickens were cut up and the platter of potatoes, turnips, carrots, and parsnips were seasoned to mouth-watering perfection. Lukas cut a huge chunk of fresh bread from one of the many loaves, forcing himself to leave enough room for the pies Miriam had also somehow found time to make.

"You were baking up a storm today, my dear," Mordecai shouted from his chair at the table, his plate piled high.

Miriam smiled. "Tobias and I had to do something while all of you were playing in the wheat field."

The ten men found a place either at the table or on the porch. Lukas gave Miriam the last remaining seat on the porch and opted to lean against the railing. Tobias had finished early and asked Lukas if he could go check on the chickens. Once gone, Mordecai went up to the porch, a mug of cider in one hand and a plate with pie in the other. He leaned against the railing across from Lukas.

"He seems happy here," Mordecai said, motioning with his head in the direction Tobias had run off. "Truth be told, I was a bit worried about him. He can be a handful sometimes, as all little boys are." Mordecai winked at Lukas, no doubt remembering the trouble Lukas used to get into at Tobias' age.

"Tobias loves it here," Miriam said, taking a sip of her own cider. "As do I."

Lukas had a hunk of bread in his mouth, saving him the chance to reply as his cheeks turned red. Mordecai still noticed and laughed.

"Good. I'm glad this arrangement is working out. Mimi, could I trouble you to fill up my cider?"

"Not at all, Uncle. I'll fill mine, too." Miriam got up and was gone before Lukas could say a word. As Mordecai turned his gaze to Lukas, his blush deepened. He had a feeling Mordecai wasn't as low on cider as he had claimed.

"I know this isn't exactly my place, but Mimi has always been like a daughter to Tanya and me. I don't doubt you're being respectful of her while she's here. Your parents raised you right." Mordecai sighed. "However, I do have a question, and I hope, from one man to another, you'll be honest with me. What are your intentions with my niece?"

Lukas swallowed. He hadn't expected to be having this conversation so soon, least of all with Mordecai. He had hoped once Hans returned, he could approach Miriam's father and make a proper request to court her. He cleared his throat.

"I'd like to marry her someday, sir."

Mordecai grinned. "I told Tanya! She owes me a few coins," Mordecai said with a chuckle.

Lukas wasn't sure whether to laugh or be mortified that Mordecai and his wife were taking bets on his feelings for Miriam.

"Have you told her that?" Mordecai asked.

Lukas shook his head. "With all my responsibilities here, I haven't had much time to think of romance." He cleared his throat. "But I intend to. Soon. I hope she feels the same for me."

Mordecai winked at Lukas. "Trust me, I don't think you have to worry about that." He put his pie down and stood in front of Lukas. "You're a good man, Lukas. You've been put to the test these last few weeks, and I'm impressed with how you're handling it. I know Miriam would have a happy future with you. I'm sure her parents would feel the same. Just make sure you talk to her father soon. I know right now this arrangement is working, but people like to talk. Gossip spreads faster than wildfire in the village, and I'm sure her parents will start to grow concerned if they hear some story making its way through the market."

Lukas nodded. "I don't want to jeopardize Miriam's reputation."

"I know you don't. I'm glad I never had daughters. Don't have to worry so much about all this with boys," he said with a laugh. He clapped his hand on Lukas' shoulder. "If you ever need any-thing, you know you can always come to me. And about more than the farm."

"Thank you, Mordecai. That means a lot." He wasn't sure how to express just how much it meant. Not with words, at least.

Miriam came back to the porch and handed Mordecai his cider. Mordecai thanked her then asked Lukas how his chore list was progressing. "Mine seems to fill up every time I cross a few things off," he said with a chuckle.

"Mine too." Lukas grimaced. "Now that the harvest is mostly done, I can start to focus on some other projects I have to get done before winter." The list was growing longer with each passing day. He tried not to think of Hans' retreating frame, leaving Lukas with weeks of work but not enough time.

"I can leave Fitz here, if you'd like. He's my best farmhand, but I have four others at home that can help me finish my work."

"Thank you, but I think Miriam, Tobias, and I will be fine. If we're not, I'll let you know."

"I know I said this at the funeral, but Tanya and I were so sorry to hear about Sarah."

"Thank you. I miss her very much."

"Speaking of," Miriam said, then went inside.

Mordecai glanced at Lukas, eyebrows raised. Lukas shrugged. Miriam came back out with one of Sarah's quilts. "Would Auntie like one of Sarah's quilts? This house is fit to bursting with them."

Mordecai looked from the quilt to Lukas. It was a mixture of green and blue fabric; it reminded Lukas of the sea, or at least what he assumed to be the sea. He had never travelled farther than the nearest village.

"She would love it, so long as you don't mind giving it to us, Lukas," said Mordecai.

"You're more than welcome to it. It's the least I can give you after all your help today."

Mordecai grinned. "Then I happily accept it. Tanya will adore it." He took it from Miriam and draped it over his shoulder.

Another hour went by. The moon was just coming out when the men finished putting the table and chairs away, and helping Miriam bring in the dishes. Each man left with one of Sarah's quilts for his family, including Brandon. Miriam had teased him about hiding it from their sister Alexandra.

"If she spots it, you'll never see it again!" she said.

Brandon was spending the night at his uncle's, and Miriam had already explained Lukas would walk her home with Tobias later. Mordecai and Brandon surprised Lukas with a departing hug before they set off for home in their wagon. Lukas watched them leave from the doorway, his heart full of good will towards the men who had helped him. He wished he had better words to tell them how he felt.

Lukas went into the kitchen to see to the dishes, but Miriam cornered him in the doorway with a cup of tea. "Dishes can wait. You need to rest."

He bowed his head with a smile. "Yes, ma'am."

They sat together on one of the couches, their cups of tea warming their hands. Tobias lay on the other couch, fast asleep. His cup of tea lay on the ground, half empty. Lukas had told him to lie down in his parents' room, but Tobias hadn't made it that far. Lukas glanced at the boy.

"I wonder what he dreams about," he muttered.

"Chickens. Or rabbits."

They both laughed quietly. "I wonder if he dreams about his parents." He took a long sip of tea. "I can usually get her out of my head during the day, but in my dreams, she's there."

Miriam held his free hand. "Are they good dreams?"

"Sometimes," he said as he ran his thumb over her knuckles. "Other times I see her coffin and I'm trying to free her. From what, I don't know. I hear her voice and think she's calling for help. Like we buried her by mistake." He shook his head. "I worry I'll always have these dreams."

Miriam squeezed his hand. "Perhaps. But that might not be a bad thing. At least not the good ones. Maybe they're her way of showing you she's with you, in the only way she can be."

Lukas said nothing and took another sip of tea. He hadn't thought of it like that.

"What did my uncle say to you earlier?" Miriam asked.

Lukas blushed. He briefly considered lying, but he was too tired to come up with something that sounded plausible. That, and he didn't want to start his courtship with Miriam by lying to her. He took a big sip of tea for courage.

"He wanted to know what my intentions are with you."

Miriam tilted her body, so she was facing him. "And what are those?"

Lukas put down his tea and met Miriam's gaze. "Courtship. Then marriage. A farmhouse of our own, with lots of sheep and a few cows. Babies, someday, when we're ready." He squeezed her hand. "A lifetime of evenings like this, where the only thing I'm thinking about is how wonderful it is to be beside you." He swallowed, unsure what came next.

Miriam grinned, wide enough so her dimples showed. "That sounds pretty amazing, if I do say so myself." She leaned closer, their lips a breath away from touching. "I suppose you'd better talk to Papa, then."

Lukas was sure he nodded, but looking back, he couldn't remember. All he could recall was his hand cupping Miriam's soft cheek as he pulled her closer for a kiss. Just as their lips met, Tobias screamed.

The pair jumped apart, Lukas' heart racing from something other than the too-brief kiss. They went over to Tobias, who was having a nightmare. Lukas gently placed a hand on Tobias' shoulder, shaking him awake. "Tobi, Tobi!"

"It's alright, Tobi, you're safe," Miriam cooed, rubbing his back.

A few seconds passed, but they felt like hours. Tobias' eyes opened and tears started to run down his cheeks. "Papa? Mama?" he whispered.

Lukas smiled sadly at the boy. "It was just a dream, Tobi. You're safe."

Tobias sat up and hugged Lukas tight. Miriam wrapped her arms around them both. As Tobias sobbed against his shoulder, Lukas met Miriam's gaze. Perhaps it would be better if they spent the night. Lukas suspected Tobias wasn't going to be in any shape to walk home later.

"How are you feeling?" Miriam asked when Tobias pulled away from Lukas' shoulder.

"Better," the boy muttered. "Can we stay here tonight? I don't want to go out in the dark."

Lukas saw just how dark it was getting outside and nodded. "You can sleep in the loft with me." He glanced at Miriam. "I can walk you home still."

Miriam waved away the offer. "I'll be fine. I know a few short cuts," she said with a wink. "Walk me to the door?"

Lukas got Tobias settled upstairs on his cot. Once his breathing settled, Lukas came downstairs and met Miriam on the porch. His hand immediately found hers.

"Do you remember when we were children and you used to go to school at the chapel? How we'd see each other in passing when I went in with my sisters for our private lessons?"

"Of course. I always liked how your mama insisted you and your sisters get an education. Not many families did back then, or do today. Mama was so mad at Papa for pulling me out of school to help him when I turned thirteen," he said with a chuckle. Hans and Sarah had argued for weeks. That was the only time he remembered his parents fighting.

Miriam stared at the barn, her gaze in the past. "The year before you left school, some of the village girls would see my sisters and I going and tease us, saying we thought we were better than them just because we had lessons."

Lukas frowned. "I think I remember Isla complaining about them."

"One day, they cornered me in the churchyard. I still don't know what they were doing there. They stole my books and one of them pulled my braids. I thought one girl was going to yank my hair out." She took a deep breath. "You were just leaving, but you saw them. Saw me. I remember you told them to stop. When they left, you helped me pick up my books they had tossed in the mud, and you let me lean on you as we went inside to find the preacher." She met his gaze. "I think that was the first time I remember loving you."

"It happened often over the years. You'd wait after my lessons were done and talk to me on the way home, or I'd see you in the market and you would offer me a sweet. The little things added up and suddenly, I'm here. On your porch. Still in love with you." She licked her lips. "I've wanted to tell you for years, but ladies aren't supposed to pursue men. We're supposed to wait for you to come calling." She snorted. "I'm not very patient, obviously. I know the timing is awful. Losing your mother is tragic, and I can only begin to imagine what—"

Lukas cut her off with a kiss. This time, no scream pulled them apart. Miriam's lips were soft against his, making his heart beat faster and faster. After a moment, desperate for air, Lukas pulled back. Miriam stared at him, her eyes wide.

"You know it's rude to cut a lady off when she's talking," she whispered.

Lukas blushed. "Would you mind if I did it again?"

She grinned. "No."

Just as they were leaning in for another kiss, frantic footsteps broke the farmyard's silence. Lukas looked in the direction the noise was coming from and saw Hans running up the walkway.

~ 20 ~

ISLA

"You know, when people said it was made of gingerbread, I always thought they meant it just *looked* like it," said Szilvia, her head tilted to the side as she looked at the witch's cottage. "Do you think it tastes like it, too?"

"Even if it does, it's probably stale gingerbread now," Erik said as he held Isla's hand, intertwining his fingers with hers.

Gumdrops lined the roof of the cottage. Candy canes made the window frames, and hardened chocolate created the door. Isla had been staring at the candy for several minutes as night turned to day. She wanted to go in, but her gut told her to run. She swallowed and squeezed Erik's hand for courage.

"The sooner we get this over with, the better," Isla whispered to herself. She cleared her throat. "Let's go in and see what we can find."

Szilvia was the first through the door. It creaked on its sugar-spun hinges. Surprisingly, nothing was rotten on the inside. There was no smell of mold, nor was there dust covering every surface. It seemed as if the cottage had been frozen in time, remaining in place from over thirty years ago when Hans and Greta escaped the witch.

Isla stood in the doorway, her eyes scanning the gingerbread walls. Although this was someone's home, there were no personal items scattered about like in a normal person's house. No pictures hung on the wall; no books littered the parlour table. Isla went into the first room on her right. It was the parlour, but there was nothing cozy to make it an inviting space. No blankets to curl up in, no clock on the wall. The couch was devoid of cushions, as if the owner couldn't bear the thought of being cozy in their own home. Isla rested her hand on the side table, her fingers coming away free of dust.

What made you who you are, witch? What changed you?

Isla hoped the cottage held the answers she needed, not only to free Constance, but to sate her curiosity.

"I found something," Szilvia called.

Isla found her friend in the witch's kitchen. Isla paused as soon as she stepped in. This kitchen looked remarkably like Constance's. The fireplace was huge and had a large cauldron hanging there, just waiting to be used. Shelves upon shelves lined two of the four walls. Jars and bags of what Isla assumed were herbs and other ingredients rested there. Isla tried to read what the labels said, but she couldn't make out the language.

Szilvia was at the large table in the middle of the room hunched over a book. Erik stood off to the side, his eyes constantly scanning the room, as if he expected something to jump out at them. *Not an unrealistic fear.* Isla brushed her hand against his arm, trying to offer what comfort she could. She knew the woods unsettled him, let alone this cottage. She flashed him a quick smile then went to Szilvia.

"What did you find?"

Szilvia moved over so Isla could see the page the book was opened to. It appeared to be a recipe, but Isla couldn't tell for sure. It was written in the same language as the labels on the jars. She squinted, trying to make it out.

"A spell?" she hesitated to guess.

Szilvia shrugged. "I found it lying here open to this page. Perhaps it's what the witch, or whoever is taking the children, used to enchant them."

"But what does it *say*? Have you ever seen this language before?"

"In some of my mother's books. The *very* old ones she got from Grandmother. I've only seen her bring them out once every few years when she gets a truly difficult case."

"Can you read it?"

Szilvia cringed. "A little, but only the most basic phrases. I barely recognize half of the words on this page."

Isla grabbed a scrap of paper on the cluttered table and bookmarked the spell. "We'll have to take it with us, then. Perhaps your mother can translate it."

Szilvia nodded and put the book in her bag.

"Can we leave now?" Erik begged.

"Not yet. We haven't checked all the rooms," Isla said. "I'll head upstairs. You two check the rest of the lower level. Maybe she had a cellar or something."

Szilvia and Erik agreed then left the kitchen. On her way out, Isla spotted the oven. She was so focused on the book she hadn't looked further than the table. It was an unassuming thing, much like Greta's stove at home. It was black and smelt like smoke and ash, even after all these years of disuse. Isla stared at it, almost expecting the door to open and for the witch to step out. Her heart trembling in her chest, Isla left the kitchen, her hurried steps carrying her upstairs.

There were only two rooms there, neither holding anything interesting, least of all anything Isla thought would help solve the mystery. In the room she assumed to be the witch's bedroom, Isla rummaged through every drawer and scanned every book title in the bookcase but found nothing worth bringing back to the others. The bed was perfectly made, and the chair positioned just right in front of the fireplace. It reminded Isla of a doll's room, the child tidying up before going down for dinner. Isla was about to leave when she noticed a trapdoor in the ceiling. She would have missed it had it not been for the moonlight shining at just the right angle.

"Szilvia, Erik, I found something!"

A minute passed and the others were soon in the room with her, staring up at the door.

"How do we get in there?" Szilvia wondered.

Erik pulled over the chair and stood on it. He attempted to pry it open, but the door wouldn't budge. "Nothing," he said with a sigh.

The crystal, which had been still since they entered the cottage, suddenly glowed.

"Let me try," Isla said, taking Erik's place on the chair. She almost couldn't reach it, but with a fully extended arm, the crystal just barely touched the door. It popped open and sliding stairs began to clink down one by one. Isla jumped out of the way before one of the stairs hit her in the head. Once the last step settled, Isla tested the bottom step. It seemed sturdy enough. She was about to head up when Erik placed a cautious hand on her shoulder.

"Do you still have your dagger?" he asked.

Isla unsheathed it.

"Good." Erik took out his and motioned for Szilvia to do the same.

"You realize a dagger won't do anything to a ghost, right?" Szilvia said.

"One, I'm not convinced it *is* a ghost, and two, a weapon makes me feel safer," said Erik.

Isla chuckled then headed up the staircase to the secret room. Once all three were up, Isla motioned to Erik to light his lantern. He grabbed it from his pack and within a minute they could make out what was in the attic. At first, it seemed like a regular attic, just storage space, but then Isla saw a massive crystal, the same colour as the one around her neck. It was on a small table, dried lavender and rosemary tied in small bundles beside it. The large crystal was roughly cut, its sharp edges glaring at Isla. She went over to the table and noticed how warm her crystal was against her chest. It glowed faintly, as if it was calling to its bigger sister. Isla reached out and touched the large crystal. The crystal immediately warmed under Isla's touch. She noticed the glow growing brighter and brighter. She stared in awe as the glow spread to cover the whole crystal.

She almost didn't hear the door to the attic close.

Isla forced her gaze away from the crystal and stared at the door. Her heart rammed against her ribs like a bird trying to escape its cage.

"Please tell me one of you shut the door," she whispered.

Erik reached out and grabbed her free hand. "I was hoping that was you showing off with the crystal."

"As was I," Szilvia whimpered.

"I hoped it would be you, Isla," a voice said in the attic.

Isla's hand against the crystal trembled. "Me?"

The voice chuckled, the crackling sound filling the room. "You took your time, though. And you brought guests."

Erik stood back-to-back with Isla, his dagger ready to strike. He grabbed Szilvia and brought her closer to them. "Show yourself."

"With pleasure."

The voice manifested into a woman, a perfectly normal-looking woman, if one ignored the fact that they could see right through her.

The witch who haunted Hans and Greta's nightmares stared at Isla, a wicked grin on her pale face.

"Hello, Isla. It's been a long time."

~ 21 ~

LUKAS

"Papa," Lukas gasped, his hands still on Miriam's waist.

Hans stared at his son. "Hello, Lukas." He glanced at Miriam, who hadn't moved from Lukas' embrace. "And Miriam. Nice to see you again."

Miriam flashed a smile at Hans, her cheeks crimson.

"I thought you were with the sheep," Lukas said.

"I left them in the far field. Not the one you harvested." Hans stood at the bottom of the porch staircase. "Nicely done, by the way. I had hoped our neighbours would lend a helping hand."

"I couldn't have done it without them. It wasn't as if I could ask you for advice." Lukas knew how bitter he sounded, but he couldn't help it. *What is he doing here?*

Hans bowed his head. "Yes, I did leave you with a lot on your plate. We can talk about it later. Right now, we have to go."

Lukas shook his head. "I can't leave Tobias alone."

Hans raised an eyebrow. "Tobias?"

"A ward of Miriam's uncle Mordecai. He and Miriam have been helping me since Mama died. He's had a nightmare and is spending the night. I can't just leave him." That, and he didn't exactly want to be dragged off by Hans, who still hadn't explained where he had been or why they had to leave so soon. "Where could we possibly have to go?"

"The witch's cottage."

It was as if every cricket and bird fell silent as soon as they heard Hans' proclamation.

"What?" Lukas whispered.

Hans stared at his feet, his hands shoved in his pockets. "I was with the sheep when I first sensed it. This . . . This *wrongness*. It felt like when I was in that cottage, trapped in a cage as the witch fattened me up. I heard rumours on my journey about the village children. My gut told me what my mind refused to accept. That the witch is back." He looked at Lukas. "So, I turned around, and here I am."

"And you want me to come with you?" Lukas took a step closer to his father. "After you left me alone here, with Mama dead, you come running back here and expect me to follow your orders? Now?" Lukas exclaimed, his anger spilling over.

Hans took off his dusty cap, twisting it in his hands. "Lukas, I know you're upset. I don't blame you. But the village is in danger. Our family is in danger. There's no time to lose. Will you come?"

Lukas shook his head. "Isla already left. She's probably there. Let her solve the mystery. She doesn't need me to meddle."

Hans paled. "Greta let her go?" He shook his head, putting his hat back on. "It's worse than I thought. Come, we have to go, *now*." Hans grabbed Lukas' hand, attempting to pull his son along.

Lukas planted his feet. "Papa, wait. What's wrong with Isla being there?"

"I'll explain along the way. We must get Greta. She knows the way."

Lukas sighed. He couldn't let his father go off into the woods alone, especially not like this. It seemed like he hadn't slept lately, or at least not enough. "Give me a moment. I need a lantern if nothing else." He went inside, Miriam close behind.

"What are you going to do?" she whispered.

"Follow him, I suppose. I don't want to take Tobias, though. The last thing he needs is to be involved in all this," he muttered.

Miriam grabbed Lukas' hand. "I'll stay with him."

"Are you sure?

She squeezed his hand. "You have to go if Isla's in trouble. We'll be fine. Just come back safe."

"I'll do my best to hurry." He glanced over his shoulder and saw through the open door that Hans was still on the porch, his back to his son. Lukas quickly kissed Miriam. "I love you," he whispered. He grabbed his lantern and a thicker jacket. Lukas locked the door then headed down the steps, walking past Hans. He heard his father's footsteps close behind.

The first part of the trek to Greta's was silent. A tense, awkward silence that Lukas had never experienced with his father before. He had hoped the walk would help calm him, but with every step, he kept wishing Hans was still with his sheep. When they rounded the bend that signaled the halfway mark to the village, Hans was the first to break the silence.

"Miriam seems well," Hans said as he glanced at his son. "She's been here a few weeks?"

Lukas nodded, his shoulders sagging. "She and Tobias have been an amazing help on the farm. I don't know what I'd do without them."

"I'm glad. I was worried about you alone out there."

"I wouldn't have been alone if you had stayed."

Hans sighed. "You don't understand, Lukas. Without Sarah, I feel lost. Broken. Everywhere I look on that farm, I think of her." He shook his head. "I can't stay there. Not yet. I can't face it."

"Aunt Greta was right about you. She said you ran away, just like you ran away from the village years ago."

Hans smiled bitterly, shaking his head again. "My sister would say something like that," he muttered. "We all have different ways of grieving, Lukas. I'm not saying mine is the best but leaving was what I had to do. I don't regret it. I'm only sorry I've caused you pain."

Lukas didn't reply. As the village lights grew brighter, he glanced at his father. "Do you even understand what it's been like for me? I lost my mother and father in the same week," he said, his voice thick with tears.

Hans grabbed Lukas' arm and forced him to stop walking. Lukas' vision blurred from the unshed tears. He could barely see Hans as his father pulled him in for a hug. They stood in the middle of the road for some time, Lukas crying on his father's shoulder and Hans rubbing his back. When Lukas calmed down, they continued together. Lukas' heart still hurt, but he didn't feel as weighed down by his grief and anger as he had before.

"Are you going to tell me why Isla shouldn't be at the witch's cottage, besides the obvious fact that it's dangerous?"

"Let's leave it at the obvious for now. I'm hoping we get there in time and I'm worrying over nothing."

The pair came up to Greta's door and knocked. Jacob opened the door, his eyes red and puffy. Lukas had never seen his uncle cry before. When Jacob's gaze fell on Hans, those eyes widened.

"Hans, what a surprise! Come in, come in. You must be exhausted."

Jacob ushered them inside. A pot of still-warm tea was on the table. Jacob poured them all a lukewarm cup. He sat down heavily in his chair by the fire, tilting his head back. "I apologize for my exhaustion. Isla left this morning, and Greta has been a wreck since. I'm worried myself, but I'm afraid for my wife. I don't want her to hurt herself."

Hans didn't sit, instead standing in the doorway of Greta's bedroom. "That's why we've come, actually. We're going to fetch Isla, and we need Greta to do it."

"I'm not going, Hans," Greta shouted from behind her closed bedroom door. Lukas sank into his chair, taking a sip of the bitter tea.

Hans turned around and stood in front of her door, his arms crossed. "If you don't, you're letting that witch win."

"She's dead, Hans! I pushed her in myself."

"Then why the children? You can feel her magic as well as I can. Better even."

"You don't know anything," Greta hissed. "Neither does Isla. I tried to stop her, but she wouldn't listen!"

"And now it's up to us to save her, and the children of the village. If we don't, you know what will happen."

"Why should I care what happens to any of them? They never cared about us when our stepmother beat us or when Papa left us to starve."

Hans sighed. "You're the only one who knows the way, Greta. We need you."

Greta said nothing for a time. Lukas stared at his lap, a twist of anxiety curling in his stomach. The tea didn't sit well with this topic. He felt like he was listening to a conversation he wasn't privy to.

"You know what that woman did. Why would you ask me to go back?" Greta said, her voice small and pinched, like she was holding back tears.

Lukas heard the door open. He lifted his gaze and saw Hans was no longer leaning against the doorframe, but inside Greta's room. The door was left open enough for Lukas to still hear their conversation.

"Because if we don't, we'll never be free of her. And I want that for you more than anything."

Lukas heard the rustle of fabric and suspected the siblings were hugging. He looked over at his uncle, but Jacob had shut his eyes, one hand resting against his forehead as if he had a headache.

Hans and Greta left her room hand in hand. Hans could use a shave and Greta's hair was the most unkempt Lukas had ever seen it, but they were ready. Lukas stood, his cup empty, and grabbed his lantern. "Ready?"

Hans looked to his sister. Greta sighed. "Ready."

Jacob stood. "What do you need?"

"Nothing. We must leave now. The magic is changing," Hans said, shifting from foot to foot. "Can you feel it?" he asked Greta.

She avoided her brother's gaze. "Just a few cloaks and a lantern. We won't be there long."

Hans and Lukas waited outside as Greta said goodbye to her husband. Jacob had offered to come, but Lukas heard Greta refuse. When she joined them outside, her hair was pulled back in her usual tight bun and she had on a pair of work boots with a thick heel, completely different to her usual pair of slippers. She pulled up the hood of her cloak.

"Let's get this over with," she muttered.

Lukas followed at his aunt's heels as she led them away from the village and into the woods. He wasn't sure where they were going, but Greta knew, and that was enough. He hoped they arrived in time before whatever Hans feared took place.

~ 22 ~

ISLA

"How do you know my name?" Isla asked, swallowing the lump in her throat.

The witch grinned, her lips painted grey against her translucent skin. "I know the names of all the children in the village. But yours especially." She floated closer to the group and Erik raised his dagger higher. The witch ignored it, refusing to break her gaze from Isla's. "You were very young the last time I saw you."

Isla gripped Erik's free arm tightly. "I've never seen you before."

"Do you remember when you ran off into the woods? It was your grandfather's birthday. You were trying to beat Lukas in a race."

Isla paled. She barely remembered that day, but it was there. She had taken a shortcut into the woods; even at that age, she wasn't afraid.

"I gave you that pendent," the witch said, pointing to Isla's crystal. "I told you to keep it close. And I'm so glad you did."

"What does the necklace have to do with the village children? And Isaiah and Aliz?" Szilvia said.

The witch looked over at Szilvia. Her white hair, pulled up in a bun, shook as she acknowledged Szilvia for the first time. "I don't care one fig for those children, especially the Chief Steward's. I just needed them to get your attention," she said, turning her gaze back to Isla. "I had to get you into my woods again."

"They're not *your* woods," Isla said, narrowing her eyes. "And those children didn't deserve what you did to them, nor did their parents. Free them!"

The witch laughed. "What right do you have to make demands of me? And they *are* my woods. When that foolish Council banished me here, they didn't count on me making it my queendom." She spread her arms wide. "These woods listen to me. When I call for children, they answer. Just like your mother and uncle."

"My mother?"

"What, you think Greta happened upon here by mistake?" The witch chuckled. "No, she heard my song and brought Hans with her. She couldn't know what I had in mind, but still she came. Her cheek still stung from her stepmother's slap, and her heart was heavy from her father's absence. I suspect she would have done anything to escape them, even lead her brother to me."

Isla shook her head. "Mama was a prisoner here. She told me so."

"I'm sure she's told you a lot of things over the years. Have you believed it all?"

She hesitated. "About this, yes."

The witch smirked. "Then you're as foolish as she was back then." She pointed to the crystal behind Isla. "I showed her my crystal, too. Hans was asleep and she managed to get out of her cage. Do you know what she did?" The witch tilted her head, holding Isla's gaze. "She touched it, just like you. I've never seen it glow so brightly. Almost brighter than when you touched it."

"What are you talking about?" Isla whispered.

"Have you never wondered why herbology comes so easily to you? How you find your ingredients faster than even your tutor? Why your potions seem so much more potent?" The witch grinned. "It's the same reason your mama's tea soothes people, giving them exactly what they need when they drink it."

The witch leaned in close, suddenly coming between Isla and Erik, almost as if he wasn't there. From the corner of her eye, she saw the witch had somehow shoved Erik and Szilvia out of the way. They stood side by side near the window, their daggers on the ground. Erik stared at Isla, trying to speak, but nothing came out.

"You're a witch," the witch whispered.

Isla took a shaky breath, reaching back to brace herself against the table that held the crystal. She thought back to when her mother fought her about working for Constance, how terrified she seemed. Isla remembered how she caught on to herbs and mixing potions early on, and how impressed Constance was.

"I'm a witch," she said, her hands trembling.

The witch grinned, her black eyes twinkling. "Just like me."

"As a witch, can I break your spell on the children?"

"You can try, but you'll fail."

Isla's shoulders sank. "I don't understand. I'm here now. Let them go." She motioned to Erik and Szilvia. "Them as well."

The witch shook her head. "We're missing someone. Someone important." She floated past Isla and placed her see-through hands on the crystal. Nothing happened. Isla saw the witch's eyes flare up, tiny flames lurking there. "It used to listen to me, but no longer. It will, though. Soon."

"What does it *do*, exactly?"

The witch grinned. "Anything you want it to. It has no limits. There's a price, though. There always is."

"What price did you pay?"

The witch spread her arms wide. "What do you think?"

"Was it worth it?"

Before the witch could reply, the door downstairs slammed open, shaking the house. "Witch!" Greta shrieked. "Where's my daughter?"

The witch's smile widened. "Finally. It took her long enough."

Isla tried to move to the trap door, but whatever spell the witch had cast over Erik and Szilvia now affected her. She couldn't move a muscle. *Mama, run,* she silently screamed.

The witch waved her hand and the trap door slid open. "You know where to find us, Greta. You always did know where I was lurking."

It wasn't long before Greta, along with Uncle Hans and Lukas, were in the attic as well. Upon seeing her daughter, the blood drained from Greta's face. "Let her go, you demon," Greta hissed.

The witch chuckled. "Demon? That's a new one. They used to call me the devil's wife." She tilted her head, facing Greta. "Come now, she's hardly a prisoner. Show her, Isla."

The spell over her lifted. Isla stumbled towards Greta. Her mama wrapped her in a tight embrace, burying her face into Isla's hair as she took deep breaths. Isla felt her mother's tears dampen her hair.

"Are you alright? Did she hurt you?" Greta whispered.

"Why would I hurt her? I need her. As I need you, Greta. I've been watching you. I know you use your little tricks for small magics, but it's powerful. It's still there, no matter how hard you've fought against it." The witch shook her head. "What a disappointment. Had you not pushed me into that oven, I could have taught you so much."

Greta looked up from Isla's hair and glared at the witch. "I told you then and I'll tell you again, I want nothing to do with your magic. Let the children go! Your problem is with me."

"While I do hold some resentment over the oven situation, I wasn't lying when I said I needed both of you." The witch crooked a finger, pulling Isla away from her mother.

"Mama!"

"Give her back!" Greta snarled.

"Not until you give me what's mine."

"I have nothing to *give* you."

"Ah, that's where you're wrong," the witch said as she used her other hand to shove Hans and Lukas to where Erik and Szilvia were stuck.

"What do you want?" Isla asked, meeting Erik's desperate gaze. She wished she had never brought him, or Szilvia, with her.

"I want my body back. And I need you two to help me."

Greta clenched her hands. "That's impossible! Your body is ash."

The witch glared at Greta. "I know what happened to it," she snapped. "I remember every agonizing moment in that oven."

"You deserved every second of it," said Greta. "You were going to eat us."

"Hans, perhaps, but not you. I had plans for you, Greta. Plans I'm sure you never shared with your brother."

Greta kept her back to Hans, her cheeks flushed. "Your plans don't matter, nor do you. You're a ghost. You shouldn't even *be* here."

The witch spread her arms. "With this crystal still here, I remain. Its power will sustain me until you do as I say. We're all here and no one is leaving until I have a body again."

The trap door slammed shut. The bolt in the window locked. Isla met her mother's gaze, dread pooling in her belly.

$$\sim 23 \sim$$

LUKAS

Lukas had never been under a spell before.

He certainly wasn't fond of being enchanted in the witch's attic, especially while his cousin and aunt were being manipulated by a ghost, something Lukas didn't think existed in the first place. As he watched Greta, Isla, and the witch in a stalemate, his mind wandered to Tobias and Miriam. He hoped they were safe at the farm.

I'm glad I didn't ask her to come. The last place he wanted her was in this witch's attic.

Greta stood straight as a pole, her glare fixed on the witch. "What makes you think we're going to help you, or even that we can?"

The witch smirked, her translucent skin puckering at the corners. Lukas cringed. She was incredibly unsettling to look at, and yet he couldn't turn away.

"I wouldn't have brought you here if you couldn't." The witch went over to Lukas and the others near the wall, unable to move. "And you're going to help because if you don't, I'm going to start picking off your family one by one. Until there's only the three of us left." The witch smirked at Lukas. "And I don't mean putting them in an enchanted sleep."

Lukas paled. Greta's hands trembled and she clenched them at her sides, her iron nerves faltering.

Isla glared at the witch, her face flush. "They have nothing to do with this. Let them go!"

"Somehow, I don't think you'll cooperate if I do," said the witch.

Isla stepped forward, placing herself between the witch and her family. "I swear to you, if you let them go, I'll do whatever you want. Mama as well. We don't need her. Like you said, she denies her powers. She barely uses them. She won't be able to help."

The witch crossed her arms. "And you will?"

"I'm willing to try."

"Isla," Greta hissed.

The witch raised a hand, silencing Greta. "Why? You know who I am and what I've done. Why help me?"

Yes, why help her indeed? Lukas tried to meet Isla's gaze, but she wouldn't look his way. She kept her back to her cousin, staring at the witch. "I don't know you, not truly. Constance mentioned you used to be a quiet, solitary woman who healed the sick. And now you're this," she said, waving her hand towards the ghost. "What happened?"

"What do you think happened?" The witch glared at Hans and Lukas. "Men decided I was dangerous. They didn't understand my faith. So, I became what they feared."

"Let them go, and I'll get your body back. Then you can do whatever you want to the Council."

The witch chuckled. "You have little love for them, I see."

"What woman with any semblance of a backbone would?"

The witch looked from Isla to the group. Lukas met her gaze, refusing to cower before the spirit. She nodded. "Two go free now, the others when the spell is done. Greta stays. Deal?"

Isla swallowed. "Deal."

No! Lukas tried to shout, but his tongue had turned to lead in his mouth. Erik stamped his foot, but that was all he could manage. From the pained expression that came over Erik's face, the movement had cost him.

The witch waved her hand and Erik and Szilvia fell on their knees. "Leave now," she ordered.

Erik stumbled towards Isla. She caught him and they clung to each other.

"Don't do this," Erik whispered.

"Trust me," she replied, kissing his cheek.

Lukas watched as Isla kissed Szilvia's cheek then sent them on their way. Tears ran down Szilvia's cheeks. Part of him wished he could have been released first, but as he stared at the witch, he knew why he wasn't allowed to go.

This was family business.

The witch nodded towards the trap door. "To the kitchen, all of you. It's time we get started."

Lukas felt the magic leave his body as suddenly as it had come over him. His hands and feet tingled like they had been asleep. He realized why Erik had stumbled. Lukas had to cling to his father's arm as they went downstairs. Although they had control over their bodies, it was clear the witch had no intention of letting them wander. Every time Lukas tried to take a step out of line, he was met by an invisible wall. He looked down the hall to see if Erik and Szilvia were hiding somewhere in the house, but if they were, he couldn't see them.

Upon entering the witch's kitchen, Lukas was struck by the similarity to Constance's. Under different circumstances, he would have liked to explore it more, but once he saw the oven, he couldn't tear his gaze away. He looked to Hans, wondering if he had seen the oven as well. His father had shut his eyes tight, his hands clenched into fists.

Lukas looked to the door, wondering where the women were, when suddenly Greta marched in. She slammed a book onto the table, her anger filling the small kitchen. Isla wasn't far behind, the crystal in her hands. She placed it on the table beside the book, but with much less force than Greta might have used. Perhaps that was why the witch hadn't let Greta carry it.

"This is ridiculous. We need to leave," Greta hissed to her daughter.

Isla folded her hands behind her back. "We will," she promised, glancing at Lukas. "We all will."

The witch floated in. "Enough whispering. Turn to the last page. The ingredients are listed there. We'll need a fire. I think you can handle that part, Greta."

Greta glared at the witch but went to the oven and began to fill it with wood. Lukas noticed her hands trembled as she fiddled with the oven's handle. Hans had opened his eyes and focused them on the crystal, ignoring the oven.

The witch had Isla fetch the ingredients. As Lukas watched her, he wondered how she planned to get them out of this mess. He wished he could help, but once again, the witch had cast her magic over him, not allowing him nor Hans to move.

When all the ingredients were gathered and the water boiling, the witch motioned to the crystal. "Now place your hands on it, both of you, and read that spell."

Isla hesitated. "What happens when we read it?"

"Do you really want to know?"

"We deserve to."

The witch chuckled. "What do you know about what you deserve? Or what anyone deserves, for that matter? Do you think I deserved to be driven from my home, named a witch, and made an outcast by men who thought they knew better than me? Did I deserve that?" the witch shouted. "All I wanted was to live peacefully on my own. But here we are, and this is what my life has come to. Or my afterlife, I should say," the witch said with a bitter smile. "Now, put your hands on the damn crystal and read the spell, or I will hunt down that pretty boy of yours and kill him first."

Lukas watched with a growing sense of dread as Isla reached out and put her hands on the crystal. The witch glared at Greta. "You know I'll do it," the witch said softly.

Greta returned the witch's glare then reached out her hands. Before she could touch it, Hans ran towards them.

"Run!" Hans shouted as he shoved the crystal off the table. It shattered on the floor, the shards flying in every direction.

"No!" the witch screeched. "What have you done?"

"Papa!" Lukas stumbled, the spell temporarily broken. He reached for Hans, but the witch got to him first. She waved her hand, slamming Hans onto the ground. Without a physical hand, she couldn't touch him, but with her powers she could still manipulate people.

Greta grabbed Lukas' arm and shoved him to the door.

"Run," she whispered. She tried to get Isla to go, but she wouldn't. Isla clasped one hand on her own crystal. She squeezed her eyes shut and Lukas watched with a mix of awe and terror as the oven door creaked open.

The witch turned her attention to Isla, eyes narrowed. "You want to play, do you? Fine. Let's see what you can do with that little crystal of yours." She raised her hand and Lukas stared as the witch sent the full, boiling cauldron flying at Isla. Isla dashed out of the way, one arm up, and the cauldron bounced off what seemed to be an invisible shield.

Lukas knew he should leave, go find Erik at the very least, but Hans hadn't moved from the ground. His eyes were shut, and Lukas didn't like the way his chest moved when he breathed. *I can't leave him. Not like Mama.*

Lukas hid in the doorway and watched as Isla shoved Greta behind her. "You lay a hand on my family, and you'll find out exactly what I can do."

The witch grinned, raising her see-through hand. "I knew I was right to choose you." She waved her hand, and the kitchen erupted into chaos.

~ 24 ~

ISLA

Isla clasped her crystal in her sweaty hand, doing her best to shield her family from the witch's attacks. Part of her mind was still attempting to grasp the fact that she was using *magic* in the first place, but the rest of her was trying not to get killed. The witch's magical knowledge far exceeded Isla's, so she knew the only way to beat her would be to distract her. She hadn't expected her uncle to break the larger crystal, but that was certainly enough of a distraction to set her escape plan into motion. The room was swirling with objects, some pelting down unexpectedly, others creating loud, distracting noises.

From the corner of her eye, she saw Lukas hovering in the doorway. She shoved her mother towards him, her gaze never leaving the witch's as she dodged the chair thrown at her head.

"Go with Lukas," she ordered. "Run while you can."

Greta glared at the witch, throwing the nearest vial towards her. It passed right through her, eliciting a slew of curses from Greta. "And leave you here with her? Never." She glanced at the oven. "Keep her distracted. I have an idea." She glanced at Hans, who stood between the witch and his son. He had gotten off the floor, but Isla suspected from his laboured breathing her uncle had at least one broken rib. Hans met Greta's gaze and nodded. The two started to move towards the oven, leaving Isla on her own.

The crystal was growing hotter and hotter in her grasp. Isla drew her arm in a sweeping arch, causing the shelves to tremble above and around her. The jars, bags, and other items flew off the shelves and pelted the witch. Although most passed through her translucent form, some did make an impact. Isla suspected those items were enchanted, but she couldn't be sure. Whatever they were, they certainly made the witch angry. Her eyes were hot coals, glaring at Isla as she sent a violent wind towards her. Isla fell back, loosening her grip on her crystal.

The witch took her chance. Isla felt like two large hands were holding her down, one pressing against her throat as the other prevented her from grasping her crystal completely, stopping her reconnecting her power.

"So much still to learn, right Isla? You had a lot of promise, but I'm sure I'll find another girl to get what I want. Szilvia has the gift. I'm sure I could convince her to work with me."

Isla glared at the witch. "Don't you dare go near her," she snarled, spitting out the words as the invisible hand around her throat constricted tighter.

Lukas tossed a lamp from the doorway. Its shatter didn't impact the witch, but it did distract her enough to loosen her grip on Isla's hand. He kept to the doorway, out of Isla's line of fire but still able to toss items as distractions. Isla clenched her jewel and forced the witch's ghostly hands off her. She pushed the witch back in the process, unknowingly getting her closer to the oven. Amidst the chaos, Hans and Greta had made it to the oven. Isla couldn't see what they were doing, but she did notice the flames from inside the oven peeking out from the door.

"Witch!" Greta yelled.

The witch paused, her hand raised but no magic used, and glanced behind her. Greta had Hans' hands bound, kneeling before the open oven. Isla squinted, wondering what in the world her mother was doing.

"I realize now I should thank you. All those years ago, you were just trying to rid me of my ball and chain," Greta said, motioning to Hans. "I should have let you eat him. You would have saved me the hassle of cleaning up all his messes."

The witch grinned. "I told you he would only hold you back. You didn't believe me."

Greta tilted her head, conceding the point. "I believe you now, though. And while I don't relish cannibalism, I think there's something else we could do." She motioned towards the open oven door. "How would you like to do the honours?"

The witch floated closer, only a few feet separating her from the oven. She narrowed her eyes. "You would sacrifice your own brother to the flames? Why?"

Greta grabbed Hans' hair and yanked. Hans cried out. "As I said, I've been picking up after him for decades. Do you know he ran off after his wife died, leaving all the work to me? He's selfish and stupid, just like every other man in that damn village. He deserves the same fate as them."

The witch chuckled. "You've become crueler since we last met. I like it."

"Before you do it, though, wouldn't you like to do it with real hands? Ones that feel?" She handed over a vial. "I remember from your book willow root can act as a temporary mask. It's not as good as your actual hands, but once we get rid of him, we can finish the spell. Those villagers won't know what's coming for them," she said with a grin, her grip on Hans' hair tightening.

The witch took the vial and didn't read the label as she poured it over her hands, her chest heaving as excitement built in her. Once her hands were coated, she closed the gap between herself and the siblings. She pressed her hands against Hans' chest, her grin catlike. "I hope you enjoy the heat, Hans. It's all-consuming."

"Now, Hans!" Greta shouted.

Hans removed his hands from his back, which weren't tied tightly, and clasped the witch's hands. Because of the willow root, he could hold them and not fall through. He spun the witch around and shoved her through the oven door.

"No!" the witch screeched.

Greta slammed the oven door shut and locked it in place. She turned to Isla and Lukas. "Run!"

The group hadn't made it out of the kitchen before the gingerbread house started to tremble. By the time they were in the hallway, the walls and ceiling had begun to crack.

Greta grabbed Isla. "We won't make it in time. Come here, all of you!"

Isla took Lukas by the arm and pulled him to her side. Greta did the same with Hans. Greta met Isla's gaze. "Think of a shield. A barrier. Anything to cover us from the debris."

Isla nodded. Greta wrapped her arm around Isla's shoulders and closed her eyes. Isla followed her mother's lead, praying whatever they came up with would hold. Isla instinctively raised an arm and spread her fingers wide. When the roof collapsed, she felt the trembling of the building, but didn't feel anything hit her head, so she took that as a good sign. She forced herself to keep her eyes closed and hands raised, afraid if she stopped something would get in.

When the shaking stopped, Isla slowly opened her eyes. Crumpled candy and broken furniture lay scattered around them. She lowered her arm, checking over her family. No one seemed harmed. That was when she realized Greta had had her arm up, too. She didn't have a crystal, but Isla could feel the magic wafting off her.

The four stood in silence as the dust settled around them.

"Did that really just happen?" Lukas asked, the first of the group to speak.

Hans sighed, his beard dusty with gingerbread crumbs. "It's over. Finally," he said, as if he hadn't heard Lukas' question.

"As it should have been years ago," Greta said.

Isla stared at her mother. "You never told me."

Greta ran a hand over her head, smoothing down the stray hairs that had escaped her bun. "Told you what?"

"The magic. The crystal. Why?"

Greta sighed. "It's a long story."

"I'd like to hear it."

Before Greta could reply, Erik and Szilvia ran to them. As soon as he was close enough, Erik wrapped Isla up in a hug.

"We heard the commotion. What happened?" Szilvia asked.

"We'll explain on the way back. We need to tell the council," Hans said.

Hans did most of the talking, letting his sister and niece recover from their interaction with the witch. Isla's body felt like it was full of live coals. She kept flexing her free hand, the one Erik wasn't clasping, trying to get the static feeling out of it. When the topic of Isla using magic against the witch came up, Erik stared at her in surprise.

"What she said was true, then? You're a witch?" he asked quietly.

Isla shrugged. "It doesn't matter what I am." She met his gaze. "It doesn't change anything."

Erik squeezed her hand. "No, it doesn't. I'm still marrying you when this is over." He blushed then looked over at Greta.

Greta smoothed the wrinkles from her dress, shaking the dust and debris from her skirts as she kept walking. "We'll discuss *that* when we get home. You need to clarify a few matters first."

Isla grinned. For Greta, that was as good as a "yes."

"She's gone, then? Well and truly gone?" Szilvia asked. Hans had still been telling his story.

Hans nodded. "With her spirit trapped in the oven, the crystal gone, and no body to return to, there's no way for her to come back."

Szilvia's shoulders relaxed. "Will the Council believe us, though?"

Hans sighed. "That I can't say. We'll just have to hope that the book you took has the answer to breaking the spell."

The group made their way slowly out of the woods. It was just past dawn when they entered the village. Instead of locked doors and unsettling silence, there was a celebration in the streets. Shops were open and loud cheering could be heard echoing around every corner.

Lukas stopped the first man that danced past them. "What's going on? What's happened?"

"Haven't you heard? The children are awake!" he said, his nose already red from too much alcohol.

Isla's eyes widened. "All of them? Even the Chief Steward's children?"

The man nodded, his straw hat revealing a few blonde curls underneath. "All of them! The preacher says it's a miracle."

Isla met her mother's gaze, then Szilvia's.

"What about the healer? Is she still under arrest?" Greta asked.

"She was released as soon as they woke up," the man replied.

Szilvia's eyes filled with tears. "Mama," she whispered. She kissed Isla's cheek then ran off towards her cottage, and her mama.

Isla felt a weight lift off her shoulders.

"Come, this calls for a celebration," Hans said as he began to lead them towards the nearest tavern.

"I should get back to Tobias and Miriam. They'll be worried."

Isla linked her arm through Lukas'. "They can wait until you've eaten and had something to drink. You won't make it ten more steps if you don't rest." She certainly wouldn't herself, either. She glanced at her mother. "And we have a story to hear."

With a sigh, Lukas followed his cousin's lead, the smell of delicious food calling them both.

~ 25 ~

LUKAS

Lukas had never been so tired before. When the soup bowl was placed in front of him at the tavern table, his head almost dropped into it face first. The tavern was packed with people celebrating the children's freedom. Lukas had spotted Uram Szabó in the crowd, but he hadn't stayed long enough for Lukas to congratulate him on the news.

Isla sat between Lukas and Erik. She had left her bowl of soup half full and leaned against Erik's shoulder, her eyes closed. Lukas smirked. *So much for me being the one to fall asleep.*

Between slurps of soup, he tried to pay attention to what his father and aunt were talking about.

"I hated that. Every minute of it," Greta said, shaking her head. She dunked a chunk of bread into her soup.

"There was no other way, and you know it," said Hans.

"Yes, and I *still* hated it. But at least it's over. For good," she sighed.

Isla opened one eye and stared at her mother. "Are you going to tell us the story?"

Greta sighed, her shoulders sagging. "Where to even begin?"

Hans cleared his throat. "I know your mother and I have never been very forthcoming with that time in our lives, but you have to understand, the time we grew up was full of strife. Bad harvests, a great deal of crime, high taxes . . . the list goes on. When our mother died after giving birth to me, our father was devastated. When our stepmother came along, he would do anything to make sure she stayed."

"Even abandon his children?" Isla asked, eyes wide.

Greta nodded. "The witch wasn't entirely wrong when she said I would have done anything to be rid of my family then. I was so angry at Papa. Over the years, Hans and I did our best to forgive him and move on, if not for our sakes but for yours, but it wasn't easy. I never loved him the same way. I think he knew about my magic, even if I wasn't ready to tell him, or anyone for that matter." She looked over at Hans. "I'm sorry for saddling you with his care in the end. I know that must have been unbearable at times."

Hans shrugged. "Sarah bore the brunt of it, if I'm honest. She didn't deserve that." He glanced at Greta. "Did you mean what you said to the witch? About me?"

Greta met her brother's stare. "Some of it. I was angry when you left Lukas after Sarah passed. It's not the first time I've had to step in for you. But I understand why." She covered Hans' hand with hers. "If Jacob died, I'd probably want to walk away, too."

Hans chuckled. "No, you wouldn't. You're too stubborn to leave loose ends." He patted her hand in return. "But thank you for all that you've done for my family. I know I'm not the best brother."

"You're the reason I have Isla safe and sound, so I'd say you're a pretty good brother. I wouldn't choose any other," Greta said with a smile.

Lukas wasn't sure how to feel about his grandfather, now that he knew a bit more about how his father and aunt grew up. But with the man long dead, it wasn't like he could ask his grandfather for his side of the story. It didn't change the fact that his grandfather had still abandoned his children.

As soon as they were finished eating, Lukas told the group he was heading home. "Miriam will be worried."

"I'll come, too. We've got a few things to discuss, and I could use a good sleep in my own bed," said Hans.

Greta hugged her brother then embraced Lukas, kissing both his cheeks. "Thank you, Lukas. Isla and I couldn't have done this without you."

Lukas doubted that very much, but he was too tired to argue with his aunt. He hugged Isla, who was still half-asleep, and shook Erik's hand. The streets were still crowded with celebrators as Lukas and Hans left the village and headed back to the farm. Their walk home was quiet, both too tired to carry a conversation, and perhaps that was for the best. There were too many thoughts tumbling in Lukas' head to sort out on the walk home. He didn't want the next conversation with Hans to be one influenced by anger or grief.

As soon as the farmhouse came into view, Lukas picked up the pace and jogged the rest of the way. When he reached the front door, he didn't even have time to get his key. Miriam flung open the door and launched herself at Lukas. He caught her just in time, lifting her clear off the ground. She wrapped her arms tightly around his neck and soon his shoulder was damp with her tears. Tobias' arms wrapped around his waist.

"Thank God you're safe," she whispered, her breath shaky as it brushed across his neck.

Lukas buried his face in her curls, breathing deep the lavender smell he so loved on her, and held her tighter. "I'm sorry I took so long."

Miriam pulled back a little and Lukas put her back on the ground. She placed a hand on his cheek. "I'm just glad you're home."

"Did it work? Did you find the gingerbread house?" Tobias asked. Apparently, Miriam had filled him in on where Lukas had gone.

Lukas nodded. "Let's go inside and I'll explain." He waved Hans over, who had hung back. He had been staring at the farmyard, inspecting Lukas' work. "Papa will, too. He can fill in the gaps."

Hans came up the staircase and smiled at Miriam. "Hello again, Miriam." He bowed his head to Tobias. "And to you, young man."

She smiled and bobbed a curtsey. "Good morning, sir. Would you like a cup of cocoa?"

"That would be lovely."

The four headed inside. Lukas and Hans went into the parlour while Miriam fetched the drinks. Tobias asked dozens of questions while they waited. Lukas was even more exhausted answering as many as he could by the time Miriam came back.

"Sounds like you had quite the adventure!" Miriam said as she came back with the tray of drinks. Tobias helped Miriam pass out the mugs. Then he sat beside Lukas again, as if he couldn't get close enough to him.

"I'm glad you're back," Tobias said, leaning his head against Lukas' shoulder.

Lukas ruffled Tobias' hair. "Me too."

Hans smiled at the boys. "Seems like you have quite the farm hand, Lukas."

Lukas grinned. "I certainly do. Tobias has been a big help, especially with the chickens."

"And bunnies!" Tobias added. "You have lots of rabbits."

Hans took a long sip of hot cocoa. "How do you feel about sheep?"

Tobias and Hans chatted about farm animals and their level of cuteness. This gave Lukas the perfect chance to go into the kitchen. Miriam followed him. With their backs to Hans and Tobias, Miriam intertwined her fingers with his. "I suppose our card game will have to wait."

"Perhaps; we'll see what Papa plans to do." He squeezed her hand. "Either way, I'm still going to visit your father this week. I have some important things to ask him."

Miriam blushed. "Would you like me to join you? My brothers and sisters can be a bit much."

"I should probably go alone, but I'll never turn down your company."

"Good, because you're going to be seeing it for a while. Possibly forever."

Lukas smirked. "Possibly."

They busied themselves in the kitchen a few minutes longer, looking for any excuse to stay in each other's circle. "Do you need anything to eat?" Miriam asked.

"No, we stopped at the tavern in the village before heading here. Isla wouldn't let us say no," Lukas said.

"Tell me what happened! I want to know everything."

"Yes, tell us!" Tobias said from the couch.

Lukas and Miriam rejoined Hans and Tobias, then Hans and Lukas shared their night at the witch's cottage. Between sips of cocoa, Miriam and Tobias heard just how the witch was finally defeated and the children released from their sleep.

"She made a point, though. The Council's suspicions drove her to the woods and that cottage. Who knows what her life would have been like if they had just left her alone and let her help others," Lukas said, finishing the last of his cocoa.

"She made her choice. She may have been driven there, but she didn't have to begin cursing people, especially children," said Hans. He shook his head. "She impacted so many lives. I'm glad she's gone."

"Did you know, then, about Aunt Greta's magic?" Lukas asked.

"I always suspected, but never asked her directly. You know how she can be. I knew she'd tell me when the time was right. Last night was certainly good timing."

Miriam took Lukas' cup and got up, carrying her own in the other hand. "I'm glad it's all over, especially for those poor children, and Isaiah and Aliz. Hopefully things will get back to normal now." She took Hans' mug as well and went into the kitchen.

Hans covered his mouth as he yawned. Tobias had curled up beside Lukas again and was fast asleep. "The boy has the right idea. Time for an afternoon nap."

"Would you like me to walk you home?" Lukas asked Miriam as he suppressed a yawn.

Miriam chuckled. "And have you fall asleep on the road on the way back?" She shook her head. "I'll be fine. I'll come back around suppertime to feed you all."

Hans waved his hand. "You don't have to do that, Miriam. I'm sure we can manage."

"I insist! You've all been through quite the ordeal. It's the least I can do."

Hans smiled as he shook his head. "I'm off to bed, then. See you all in a few hours."

Once alone, Lukas grimaced. "I should check on the cows."

"Tobias let them out to pasture, and the chickens are happily in their pen. I sent one of Uncle's farm hands to stay with the sheep."

Lukas took her hands in his and squeezed them gently. "Thank you, Miriam."

She pulled her hands from his and wrapped her arms around his waist, resting her head against his chest. "No need to thank me, Lukas. I'm just glad you're back."

He kissed the crown of her head as he hugged her in return. "Me too. I missed you terribly." He yawned, giving his body a little shake to try to wake it up.

Miriam chuckled. "Time for you to rest."

Lukas sighed. "I was hoping to get the crops in before all this happened. Threw off my plan completely."

"Uncle said he'll stop by to gather them. They should be dry by now." She gently pushed him towards the ladder. "No more excuses. Off to bed!"

Before she could push him too far, he kissed Miriam lightly. "I'll see you for supper."

"Have a good sleep," she said, then placed a blanket over Tobias as he continued to sleep on the couch. Lukas headed to his cot, never so thankful to see it in his life.

~ 26 ~

ISLA

Isla stared at the Chief Steward's castle. Erik stood beside her, his hand wrapped around one of hers.

"Are you sure you want to do this? It can wait until tomorrow," he said.

"The sooner I see him, the sooner I can leave."

Erik stared at her a moment longer, then nodded. The couple went inside the castle then separated at the door of the Chief Steward's office. Erik squeezed her hand. "I'll meet you at the front door in twenty minutes."

Isla agreed and let him go. She suspected he was going to check on Isaiah before collecting his things from his chamber. Isla watched Erik leave then knocked on the Chief Steward's door.

"Enter," a voice called from inside.

Isla's tired feet were glad of the plush carpet underfoot and the warm fire heating the small room. When Greta suggested she rest before making the journey to the castle, Isla knew if she had she wouldn't have woken before dawn the following day. The business she had couldn't wait another hour.

The Chief Steward stood in front of his fireplace, a glass of brandy on the mantle as he stared at the flames. The fire high-lighted the crow's feet by his eyes and his sagging jowls. His hair was far greyer than she remembered, but his presence still took up the whole room, intimidating Isla more than she cared to admit.

She paused a few feet from the older man, her arms folded across her chest. She was cold and exhausted and desperately in need of a bath, but she refused to look away from the man. Finally, he drew his gaze away from the fire and met her stare. She met his frown with an impassive look, doing her best to hide the animosity still rolling through her after all these years.

"I suppose I owe my children's state of rejuvenation to you, young lady."

"And my mother. But you can settle your debt with me."

The Chief Steward smirked. "What are my children's lives worth to you?"

"The better question is, what are they worth to *you?*"

Isla waited as the man continued to stare at her. He turned away and finished his brandy. He left the empty glass on the mantle then went to his desk. She saw him pull out a bag from one of the many drawers. It clinked when he set it down on the desk. He brought out a scale and started piling gold coins on one side as the other held a weight. She couldn't make out how heavy the weight was.

After about a minute of adding coins, he paused. The Chief Steward looked up at her and gestured to the stack of coins, far more than she had ever seen in her young life. "Will this suffice?"

Isla stared at the coins for a long moment. *It could buy a house in town. A big one for Mama and Papa.* She glanced at her callused hands, ones that had always loved time at Hans' farm. *Or enough land to carve out a living.* She met the Chief Steward's gaze. "It will do."

He bagged the coins up and slid them across the table to her. She put the bag in her larger satchel. Before she turned to leave, she stared at the Chief Steward. "I have a question that's been bothering me for years."

The Chief Steward grabbed the bottle of brandy and placed it beside his scale. "Ask, although I may not answer."

"Why did you force Isaiah and Aliz to stop spending time with us? What was so wrong with me, with my cousin, that you sent your children away so they wouldn't see us any longer?"

The Chief Steward was silent for a time. He sighed. "I didn't even know you were playmates until your mother came to me with a request."

Isla's heart paused mid-beat. "What did she want?"

"She wanted me to take you with Aliz when they left to spend the winter in Budapest. She wanted you to have more opportunities in the capital, so she claimed. I always believed she wanted to get you away from the woods and the witch's curse." The Chief Steward sipped his brandy. "I said no, of course. Greta did, however, make me realize I had been ignoring my children's needs longer than I should have. Grief muddles things, as we all know. So, I sent them away." He levelled his stare at Isla. "I pray this is the last time I see you, daughter of Greta."

Isla bowed her head. "You can count on it, Sir."

Chilled with the new information, she desperately wanted to leave. Isla would have beat Erik to the front door if she hadn't spotted Isaiah's chamber on the way out. His door was partially open, and he was lying in bed. A book laid on his chest, but he was staring out the window instead of reading it. She thought of her promise to his father. *I should say goodbye, at least. For Erik's sake.* She suspected once they were wed, the Chief Steward wouldn't welcome Erik back any more than he would Isla.

She nudged the door open further, letting the hinges creak to signal her entrance. Isaiah looked at her, his face pale. He had dark circles under his eyes, but besides that he seemed none the worse for wear.

"How are you feeling?" she asked.

Isaiah shrugged. "Strange. I slept so long, and yet I'm still tired. Besides that, I can't complain." He waved her over towards the chair beside his bed. "Have a seat. Erik just left. You've got time before he's packed up."

"He told you, then," she said as she did as she was told. At least the seat was comfortable.

"About your plan to marry and live happily ever after? Yes, I know he's leaving. I'm sure you'll both be deliriously happy together."

Isla rolled her eyes. "Only you could make a congratulatory message so sarcastic."

"Oh, my apologies, did I not have my smile on? I do forget to fake happiness at the worst of times."

"Why do you hate me so much, Isaiah? I truly wish to know what I did to offend you."

"What makes you think I hate you?"

Isla snorted. "You can't just treat me so rudely simply because your father told you to. I know you have more of a mind than that." She narrowed her eyes. "Or did your time among the court suck you dry of your conscience?"

Isaiah stared at the ceiling of his room. "It's not my mind that troubles me. If I could cut my heart out, I would," he muttered.

"What does your heart have to do with this?"

"Must you ask?" he snapped.

Isla stared at him, her eyes slowly widening as his words finally made sense. It certainly explained why Erik was allowed back to Isaiah's side. She leaned forward, her satchel jingling as the coins shifted. "All this time?"

Isaiah drew his gaze from the safety of the ceiling and met Isla's stare. "I had hoped over time, and knowing how much he loved you, I'd stop loving him, but we can't always get what we want."

"Why didn't you just *tell* me? If I had known you loved Erik, I—"

"You what? Erik has never felt that way about me, or any man. He loves *you*. Ending your relationship with him certainly wouldn't have sent him running into my arms."

Isla paused. Isaiah had a point. "Have you ever told him?"

"No, and neither will you. Erik is too good of a man. He would do something silly, like apologize." Isaiah shook his head. "I promised him I would come to the wedding, but after that, I'm going back to Budapest with Father."

"You're leaving? Aliz too?"

"No, Aliz is allowed to stay, on the condition that she meets with the suitors Father sends from court. She managed to avoid marriage while in Budapest, so I'm sure she'll manage the same here. Szilvia won't have to worry."

"Aliz told you?"

Isaiah smiled sadly. "My sister isn't good at keeping secrets from me. Don't worry, Father doesn't know. Or if he does, he's chosen to ignore it." Isaiah took a deep breath then let it out slowly. "This is goodbye, Isla. Take care of Erik for me, please."

Isla got up, her satchel sagging, and leaned over Isaiah's bedside. "Goodbye, Isaiah. I hope you find happiness in Budapest." She kissed his cheek then left the room, hoping Erik was ready to leave.

~*~

Isla didn't remember the walk home, nor crawling into bed. She suspected she would have slept into the following day, had it not been for the delicious smells coming from the kitchen. Her hunger was enough to wake her up. She sat up in bed and rubbed her tired eyes. The sun was just setting.

She undid her loose ponytail, ran her fingers quickly through the knots, then braided her hair. Isla smoothed the wrinkles from her skirt then slipped her feet into the closest pair of slippers. She went straight to the kitchen. Her father had his back to her as he fried bacon on the stovetop. Fresh bread was cooling on the counter and eggs were sizzling alongside the bacon.

Erik sat at the table, a cup of tea before him. Greta sat across from him. Isla was surprised to see him back at her house so soon after leaving him at his parents'. She thought after his goodbyes at the castle, he would need some time to rest and catch up with his family.

Jacob turned around and smiled at her. "Good evening, Sleeping Beauty!"

Isla passed Erik and kissed his cheek before heading to her father. She hugged him tight. "This smells delicious, Papa, thank you." She glanced at her mother. "How did you sleep?"

Greta looked much more rested than when Isla had left her for the Chief Steward's castle earlier that day. She had changed into a different dress and her hair was still damp from a bath she must have taken. *I should do that, too.* A bath would be wonderfully relaxing after everything that had happened the last few days.

"Very well, thank you," Greta replied. She wrapped her hands around her steaming mug of tea but didn't take a sip. She still held Erik's gaze. "Your beau and I were just having a conversation."

Isla went to the kettle and poured herself a cup. "A pleasant one, I hope."

"They haven't killed each other yet," Jacob teased, putting the eggs and bacon onto a large plate.

"Oh good, nothing has changed then," Isla said dryly, trying not to roll her eyes.

Greta shook her head. "See what you're getting into? She really does take after him."

Erik grinned. "Oh, trust me, she's your daughter through and through."

"What's that supposed to mean?" Greta said.

Isla narrowed her eyes at Erik just as her mother did the same. Jacob, breakfast in hand, laughed alongside Erik. Isla looked at her mother and the ladies joined in the laughter.

"See what I mean?" said Erik. Isla sat down beside him, and he squeezed her hand underneath the table. "I'm a lucky man no matter who she takes after."

"*That* we all can agree on," said Jacob. He grabbed a stack of plates and started handing out the food. Greta brought the kettle and bread over, refilling Erik's cup. Isla sliced the bread and gave herself an extra piece. She hadn't realized how hungry she was.

After the first few bites, conversation began to flow around the table. Isla explained the gold coins from the Chief Steward.

"Erik and I thought we would ask Hans if we could buy a portion of his land. We could live out there and farm, just like we talked about. What do you think?"

Jacob nodded. "You know I'm happy so long as you're happy."

Greta focused on cutting up her egg, refusing to meet Isla's gaze. "I'm not exactly thrilled at such a rushed wedding, but I know you'll be happy out in the country. I know how miserable the village makes you." She met Isla's stare. "And you can continue your training under Constance."

Isla remembered the Chief Steward's story. "Isaiah's father told me about your request to take me to Budapest when I was younger. Does this mean you won't try to send me to your family there, or ask the Chief Steward again?"

Greta blushed. "I had hoped he had forgotten that." She met her daughter's gaze. "I only ever wanted to keep you safe, Isla. I thought if you were in Budapest, the woods wouldn't be able to claim you. Or perhaps your magic wouldn't surface as it did. I know now that I was wrong to try to keep you from what – and who – makes you happy."

Isla got up and hugged each of her parents. "Thank you," she whispered.

Greta held her longer than Jacob had. She kissed Isla's cheek. "Just be careful. And come visit."

Isla pulled back, laughing. "Of course we'll visit! It's not like we're moving halfway across the country."

"And we'll be close to Lukas and Miriam," Erik added. "It'll be nice to visit them, too."

The rest of the evening passed pleasantly. Isla and Greta volunteered to do the dishes so Jacob could put his feet up and rest. Erik offered to help, but Greta urged him to head home.

"Your parents will be wondering where you are. And you have quite a bit of news to share with them," she reminded.

Erik conceded her point. Isla walked Erik to the front door. With Jacob snoring in the parlour, they shared a quick kiss.

"I'll see you tomorrow?" Erik asked.

"I'll meet you in the market. I'm going to stop by Szilvia's in the morning."

"It's a date."

Erik left, letting in a chilly fall breeze. Isla shuddered then went back to the kitchen, grateful for the hot, soapy water. She and Greta worked quietly side by side for a few minutes.

"Anymore family secrets I need to know about?" Isla asked.

Greta dried the large platter, avoiding Isla's gaze. "I'm fairly certain we've gone over every unpleasant aspect of our family."

Isla smirked. "It's not all bad. We have magic."

"Magic has never brought any happiness into my life. The last thing I wanted was for it to make you a target. It did with the witch and it almost did with the Council. Going forward, you have to be careful."

"Maybe it hasn't made you happy because you've been using it for the wrong reasons."

Greta glanced at Isla, eyes narrowed. "What do you mean?"

"You only ever use it in your tea. Just to add a little sweetness, or calm a person down, right?"

"That's all it's safe for. It's so easy to lose control."

"How do you know? Have you ever really tested your powers?"

Greta snorted. "And find myself driven from my home like that witch was? No."

Isla slid her soapy hand over her mother's. "You should come to Constance's with me tomorrow. Talk to her. Perhaps she can help you unlock your magic and find a way to use it for its purpose. In a safe way, of course."

Greta stared at their hands then slowly nodded. "What time are you going over?"

"After breakfast. Then Erik and I are going to the market."

"Don't stay out too late. We have a wedding to plan, and it's going to take longer than you think to do it."

Isla withdrew her hand, rolling her eyes as she smiled. "Oh, Mama, I just want something simple. Can't I wear your dress and just pick some wildflowers for the bouquet?"

"*My* dress? What makes you think that ratty old thing will suit you?"

"I don't care what it looks like. I want to wear it because it's yours."

Greta didn't say anything for a moment. Isla looked over and saw tears in her mother's eyes. Greta shook her head and got back to drying. "We'll look at it later. Perhaps Erik's mother still has hers. I remember going to her wedding back in the day. Now *her* dress was stunning. I was so jealous," Greta said with a chuckle. "I told your father I wanted to get married again in that dress, but he said no. The first one cost too much."

Isla and Greta laughed. The dishes were almost done when Isla looked over at Greta again. "What made you change your mind about Erik?"

Greta opened the mug cupboard and put away the cups from supper. "I saw how much he cared about you. He was so determined to rescue you – you, who hadn't needed rescuing since you were six!" She shook her head. "I knew then that no matter what trouble you got yourself into, he would walk through it with you. And that's all I can really ask for in the end. Your father is the romantic, in case you haven't realized," she said with a smirk. "You two are well-matched. You'll find your way, just like your father and I did."

Isla unplugged the sink and dried her hands off on the nearest towel. She kissed Greta's cheek. "Thank you, Mama."

Isla did a last sweep of the kitchen, making sure they hadn't missed anything, then linked her arm with Greta's. "How about a game of cards? It's been ages since I let you beat me."

"*Let* me?" Greta snorted. "Grab the deck. We'll see who lets who win."

Jacob slept through the first few games, but he joined them for the last round before bed. It was one of the most relaxing nights Isla could remember having in years.

~ 27 ~

LUKAS

Miriam added another log to the fire. "You can't avoid it forever, you know," she said as she sat beside him on the couch.

"I can try," Lukas muttered, nursing a lukewarm cup of tea in his hands as he stared at the fire.

"Your papa will still be on the porch whether you hide in your loft or not," she pointed out.

"Must you be so logical?" he said with a smirk. He sighed as he stood, mug forgotten. Miriam took it from him. "Wish me luck," he muttered.

Miriam grabbed his hand before he could get too far and pulled him down for a quick kiss. "Good luck," she whispered.

Lukas squeezed her hand then grabbed a mug of hot cocoa for Hans. He considered another cup of tea, but grabbed a clean cup and poured himself a fresh cup of hot cocoa as well. He nudged the front door open with his hip and let it slam shut behind him. Hans didn't turn from his position on the porch steps. His back was to Lukas as he stared up at the night sky. The stars had come out and the moon lit up the farmyard. Bella and her calf bayed from their stall in the barn, wanting a second helping of supper. Lukas went over to the steps and sat beside Hans. He handed over one of the mugs.

Hans nodded his thanks. The two sat in silence for some time, enjoying the peaceful night. For once, Lukas wasn't keeping one eye

233

towards the road, expecting someone to come racing up, warning him of more missing children. He let out a deep breath, relaxing his shoulders. He certainly wasn't going to miss that.

"I love sleeping under the stars. It's probably my favourite thing when I'm with the sheep," Hans said quietly. He took a sip of his cocoa. "Although I do miss the cocoa. Not quite the same over a campfire," he said with a chuckle.

"I don't know how Miriam does it, but hers always tastes better than mine."

"Your mother's did, too. I think she added cinnamon."

"Nutmeg, too." Lukas took a sip. "I don't know why she bothered writing recipes down when she never followed them."

"She didn't write it down for herself; she wrote it down for you, or your wife." Hans glanced behind them towards the parlour. "Although, I don't think Miriam needs any help in the kitchen. She certainly can cook. Be careful, or you'll have to have your trousers let out at the waist," Hans teased, patting his own stomach. Miriam had prepared a feast for supper that night. The men both had their fair share, and then some.

Lukas cleared his throat. "I wanted to talk to you about that, actually. I'm going to approach her father about courtship. She's planning to stay on at her uncle's, but she agreed to keep helping here, too. If she was needed." Lukas met Hans' gaze. "We weren't sure what your plan was."

Hans sighed. "I'm not sure, either," he muttered. "It's good that you're going about this the right way. I like Mordecai and his sister runs a tight ship in the city. Miriam has a good head on her shoulders. I know she'll do well here. You both will. You've already proven that."

Lukas could hear the unspoken words. His stomach sank. "But you're not staying."

Hans slowly shook his head. "I can't, Lukas. Not yet."

Lukas took a sip of his cocoa. "Where will you go?"

"I think I'll wander, like the good Lord did back in his day. Maybe that will settle my mind and heart." Hans stared at his mug. "I don't know when I'll come back."

Lukas fought the acidic anger boiling in his belly. He wanted to rage at Hans, but part of him understood why he was leaving again.

"But you will come back? You promise?" He couldn't stand it if Hans abandoned him completely.

"I promise." Hans placed a hand on Lukas' shoulder and gave it a tight squeeze.

Lukas nodded. "Good. You won't want to miss the wedding," he said with a smile, trying to lighten the mood.

"I'll send letters from every inn I stop in. We'll keep in touch." Hans drained his hot cocoa. "Your mother's wedding ring is in her jewelry box in our room. She would want you to have it."

Lukas had always loved the simple gold band Sarah had worn. "Thank you, Papa. I didn't realize you saved it."

"I couldn't let it go with her," he said quietly. "It was hard enough knowing she couldn't wear it any longer while alive."

Lukas looked up at the stars, tears flooding his eyes. "I miss her," he whispered.

Hans wrapped an arm around Lukas' shoulders. "Me too."

They stayed outside for a time in silence, watching the stars and sipping cocoa, until Lukas realized he would have to walk Miriam home. He dumped the dregs of his mug in the grass then got up off the steps. "Are you coming inside?"

"In a while. I'm in no rush, now that the sheep have settled." Hans had checked on them in the field after supper. "Speaking of, can you manage them for the winter? I know it's more work than you need, but I can't take them with me."

"I'm sure I can teach Tobias how to care for the sheep. We should be able to handle it together. When are you leaving?"

"In a few days. I'll help gather up the wheat and try to tidy up my shop for you, in case you need anything while I'm gone."

Hans got up and hugged Lukas, his cup bumping against Lukas' back. "I'm proud of you, son. You've really shown me you're ready for the responsibility that comes with running this place."

Lukas squeezed Hans tight. "Thank you, Papa. I hope Mama is proud, too."

"I know she is," Hans said, his voice strained. He pulled back and quickly wiped his eyes. "Don't wait up for me."

Lukas took his father's cup then headed inside. He heard Bella bellow when Hans opened the barn door.

He had just put the mugs on the counter when Miriam came over, his jacket in hand. "Still planning to walk me home?"

"Of course. One does not let a fair lady go off on her own!"

Miriam snorted. "This fair lady can handle herself just fine, thank you."

Lukas kissed her cheek. "This gentleman will also take any excuse to be alone with his fair lady, even if that means a moonlit walk before curfew."

Miriam laughed as she helped Lukas do up the buttons on his jacket. "Good thing my uncle trusts you, or these walks would be few and far between."

The pair left the farmhouse and headed down the familiar lane to Mordecai's property. Hands held, Lukas gathered the courage to share his father's news.

"Papa's going away again."

Miriam squeezed his hand. "That was quick."

"I know, but he's determined."

"How soon?"

"In a few days. He approves of the courtship, though. I told him to be back in time for the wedding," Lukas said with a wink.

Miriam chuckled. "Now you just need my papa's approval. Do you still want to go over tomorrow?"

"I think that would be best. With Hans here, I don't have to worry about the farm."

"I'll come by with Tobias after breakfast. The chickens and rabbits will keep him entertained while we're in town. If all goes well, perhaps you'll even want to stay for lunch!"

"If your brothers and sisters save me anything," Lukas teased.

The pair walked in contented silence for a minute before Lukas remembered the sheep. "Do you think Tobias can learn to herd sheep?"

"Tobias is quite special, especially when it comes to animals. I don't think it'll take him long." Miriam grinned. "I'm especially fond of the lambs. I know there won't be many babies right now, but I don't mind helping with them, either. The three of us shouldn't have any troubles."

They reached Mordecai's far sooner than they wished. Lukas walked her up to the front door and hugged her tight. "See you tomorrow?"

Miriam pulled back just far enough to kiss Lukas. "Tomorrow," she promised.

Lukas was about to leave when Aunt Tanya opened the door. "Lukas, thank you for walking Miriam home! Would you like to come inside? Mordecai and I were just about to play a game of cards, but it's more fun with more people."

He thought about Hans at home, reacquainting himself with the farm. He should go back, but Tanya's fire was roaring, and he could hear Tobias up past his bedtime, demanding another card from Mordecai.

"One game won't hurt," he said with a grin.

Tanya beamed as she opened the door wider to let him inside. She sat Miriam down closest to the fire and offered them both tea. Lukas accepted while Miriam declined. Lukas could see the excitement of the day had worn her out and she could barely keep her eyes open now that she was inside the warm farmhouse. Lukas sat beside her and did his best not to blush when she leaned her head against his shoulder, quietly dozing. He tried to win against

Mordecai, but the farmer was a champion at Noddy; Lukas had never had such fun losing.

EPILOGUE

Greta grunted as she ground the bay leaves into a fine powder. Constance looked over her shoulder, hands on her hips.

"You're getting better. Almost as good as your daughter," Constance said with a wink.

Greta glared at the woman. "Don't you dare tell her that. I'll never live it down."

Constance chuckled as she wiped her hands on her apron. "I wouldn't dream of it. The last thing we need is those two teaming up and nagging at us to retire."

Greta shook her head. "What, and deprive the farmers of my well-ground bay leaves? Never!"

The women laughed then got back to work. Greta glanced at the clock and ground faster. Isla and Erik would be there soon.

Six years had passed since the witch of the woods was defeated, freeing the village children from her cursed clutches. Only four years since Greta became a widow. She didn't like to think of that dark year spent nursing Jacob, whose sudden illness perplexed even Constance and Szilvia. Isla had spent more time in her childhood home than at her farm, leaving her husband Erik to manage as she did all she could to nurse her father back to health.

In the end, his death was a blessing. Greta could see from the dark circles under his eyes and his laboured breathing that his days were full of pain. Constance, when confronted, agreed. When Isla slept in her old room, Greta and Constance gave Jacob a tonic that would end his suffering. Greta still hadn't told her daughter the truth of what happened early that final morning. How could she explain to her daughter that sometimes, the best way to prove your love for someone was to let them go?

After the funeral, Greta managed to stay in the village only another week, just long enough to sell the house. She couldn't stand the whispering housewives and their snoopy servants a second longer. She initially thought of going to live with Isla, at least temporarily, but when Constance came by one night for a visit, they came up with another idea.

Since the witch's second banishment to the oven, Greta had tried to take her daughter's advice. Using her magic in small doses on more than just tea hadn't yet harmed anything – or anyone. Constance didn't seem to mind answering the dozens of questions Greta had, nor did she hate the company. Before Jacob's death, they had formed an unlikely friendship. As she sat across from Constance, sipping her tea, she waited to hear the woman's plan. Constance always seemed to have one, much like Szilvia.

"Why don't you live with me? Szilvia has her own cottage now, and it gets a little lonely out there. I could teach you more about your magic, and herbology, too."

Greta had hesitated. "I don't want to be a burden."

Constance had snorted. "Since when are you a burden? You're my *friend*, Greta. I want to help."

So, Greta let her. That was four years ago. Now, Greta and Constance were quite the team. It turned out Greta had a knack for herbs and plants, much like Isla did, although she was better at mixing them into teas than making potions. She had even learned enough from Constance to help with difficult births. Greta had yet to take any of those calls on her own, but Constance insisted she was ready.

Constance hung up her apron and tapped Greta's shoulder. "Come on, we had best get ready. They'll be here soon."

Szilvia had moved into her own cottage a year after Isla married Erik. She wasn't far from Isla's farmhouse, and the girls got together regularly, along with Aliz whenever she came by for a visit from the castle. The Chief Steward had given up on marrying her off years ago, and since then, Aliz had lived comfortably as a young spinster.

That day, Isla and Szilvia were bringing a picnic over to their mothers' cottage to enjoy an afternoon in the sun. Hans, Lukas, Miriam, and Tobias had been invited as well, but they declined. Miriam had just given birth to her daughter, and Lukas didn't want to leave her alone on the farm. Hans' excuse didn't sit well with his sister – she didn't believe he couldn't put off taking the sheep to a new pasture until tomorrow – but she had learned not to fight him on certain things. She was just glad he returned home. She had half-expected him to never return, too lost in his broken heart and his wanderings to return. But, true to his word, the following spring Hans came back to the farm. By then, Lukas had already proposed to Miriam, who happily accepted. Hans arrived just in time for the wedding. As a present to the couple, he gifted them the farm. He still helped with the daily tasks, but he left the farmhouse to Lukas and Tobias, his helpful farmhand and almost-brother. After months of constant sleepovers, by the time Hans returned for the wedding, Tobias was living at the farmhouse full time. He took Lukas' old loft when Lukas and Miriam moved into Hans' old room.

Greta had been to Hans' new home, one Lukas had helped him build. It was essentially a shack in the woods, and she had no desire to return, but at least he was easy to find. These days, Hans reminded her too much of their father.

Greta took off her apron and set the bay leaves aside. They were ready for their satchel, but she would deal with it later. She pulled her loose hair back in a quick ponytail and brushed the cat fur off her dark green skirt. Anna had died a few years ago, but Greta and Constance were never without a cat curled up by the fireplace. She grabbed the tea tray and set the cups, pot, and jar of honey on it. Constance got the door for her, a loaf of fresh bread in a basket hanging off her arm and the picnic blanket wrapped around her neck like a scarf, and the two went outside.

The old oak tree provided just enough shade for an afternoon picnic. Constance laid out the plaid blanket, smoothing the edges as Greta set out the tea. She considered pouring herself a cup while they waited when she heard a commotion cresting the nearby hill. Greta saw Erik first. She smiled despite herself. Over the years, she had grown to enjoy her son-in-law's company, almost more than Isla's.

Riding on Erik's shoulders was his son, Jax. At five years old, the blonde boy was a troublemaker, just like his mother had been at that age. Grandmothers weren't supposed to have favourites, but it was hard not to fall in love with the rascal. Beside Erik was Isla, carrying their three-year-old daughter Halina. Greta's smile grew as she took in her granddaughter's white-blonde hair, the ponytail swaying in the breeze.

Szilvia was on Erik's other side, a basket laden with treats in hand. Aliz had been invited, but she was entertaining company at the castle and had declined. Szilvia and Isla were laughing about something, while Erik tried to convince Jax it wasn't a good idea to leap off Erik's shoulders.

"But Grandma's right there!" Jax whined.

"You can wait another minute," Erik said with a chuckle.

Greta got up and met them halfway to the tree. Jax stretched out his arms, reaching for Greta. "Grandma!"

Greta grinned and picked him up. She hugged him tight and spun him around, causing the little boy to squeal.

"How's my favourite grandson?"

"I'm your *only* grandson!"

"So much the better. One of you is enough," Greta teased, kissing his cheek. She put him down so he could run to Constance. He viewed her as a second grandmother, and Constance loved to spoil Isla's children. Szilvia didn't seem to have any interest in having children of her own, so Greta was more than happy to share her grandchildren.

Isla kissed her mother's cheek. "How late are we?"

"You're on time for once. What happened? Did you cast a spell?" she teased. Greta plucked Halina from her mother's arms and gave her a gentle hug. "Well hello, Lina. How are you today?"

"Good," she said quietly, smiling at Greta. "I got to play with Tobi today."

Greta met Isla's gaze. Isla shrugged. "We went over for a visit."

"Lukas looked dead on his feet," Erik said with a chuckle.

Greta put Halina down and nudged her towards Constance. "Go see what treat Grandma Constance has for you."

Halina did as she was told and raced off to the oak tree. Isla linked arms with her mother and the four adults followed the little girl's lead.

"How is Miriam? It happened so fast. Constance and I arrived, and Sarah was already born."

"According to her, it was so quick she barely remembers it. Although if I ask Lukas, I'm sure he can recall every detail," Isla said. "Mother and daughter look well, though. Healthy and happy, a picture-perfect family."

"Good. I plan to visit tomorrow. I have some tea Miriam would like."

Szilvia went ahead of the others and sat beside Constance, hugging her tight before bringing out the goodies from the basket. As Greta settled in beside her friend, Jax climbed on her lap. Holding him close, she wished, not for the first time, that Jacob was there to see this. At least he had held Jax before he passed. The loss had gotten easier to manage over time, but the ache was still there.

"Grandma!" Jax said, bringing Greta out of her thoughts. "I want a muffin."

Szilvia had made blueberry muffins for the picnic. Greta and Jax shared one in the shade of the oak tree, their fingers stained dark purple.

THE END

ACKNOWLEDGEMENTS

I'm still in disbelief that this is the fourth book I've published. One always hopes to keep releasing books after their debut, but it doesn't always happen. I'm grateful to every person that has helped turn this novel from a manuscript languishing on my laptop to a book I get to hold in my hands and share with readers.

Special thanks to my publisher and good friend Annabel Townsend at Pete's Press. When we initially discussed you starting a hybrid publishing company in March 2024, I don't think either of us expected you would have so much success, and that I would be as involved as I am. I'm so thankful for all your support, tips, and guidance as we put this book together. I can't wait to see what 2025 holds for Pete's Press – and the books we release!

I would also like to acknowledge Creative Saskatchewan and thank them for their support of publishing companies and authors in our province. The funding received from this organization was instrumental in releasing my book. Although our province is small compared to creative hubs like Ontario and British Columbia, there are many wonderful authors and other creative people who would not be able to do what they love without support from Creative Saskatchewan.

Thank you, as always, to my wonderful family and friends who have supported me since before my first book even released and continue to do so during the dry spells. Your encouragement, love, and patience are always appreciated. I hope you enjoy reading the adventures of Lukas and Isla as much as I enjoyed writing them!

A final thank-you to a special person whom the book is dedicated: my aunt Marcia. An endless source of wisdom, our conversations always leave me feeling rejuvenated, and our visits are something I look forward to every week. Marcia, you are an inspiration to me, and I hope this book brings you joy as you read it on your back porch. I look forward to our discussions about it!

About The Author

Robyn Dansereau, who publishes her novels under her maiden name Robyn Tocker, has been publishing novels in her Ever After Tales collection for over fifteen years. Inspired to write the real story behind happily ever afters, she earned a Bachelor of Arts degree and works as a freelance editor and personal training specialist. In her free time, she reads copious amounts of books at her acreage near McLean, Saskatchewan, where she lives with her husband and two dogs.

www.ingramcontent.com/pod-product-compliance
Lightning Source LLC
Chambersburg PA
CBHW051442050726
47593CB00005B/1897